THE TASKMASTER

Books by Harold King

Paradigm Red
Four Days
The Taskmaster

THE TASKMASTER

HAROLD KING

Coward, McCann & Geoghegan, Inc.   New York

For Henry

The epigraphs throughout are from *Che Guevara on Guerilla Warfare*, introduction by Major Harries-Clichy Peterson, © Frederick A. Praeger, Inc. 1961: "The Publisher expresses appreciation to the Office of Assistant Chief of Staff for Intelligence, Department of the Army, and to the Marine Corps Association for their cooperation in making their translation of *Guerilla Warfare* available for use in this book."

SBN: 698-10827-2

Library of Congress Cataloging in Publication Data

King, Harold, 1945 (Feb. 27)-
    Taskmaster.

    I. Title.
PZ4.K52165Tas   [PS3561.I476]   813'.5'4   77-3529

PRINTED IN THE UNITED STATES OF AMERICA

St. George he was for England,
And before he killed the dragon
He drank a pint of English ale
Out of an English flagon.

GILBERT KEITH CHESTERTON
"The Englishman"

I would like to express my appreciation to Praeger Publishers, Inc., for allowing me to use certain passages from its translation of Che Guevara's book on guerrilla warfare which appear as epigraphs before each chapter. Some epigrahs are literal quotations from that text while others are paraphrased to conform to the spirit of the chapters. In those few deviations from the translation, I believe I have respected the intent and spirit of the original text.

I. IDENTIFY

Popular forces can win a war against any army. It is important that the popular force be suitably informed, whether by intelligence or observation, of the enemy's weaknesses and have the capability to identify the enemy at all times.

Fundamental One, Che Guevara

1

All who have written about war concur that it is subject to certain strategic rules and those who violate these rules will be defeated.

Gunther found the yellow envelope stuck in the doorjamb, with a note from his landlady scribbled on the outside: "This came today."

He'd been out late again. Drinking rum.

ALEC GUNTHER 156 W 73 ST NEW YORK NY
MUST TALK SOONEST. EXTREMELY URGENT. REGARDING
OP JUPITER. CALL MIDNIGHT THIS DATE. 602/555/5303.
HARRY PHILLIPS

Harry Phillips. It took Gunther a moment to remember.

Tall man, angular face.

Competent.

Trustworthy.

Worked together in the sixties. Early sixties. Retired now. Lived in the Southwest, last he'd heard.

Harry Phillips was a long time ago.

Gunther stared at the message again. The rum had fuzzied his thoughts. He had to concentrate on each word.

"Must talk . . . urgent. . . . Call midnight . . ."

He looked at his watch. Two-fifteen.

"Jupiter."

It took some time to register. Jupiter . . . Jupiter! His brain was working. Slowly, finally, it came to him.

Operation Jupiter . . . the invasion.

It was an Arizona area code and the number rang half a dozen times before someone answered.

"Hello."

Gunther tried to picture the man at the other end. It had been more than fifteen years. "Harry?"

"Alec. You got the telegram." The voice was nervous, edgy.

"Yes, late I'm afraid. I've been out."

Phillips's breathing was slow, slightly irregular. Gunther wondered if he might have been drinking, waiting for the phone to ring.

"I'm in trouble, Alec," Phillips said quietly. "I need help."

"What kind—"

"Just listen, Alec. I'm not at home. I'm at a pay phone in the bus terminal. I've been waiting hours for your call."

"Sorry, I—",

"Someone has been in my house . . . last week. Not a burglary. I'm being followed, have been for days. I didn't know who to call . . . I'm scared." Phillips sucked in a short, frightened breath. "Things have been moved in the house, little things . . . like *we* used to do. Whoever it was didn't leave wires, I've checked everywhere . . . nothing. It's some kind of setup, Alec. *I know it is.*"

Gunther was silent a moment, waiting to be sure he'd finished. "You've called Central?"

"Christ, yes."

"And?"

"Nothing. What's happened to everyone? They're all new."

"Things change," Gunther said.

"I finally got Greer, Bill Greer. He's doing something for Historical Staff up on the second floor. Bill Greer!"

Gunther didn't know why that should be so amazing. Greer was past fifty. Younger men worked the field now. The relics retired; the lucky ones were kicked upstairs.

"He said my imagination was hyperventilating," Phillips continued. "That son of a bitch."

"Why call me?"

Phillips exhaled a long breath, cleared his throat. Gunther remembered he was a heavy smoker. "Habit, maybe. You used to be my control."

"A long time ago, Harry. I'm out of fieldwork. I don't know how I can be much help."

"*You're* out?"

Gunther took it to be a compliment. "You didn't read about Berlin?"

Phillips paused. "Jesus, Alec . . . that was you?"

"I'm in disbursement now," Gunther said. "Paymaster for Gibraltar Service Company." He closed his eyes to the words. "Administrative Staff."

"Jesus fucking Christ!"

"It isn't so bad," Gunther said. He wondered if Phillips believed it.

"I called you because I know you . . . trust you," he said, emphasizing the words. "I have a family now. If it was just me, you understand?"

Gunther said he did.

"I'm afraid for my kids. Christ, Alec, my kids!"

"You mentioned Jupiter."

He heard the dull, tinny click of a lighter, the scrape of the wheel on the flint, the snap of the cover closing. Phillips exhaled again. "Yes," he said thickly. "I saw someone from the operation here in Phoenix."

"Coincidence?"

"Did you ever believe in coincidence?" Phillips said angrily.

"Who?"

"Big guy. Black. Name was Valdez or something. *V* like *victory.* You pointed him out to me the time I was up in the jungle camp from Puerto Cabezas. We reviewed the landing strategy. Remember him?"

Gunther thought he did. "You're sure it was him?"

"I'm not sure of anything right now."

"Frankly, Harry, it sounds too thin. You've been retired now, what, eight, nine years? I don't see it. What would be the motivation?"

"I only know I'm under surveillance," Phillips said quickly. "Someone's been in my house. I believe that. I don't like it, Alec. It scares the shit out of me, after all this time. I'm not any good at the game anymore."

"Then leave," Gunther said. "Pack up your wife and your kids and take a holiday. Go somewhere. Let someone at Central know where, then go. I'll tell them I talked to you."

"I don't like running," Phillips said sourly. "Not with my family."

"Jesus, Harry, go, stay. . . . You called me, remember?"

"All right, all right. I'm sorry. It's just . . . I'm a little edgy."

"I'll do what I can," Gunther said. "You'll probably think all this is very funny next Sunday . . . nothing to it. And you sitting around in a bus terminal."

"Maybe."

"Call me in a few days. If you're not too embarrassed," Gunther added. "We'll have a good laugh."

Sometimes retirees got a little nervous, a little paranoid after a time. Phillips was sincere enough—frightened men usually are—but Gunther did not think it would amount to anything. He reported Phillips's call to Johnson, his case officer, one of the new officers who was still so impressed with having the great Alec Gunther under him that he forwarded the message up the chain promptly. Gunther would hear if something came of it. He didn't expect it to, and after a few days he forgot it. Phillips simply had had a case of retiree's jitters.

Later, he changed his mind.

Someone tried to kill him.

Gunther was standing on the BMT platform at Times Square. He was irked with himself for coming down to the trains during the five o'clock crush, but empty taxis were just impossible to find. He'd barely missed the last express uptown and was standing in the front row of the crowded platform when he felt the poke of something hard at his back. Then there was the sound of the train and the stale breeze as it appeared, pushing a mountain of air ahead through the tunnel. Gunther saw the train coming, the pressure at his back increased, he started to turn, then he was falling.

He was lucky only because his executioner was a fraction too anxious. Gunther hit the rail nearest the platform and rolled back against the wall, seconds before the first subway car passed over, long before it stopped.

He would never forget the look on the boy's face pressed against the window at the front of the first car, eyes wide, mouth screaming. That was when he decided to call Burdict.

2

There is a saying: The guerrilla is the maverick of war. Thus circumstances and the will to win often oblige him to forget romantic and sportsmanlike concepts.

Burdict was one of the old men like Gunther, but he had changed with the changing times. Obviously, he'd known the right people and had made a secure and comfortable place for himself in the Operations Directorate after his stint in the field. He and Gunther and Miles had been good friends once. But Miles was dead now. And Gunther was, at least, alive. Only Burdict had moved up the steps to some post on the fringe of the executive staff. Gunther didn't begrudge him that. It was reward enough for a man with only one lung and the scar of a Hungarian submachine gun bullet on his chest, proof of a mistake back in fifty-seven. He was a man who learned and profited by his mistakes. Not at all like Gunther, or so it seemed.

They met in the Blue Cheese Bar, a dim and seedy little pub on the lower West Side that made promises of air conditioning from the street, but could not keep them, inside.

They sat in a booth on the end of a row against the wall, figures not clearly seen or recognized. Gunther drank rum and Coca-Cola these days because he'd lost his taste for whiskey. Burdict nursed his usual Haig & Haig and listened as Gunther reeled through the story.

"How much of this did you tell your case officer?" Burdict inquired after Gunther had finished.

"Johnson? Only that Phillips called . . . wanted an assignment petition run. Nothing about the subway."

"He knows nothing of the details of Harry's call, then?"

"That's right."

Burdict sipped his scotch. "I'm not sure I know what you want me to do, Alec."

"You're in operations. Find out if Harry's okay."

"By rights you should be taking this up with your case officer, not me."

"You're covert staff, Marty. Johnson isn't. He doesn't understand this sort of thing. He's never dealt with fieldwork before. Besides, it may concern the Jupiter operation and he doesn't have clearance for that."

Burdict nodded. "And the subway?"

"Maybe it *was* an accident . . . maybe. I don't want to look like a fool if all this comes to nothing." Gunther finished his drink and signaled the girl to bring him another.

"That's your third," Burdict observed.

"I can handle it."

Burdict waited while the girl brought the drink, watched silently as Gunther took a long swallow.

"You could use a shave, Alec. And a change of shirt. Must you tramp around looking such a mess?"

"It's my day off."

"I wonder if you should drink so much."

Gunther eyed him a long moment then gulped down another swallow. "Look, Marty, since they took me out and slammed me into disbursement, you've dropped in from time to time. I appreciate that. But you've always said if you could help with anything—" He finished the drink and pushed the glass away. "Now I'm asking you, for Harry. Okay?"

"I was thinking it was odd that you came to me." Burdict arched his eyebrows in a way that made his eyes seem too narrow for his long face. "Still the loner, aren't we, Alec? I'd have thought by now you'd have changed somewhat, mellowed, I suppose I mean. This isn't the field anymore."

Gunther had to agree, but he only nodded.

"I do worry about you, Alec."

"You needn't bother."

"Sometimes I wish you'd wash with the tide a bit . . . but only sometimes. This business you're into doesn't suit the old Alec I've always known and cherished."

Gunther avoided looking at him. "They broke the old Alec in Berlin, or haven't you heard?"

"I wonder how true that is?"

Gunther said nothing. He stared at his empty glass.

"I wonder if you need some other sort of taskwork to keep you busy?"

"Like you?" Gunther raised his glance to Burdict's face. "For a former field man, I can't say that I can see that you have anything to complain about. But then you were always adaptable."

"I manage, Alec," Burdict said with a conspirator's grin. "I'm looking forward to a step up, as a matter of fact. But at the moment, I'm concerned about you. How is your health?"

"Terrific."

"Truly?"

Gunther nearly lost his temper. "Look, I'm fine I tell you! I don't need anyone coming round to thump my chest."

"You needn't take offense, Alec."

"Just tell me if you will help," Gunther said angrily. "A simple yes or no will do."

Burdict smiled, but Gunther refused to look at him.

"Yes," Burdict said. He took out his pipe. "You'll hear from me."

A few days later a cloudburst caught Gunther as he hurried along Broadway, past Lincoln Center. By the time he'd reached the brownstone on Seventy-third, his raincoat was useless.

Gunther tramped heavily up the worn stairway to his apartment. He noticed at once the *Times* was not at its usual place against the jamb, and when he quietly unlocked the door he was aware of the dry, stale odor of pipe tobacco. He made a fist with his keys splayed out from the slits between his fingers and stepped inside.

"Burdict?" he said softly.

Gunther moved to the wall beside the kitchenette. He could hear only the wash of rain against the building.

"Burdict?"

He slid his hand into the top drawer of the small desk in the hallway and drew out a Colt Cobra. "Don't play games with me now," Gunther said. He thumbed back the hammer until it clicked.

"It's only me, Alec," a voice said. "No reason to bring out the artillery battalion."

Gunther stepped across the hallway to where he could see the sofa and the man sitting on it. Burdict sat with his feet propped on a stool, a dry raincoat neatly folded beside him, the *Times* in his lap. He'd made himself a drink.

Burdict took the pipe from his mouth. "It was important," he said solemnly. "I let myself in."

Gunther was still a moment, then eased the hammer down. Rain had matted his hair, streaked his face. He let the revolver drop into his coat pocket.

"Phillips?"

Burdict nodded.

"Dead?"

"Quite," Burdict said.

Gunther let out a breath, nodded.

"They told me you still had the instincts, Alec. I didn't even hear you . . ."

"When did it happen?" Gunther asked.

"More than a week ago," Burdict said. "Car crash . . . in the mountains. They just discovered it." He took a deep breath, stood up. "I guess he was right."

"It must be comforting to know now," Gunther hissed.

"I'm sorry, Alec."

"Yeah."

Gunther walked to the window. White chalk from a children's game washed around a stone in the alley below. Gunther wiped a hand across his face and glanced at Burdict. "Now, what?"

"I'm to take you to a meeting with the head of Special Ops," Burdict said. There was a brief silence. Gunther turned back to the window. "I am sorry, you know."

Gunther stared at the pitted alley a long while. Pages of a coloring book floated in the rain gutter, left behind. He suddenly realized he had never known how many kids Harry had.

"He's waiting, Alec."

"Mackensen, is it?"

"Yes, the main man himself. It must be important. Mackensen doesn't often leave the Langley palace, particularly not to take up with a field ex."

Gunther said nothing. He heard a rustling of clothes as Burdict got into his raincoat.

"Shall we, old boy? I don't see the weather letting up anytime soon."

He stood there a few moments longer, staring blankly past the window, then turned toward Burdict. "Yes," Gunther said, "we don't want to keep the man waiting."

3

Different geographic and social factors in individual countries may call for different methods and forms of guerrilla warfare, though the basic laws apply to all campaigns.

They drove in Burdict's car to somewhere on Forty-first Street near the Billy Rose Theater.

"This is it," Burdict said, nodding at the building across the street.

"You're not coming?"

"Wasn't invited." Burdict sat passively behind the wheel, the picture of contentment, sucking his pipe. He seemed perfectly happy not to know what was on. "They're going to miss you down at Gibralter Service Company, Paymaster's Staff."

"I doubt it."

"So do I." He motioned toward the building. "Ninth floor, Olympics."

It was still raining as Gunther climbed out of the car. He stepped into a swirling puddle below the curb.

"Good luck, Alec. Be careful, will you?" He leaned across the seat and touched Gunther's sleeve through the window with his gloved hand. "There aren't many of us left."

Gunther remembered Miles and how it was among the three of them. "I will, Marty. Thanks."

Burdict waved and was gone. Gunther watched until the car disappeared into traffic on Seventh Avenue. Then he walked across the street in the rain and thought about Nathan Mackensen waiting on the ninth floor.

The last time he'd seen Mackensen, Gunther hadn't exactly been in top form. But that was after the GDR mess. Mackensen had been running the European account then. Gunther stepped off the elevator at the ninth floor and found the door marked OLYMPICS SHIPPING, INC. and let himself in.

Mackensen was seated behind a large executive desk in the main suite, waiting. He was turned away from the room, sitting with his crossed legs propped on the sill of the window. The room was dark except for the light that shone through from the receptionist's foyer. Mackensen was staring out the window at the sea of buildings, and probably had been for some time, thought Gunther. He noticed Mackensen was wearing a coat, still wet. Mackensen was older than Gunther, slimmer, a bit shorter, but a man who carried himself well, like an elder statesman. Some said he resembled Attlee. His clothes always fit him properly and handsomely. It was an envious distinction to Gunther because, while Gunther's legs were not quite short, they were muscular, though hardly agile, and bulged slightly at the calf. Generally, the cut of his clothes hung on him awkwardly, Gunther being one of those creatures on whom tailors thrive: without alteration his between-size shirts and coats hung too long at the sleeve cuff, and his pants, straight off the rack, would drop in curious breaks over the tops of his shoes. Mackensen was almost aristocratic in look and manner, while Gunther, slightly pudgy, with a thick neck and a broad face (even broader when he wore his glasses), more resembled an aging athlete whose prowess had faded proportionately with the years. But despite his appearance, Gunther was a man, not unlike Mackensen, who knew what he was about. He lived by his instincts and played at a game that only the careful and untrusting survive.

"Have you ever noticed, Alec, that no matter how hard or long it rains, this city never seems to come clean? Probably an Indian damnation as retribution for Minuit's bargain. I think of it whenever I come here."

Mackensen had not moved. Not one to stand on formality, he acknowledged Gunther's presence neutrally, rhetorically. It was not meant that Gunther should answer. His elbows rested lightly on the chair's arms and his interlaced fingers supported his chin. Like Gunther, he had no distinguishing physical features except that he was short and sometimes wore a hat. Years ago he had sported a crew cut.

"How long has it been, Alec? Fifteen, sixteen, eighteen months?" There was a brilliant burst of lightning that illuminated the office for an instant. Gunther flinched.

"Closer to eighteen, I suspect."

"Debriefing, as I recall."

"Yes."

Mackensen's feet dropped with a thud and he turned to face Gunther. The lightning's thunder reached the building and broke with a long rumble, like far-away artillery. "Nasty weather. It's going to be a tiring drive," he said, nodding toward the window. "Sit down, Alec." Mackensen switched on a small table lamp that was adorned with a frilly shade. "We'll be driving to New Jersey tonight. Would you like to take the wheel?"

"I haven't driven for quite some time," Gunther said. "I haven't need for a car here."

"You don't own one?"

"No." Gunther glanced out the window. The rain was coming harder. "What kind is it? Automatic?"

Mackensen made a face. "No. Volvo . . . the new one. All right?"

"Yes, I'd like that."

"Good." They were facing each other over the large desk, Mackensen seated behind it, and Gunther in a high-backed bentwood chair opposite. Mackensen looked pale from the light on the desk, and Gunther supposed that he didn't get outside often. The man's hands revealed him to be an indoorsman, for he wore three rings and his fingernails were clean and groomed. A cardplayer's hands. Gunther remembered Mackensen was quite fond of bridge.

"Burdict told you about Phillips?"

"Yes, that he is dead."

"Were you friends?"

"I haven't seen him in fifteen years."

Mackensen glanced at the desk. He looked bored. "Were you friends?" he repeated.

"I didn't—not close friends, no," Gunther said. "I knew him."

"But he called you."

"Yes."

"Why?"

"I was his control once," Gunther said uncomfortably. "He didn't get satisfaction from his call to Central . . . I don't know why he called me."

Mackensen nodded. "When did he call?"

"About two weeks ago."

"And you haven't discussed it with anyone?"

"What do you mean, discussed?"

"Specifics. Johnson?"

"Johnson doesn't have the clearance to relay anything concerning the Jupiter operation."

Mackensen made a church steeple with the thumbs of his interlaced fingers and touched it to his chin. "I see. So you contacted Burdict?"

"Yes."

"Why Burdict?"

This was not at all what Gunther had expected. He wondered what was in New Jersey, why Mackensen was grilling him this way. "Burdict is still in operations. I—I don't know anyone here that could relay the information to the covert staff"—Gunther breathed deeply, exhaled—"since I'm not on that staff myself, presently."

Mackensen nodded.

"Why are we doing this," Gunther finally said.

"This?"

"This game . . . this probing."

"There may be something for you, Alec," Mackensen said with a trace of a smile. "Because of Phillips. Special Ops . . . fieldwork of a different sort than you're used to. But I haven't made up my mind. Frankly, you haven't many friends left on the top floor. A lot of people are high on having you put out altogether. Because of Berlin." He studied Gunther a moment. "You can see how they might react to putting you back in?" He waited for Gunther's response by unbuttoning the middle buttons of his raincoat, exposing his tie below the knot.

"Yes," Gunther said to fill the pause.

"The trouble is, you see, Alec, that you may be the only one who can take on this task."

"Me? You mean me, personally?"

"They've left it to my judgment."

Gunther remembered the last person who had said that. It was Ernst Landser in Bonn. They were standing in the shadow of the Münster cathedral in a park and Ernst's wife was with him. She thought he was an aide to a member of the Bundestag lower house.

"It isn't at all that I don't know you," Mackensen continued. "I've never for one minute had doubts about you, even when they had you over there." He made a nodding gesture toward the door. "But you have been away from us for some time, and now things have changed."

"So I've read," Gunther acknowledged.

"And what do you think about what you've read?" Mackensen asked conversationally.

Gunther took it to be a sore spot. No need to inflame it. Besides, he *had* been away for some time. "I guess it sells newspapers," Gunther said.

"I should say so," Mackensen said, in a confiding aside. "How do you find this—this work you're into? Satisfying?"

Gunther shrugged. "I haven't complained."

"You don't feel abandoned here, I suppose?" There was another bolt of lightning, closer than the last. The lamp flickered slightly. The boom of thunder sounded as if it must have been directly outside the building.

"Not particularly. It gives me quite a bit of leisure time. I've been reading."

Mackensen laughed. It was the short cackling sort of giggle reserved to men who aren't accustomed to it, who aren't often amused. "Ha! Reading, is it? Ha! You don't seem the bookworm type."

"I try to keep it light." Gunther smiled because Mackensen was smiling.

"And what do you say to coming back to work for me?"

"I'm available."

Mackensen swiveled his chair so that he faced the wall between Gunther and the window. He took up his chin-on-knuckles pose. "I'm a bit concerned about putting you back in the field after all this time. I was wondering if you were tired, burned out." He glanced out the window. The rain was slackening. He didn't seem concerned about the question.

The light of the lamp was at Mackensen's back, casting a shadow across his face. Gunther couldn't make out any expression.

"Do I look tired?" Gunther said, and knew immediately it was the wrong reply. "No, I'm fine. Really."

"But are you still any good?"

"I doubt if I'd be of much use in Germany these days . . ."

Mackensen glanced his way, then looked back at the window.

"Probably not Paris or London Station either," Gunther continued. "I seem to have limited mobility lately. Apparently, I'm marvelous with figures."

"It's your own doing, Alec," Mackensen replied unkindly. "You've no one to blame but yourself for your predicament."

Gunther said nothing. He assumed Mackensen was speaking of Berlin.

"How is your Spanish?"

"Passable," Gunther said. He knew it was very good. Two years as chief of station at Cadiz hadn't all been for nothing. "Probably better," he added.

"You know the Latins still?"

"Some of the Centrals—Nicaragua, Honduras, Guatemala, the Zone. Peru and Bolivia in the south. And Cuba, of course. But it's been a while. Fifteen years." Gunther pushed his glasses back on his nose and crossed his legs. "Is it the Latins, then?"

Mackensen waved his hand, indicating he wasn't ready to answer any questions just yet.

"Do you know Peter Rockwell?"

Gunther said he didn't.

"Peter is an assistant of mine. Came from NSA."

Gunther nodded. "One of the technological breed, is he?"

"He's anxious to meet you. He worked with Miller Beadle for a time . . . in crypto, as I recall. You remember Miller?"

Miller Beadle was a colorless, unimaginative relic from the OSS days who had an undeniable facility with codes. Several years ago he had gotten himself transferred to a covert operation that Gunther was handling in Hamburg. The man was simply an incompetent in the field. Gunther managed to have him transferred back to his own realm in NSA before Beadle could get himself, or worse, someone else, killed. Beadle always spoke of the time he had worked with the great Alec Gunther in the Clandestine Service before his greatness had come crashing down around him in the Berlin fiasco.

"Yes, I remember Miller," Gunther said. "Foolish little man who talks too much."

"Yes, yes," Mackensen said with a shortness that marked his irascibility. "Of course, Beadle is not one of us." A reference to the quality of the men, as a whole, in Special Ops, Gunther thought. It must be quite a department, but, then, Mackensen was quite an operator. Gunther was familiar with his impressive record. Mackensen had been solely responsible for turning more than a dozen Communist satellite deputy heads of state into double agents in the late forties, including Marshal Nicolae Wladyslaw in Bulgaria. He'd earned his promotions as much as anyone earns a promotion in the business, Gunther supposed. He thought about Burdict. Everyone was moving up. Everyone but Gunther.

"Have you heard from Judith?" It was an abrupt change of subject, to a topic Gunther had put back in the far reaches of his mind. He didn't like dredging up the painful memory of his wife.

Former wife.

"No," Gunther said.

"Not since you returned?"

"Not since then." Gunther sighed heavily. "She's moved," he added, and was sorry he remembered it.

"Oh," Mackensen said with a nod, as if he hadn't known. "So you don't correspond?"

"It isn't polite to write to your ex-wife," Gunther said, not caring if he sounded angry. "Besides, I don't even know where she lives." Gunther had seen her, the last time, in an attorney's office somewhere on Lexington Avenue. Her attorney. The divorce was final, but needed signing. It was only an accident that she'd come in the same day. She was immaculate as always, with gloves and some sort of large-brimmed hat, and beautiful as ever. They were courteous and both were embarrassed and Gunther had acted stupidly by asking her to lunch. She had declined gracefully and Gunther had felt like a fool. Some months later, the attorney had sent Gunther a note that Judith was **doing** very well, now, selling real estate, he said. He was a cruel bastard, the attorney.

"Never had any children, did you, Alec?"

He made it sound like it was his fault.

"No."

"Are you depressed at all? I mean, what with Judith gone and you out of the field and"—Mackensen couldn't find the words immediately—"this job."

"It's been more than a year. No, I'm not depressed or despondent, I've not executed a will and I sleep soundly, nights, thank you. I've always been fairly adaptable." Gunther sat stiffly upright in his chair. He was getting edgy and irritated with this whole line of Mackensen's. If he had something, Gunther wanted to get to it, otherwise he'd like to go home and change his socks.

"You needn't be touchy. I'm wondering about your frame of mind."

"My frame of mind is just dandy. Look, what is this?" Gunther asked hotly. "What are you getting at?"

"I'm considering you for something. Something unusual." Gunther wondered what in Special Ops wasn't unusual. "I'd like to get to it, then."

"Marty tells me you're moody."

"For Chrissake!"

Mackensen looked up with a frown, then swiveled around to face the window. The rain had stopped, but the sky was black. There weren't any stars.

"Marty is concerned. He says you are moody." Mackensen's seat squeaked as he swiveled back to face the desk. "Why?"

"Anybody is moody to Marty who won't swap tales of the good old days when we fought the good fight against the pinkos and college professors. We're different sorts, Marty and I."

"He tells me you drink too much."

"We all drink too much."

"He mentioned something about a nasty fall . . . subway, he said." Gunther felt Mackensen's eyes on him. "Carelessness, was it?"

"I hadn't had a drink yet," Gunther said sourly. He refused to look at Mackensen. "Obviously, I'm steadier with a drink."

"A bit of a bore sometimes—this job of yours, I mean?"

"Sometimes." Gunther was staring at the floor between his feet.

"Perhaps I can arrange for you to leave it—go back to something more demanding. I take it you'd be interested."

Gunther shrugged without looking up.

"You haven't anyone to miss you if you decided to leave for several days, have you, Alec?"

"There's the Gibralter Service Company."

"Never mind that. Any girl friends, pets . . ."

"No one regular."

"I see."

Gunther wondered if he did.

Mackensen nodded and glanced around the room as if noticing it for the first time. When he'd resettled his gaze on Gunther, he looked like a different person. "I want to use you, Alec. You're stubborn and mean and you don't give up. There is something to be done and done quickly. It has to do with the Latins . . . and, well, Harry Phillips." He buttoned two buttons on the front of his coat. "I'm up against something. You're the man who can do the job."

Gunther tried to follow, but Mackensen wasn't laying it out plainly. "What do you mean?" he asked.

"I'll explain when we get to New Jersey. But this is going to be your nut, Alec. After tonight you are to contact no one but me or Peter Rockwell, who's waiting for us. You've always preferred the lone-wolf role, so here it is. I'm going against almost everyone in Special Ops on this, Alec. Like I said, you're not too popular, but you have special qualifications that make you the obvious choice."

"Obvious to everyone but me. What does it have to do with—"

"Cuba. It has to do with Cuba," Mackensen said. "The Bay of Pigs."

4

Know yourself and your enemies and you will win a hundred battles.

Operation Jupiter is what they had called it officially. Gunther remembered it because no one forgets the failures, least of all a man who has two marked against his name.

Driving north on the Palisades Interstate Parkway with the smell of the country freshly revitalized by the rainstorm had a liberating effect on Gunther's senses. The clouds had passed, leaving behind a sea of stars and a coolness that was irresistible.

Of course (was it really sixteen years ago?) the island resort at Useppa, on Florida's west coast, had a different climate in November. And the training base at Fort Gulick in the Panama Canal Zone was hot and sticky, and the bugs ate you alive at Base Trax, the secret Guatemalan camp in the Sierra Madre Mountains. It was all coming back now, jelling in Gunther's mind. He could remember faces and put names to some of them. Merchants and field workers, bankers and bakers, they all believed solidly in what they were preparing to do in those long, sweaty months of training.

La Brigada.

The Brigade, they called themselves. The assault force. And every man had been as proud of his unit as if it were a rank in a holy crusade. To many it was.

28

It was almost too much to expect, but the early trainees passed on to those that came later an esprit de corps that infected even the American advisors. It was a game that combined all that America had stood for since San Juan Hill: it was storming the beaches at Normandy and crossing the Rhine River and throwing Hungarian wine bottles filled with gasoline at Russian tanks and beating back the Communists to the 38th parallel, all in one exercise.

Gunther remembered landing on the beach with them, strictly against orders. Absolutely no participation by United States personnel. Gunther was in a position to interpret it in a way that pleased him; he wasn't with the United States, he was with the CIA.

Gunther found the house with no help from Mackensen. Just off a lightly traveled rural road, it was a two-story white frame on half an acre. No country estate, the house was nestled neatly in the trees with a gravel drive that ended in a garage. Gunther pulled up short of a budding rose bush and switched off the engine.

"Nice place," Gunther said. "Rustic."

"Belongs to a writer who's traveling in Kenya at the moment. Picture-taking safari." Mackensen got out and slammed the door with more force than necessary. "The place used to be a general store." He started toward a side porch. "I'll get Peter to let us in."

The house inside was a big one with lots of room and high ceilings. The kitchen, down a short hall from the garage entrance, was country-style and large. Copper-bottomed pans and pots hung from pegs on a brick wall, and the wide rectangular table was heavy enough to serve as a cutting board and bore the scars to prove it. Around the corner from the kitchen was a separate dining room with a table that could comfortably seat ten. Gunther wandered around the place until he found the living room, spacious and informally furnished. To one side of an unpretentious fireplace and mantel was a large built-in bookshelf that started about cabinet level and went to the ceiling. Whoever lived here was unmoved by the plastic and vinyl inroads of progressive furniture design. The sofa and matching chair were covered in a plain tan velvet. There was also a high-backed wing chair and a battered black leather lounge chair with a square ottoman. By their arrangement, Gunther gathered there would be four people involved in that night's conference. No more than five. The floor was polished hardwood, covered in the living room by a massive multicolored Persian rug.

When Mackensen entered, Gunther was inspecting the third row of books in the bookshelf.

"What will you have to drink, Alec?"

"Coffee will be fine. Light, no sugar."

Mackensen nodded. "Peter will be down shortly. We'll fill you in; then, we have a special interviewee. After you and Peter and I have our little briefing, the project is all yours. You call the shots, handle it any way you like. That's the way I want it. Our guest doesn't know me or Peter, but he knows you. I want him to know you are the boss from the beginning. All right?"

Gunther recognized that Mackensen was not asking anything, just setting the record straight.

"Fine. Who's the guest?"

"A scab." Mackensen wrinkled his nose with distaste. "Simon Pelado. I think that's how you knew him. He has several other names: Simon Cueto, Paca Pelao, and as a Saudi he was Nuri Kowal, and as a Turk, Gabi Kalkavan. Lately he's been calling himself Maximilian Koenig, of German-English-Spanish extraction. But he has an interesting story to tell." Mackensen checked his watch. "That's what this is all about."

Gunther remembered Pelado, or whatever he was calling himself these days. An Argentine from the slums of Buenos Aires originally. Coming from a fatherless family that kept growing after his dock-working father was bludgeoned to death during a bar fight, he'd had a keen street sense. When he was fourteen, he jumped a freighter bound for Lisbon and eventually made his way into the French Foreign Legion where he learned French and German. By the mid 1950s he was a well-trained mercenary with experience in Africa and the Mideast. When he learned things were boiling back in Argentina, he returned, but joined the wrong side, and, like many others, wound up in Cuba. He'd earned a rank of captain in Batista's army when Castro's force was defeating it at every turn. He barely escaped with his life from an ambush at El Hombrito and didn't stop running until he got off the fishing boat in the Florida

Keys. Three years later, when he heard of the plan to take Cuba away from Castro, Pelado saw an opportunity and grabbed it. To Gunther, Simon Pelado had then been only one of a thousand expatriated Cubans fighting for something he believed in. Gunther had had no way to know Pelado was different than the rest.

"So," Gunther sighed. "Little Simon returns."

"He wants to make a deal, Alec. He's hot. Half a dozen countries would like his head. He's run out of places to go. He's blown every job he's had in the last five years. Personally, I don't trust him."

"Things are tough all over," Gunther said, not intending to be funny. "What's the deal?"

"Let's wait for Peter."

The book was titled *Restless*. It was one that caught Gunther's eye on the shelf and he thumbed through it while Mackensen went to get the coffee. Some day, Peter Rockwell would show up. Gunther guessed he was upstairs with their guest. Probably there was a babysitter, someone large and persuasive to hold Simon Pelado's hand while the three of them discussed this mysterious deal.

On the title page was a dedication written in a scrawl with a felt-tipped pen. "To the Closters: In warm memory of those passionate nights in Casablanca—all very bestest—y'r fellow laborer in the salt mines—Evans Mallory." The name on the jacket was Evans Mallory. Gunther wondered if these writers were really sane people. Mackensen appeared at the door with a tray of coffee cups and a full pot.

"Peter will be down in a minute. Might as well have a seat."

Gunther picked the leather lounge chair. If it was going to be a long night, might as well be comfortable.

Mackensen set the tray on the low trestle table centered in the middle of the chairs and sofa. There were four cups, plain white with small, curved handles. They were the kind some men have difficulty in deciding how to hold.

"Is there a babysitter?" Gunther asked.

"Yes." Mackensen poured three cups of coffee. "Michael something. Very quiet." He raised his eyebrows as he set the pot down. "Very muscular."

"What about the fellow that owns this place? The writer."

"What about him?"

"What's his connection? I mean, how did you come to use the house?"

"Friend of a friend," Mackensen said.

"Ever use it before?"

Mackensen shrugged diffidently. "Perhaps once."

It was like pulling teeth. "Is Peter coming?"

Mackensen finished fixing the coffee. "Yes. I'll get him. It's time we got started."

"Are you enjoying your role as paymaster, Alec?" Peter Rockwell asked. They were all seated around the trestle table, Rockwell to Gunther's right, in the corner of the sofa, and Mackensen to the left, in the wing chair. Between them, and opposite Gunther, was the empty armchair that matched the velvet sofa. Pelado's spot, when he came, Gunther thought. "Do you miss it?" Rockwell was saying. "The field, I mean. I would think so, if it were me."

Peter Rockwell was a graceless string bean of a man with long slender fingers. He was younger than both Gunther and Mackensen and had had no time as an agent in the field. His knowledge of clandestine fieldwork was of a vicarious nature, while Gunther's was by experience. There was something unpleasant about working for a man who hadn't been in the trenches, so to speak, Gunther thought. He'd heard Rockwell was a Princeton man, like himself; but, unlike himself, he was the nephew of a high-powered Senator. Obviously, it made a difference.

"It's been very restful," Gunther replied. He took the coffee cup from the table and sipped at it. He tasted the sugar first thing. It suddenly reminded him of Judith, except she used Saccharin.

"Are you eager to come back to work for us?" Rockwell had an enviable voice, deep and rich; probably he'd been a great college orator, Gunther thought. Why did he insist on referring to Special Ops as "us," as if he had some integral part to play?

"Mackensen tells me there is a problem. Something I may be able to help with."

Rockwell had restless fingers; he kept tapping them on the rim of his saucer like a man who'd recently given up smoking. "Mr. Mackensen thinks you are best suited to work with us on this project."

"Help," Gunther thought. He could have said "help us." He should have.

"Frankly, Alec, I have my doubts. You've been away, you know." He sipped his coffee.

Mackensen had said he wasn't popular. "Yes, I know," Gunther said coolly. "But it's a little like bicycling, if you know what I mean. Once you're past the training-wheel phase, you never forget. Experience is the thing, you know."

Rockwell's face turned an angry crimson. For a moment Gunther thought he would spit up Mackensen's syrupy coffee.

"Look, Gunther, I'm not here to take any crap from you. Do you hear me? You're no special case to me. Putting you on this assignment isn't a favor to *me*. I know about your record, and don't think I haven't been over it very carefully." Even when aroused to anger, Rockwell's expressions were boyish, Gunther thought. It was interesting to observe men under different conditions of stress. Plainly, Rockwell felt intimidated by Gunther, a subordinate. Even Gunther felt silly. Where did they get such men?

"Did you read everything in my records?" Gunther asked casually.

"Of course I did."

"Then you must have noted that I work best when I work solo." Gunther set his coffee to the side. "And frankly, Peter," he said, trying to catch the resonant qualities of Rockwell's voice, "I have my doubts about working with you on this project. You bother me."

Rockwell's eyes bulged wide. He'd never been talked to like this. "Mr. Mackensen!"

"Why *is* Peter here?" Gunther said.

"All right, gentlemen, all right. That is enough. Quite enough," Mackensen said, but he was looking at Gunther. "I had expected something like this to happen, and I want it finished before Pelado gets here." He turned to stare at Rockwell. Rockwell responded to authority, Mackensen was his superior, after all. "Peter, let me tell you something about Alec Gunther that you didn't read in the file. He is a first-rate agent. One of the best ever turned out by this government." Gunther was embarrassingly self-conscious; he wondered if he should leave the room. Mackensen wasn't known for his laudatory style.

"The Berlin affair—we're rather prone to call them that, aren't we? Disasters, I mean. When we have a failure in the field, we call them affairs." Mackensen was watching Rockwell intently, Gunther noticed. Even as he talked, he watched for signs that his words were being acknowledged; the movement of the eyes, the placement of the hands, expressions. It was all much like a school teacher, Gunther thought.

"Berlin has been Gunther's black mark, you see, Peter. He was a controller running more than a score of agents. Some Americans, of course, but mostly doubles and scabs. It's a very risky business. One of his people got in trouble on the East side and had to be gotten out quickly. Gunther is not untypical of our responsible agents, especially since he was a controller. A man gets emotionally attached to his work—pride I suppose—but attached, nonetheless. It's an occupational hazard to this clandestine work. Coupled with the dangers and hardships they willingly put up with, agents like Gunther drive themselves to support extreme causes and sometimes try to reach further than their grasp." Mackensen made a sweeping gesture with his hand. Gunther had the strange feeling Mackensen was talking about himself. "In that regard—the job—takes on a romantic quality. Duty and country, that type of thing.

"Anyway, back to Berlin. Gunther decided to go in himself rather than send someone else. Looking back, it likely wasn't the prudent thing to do. Looking back, it usually isn't. Gunther was caught, as you know. The whole operation went sour in a matter of months. There was the trial, the executions, the press coverage, all a nasty and costly blow for us. After his release Gunther was treated rather shabbily, I think. He's done excellent work for our side, all things considered, and shunting him off to a drudge job paying checks has not been fair to this considerable ability. The point I'm trying to make, Peter, is that our Alec Gunther is wasting away in that city." He nodded in the general direction of New York. "We now have an opportunity to use him once again. He deserves that, I believe. If nothing else, Alec deserves your respect. He's a professional. You're an administrator. I'd advise you to listen to him. I *expect* you to listen. Do we understand one another?''

Rockwell had cowered into the deep recesses of the sofa's corner, hammered there by Mackensen's depreciating pronouncement. It is almost always interesting to see a man go limp with fearful embarrassment and lose his composure, as the accused on trial are wont to do. It is a maudlin preoccupation reserved to the likes of spectators and juries, accompanied by the urge, but not the will, to look away from the subject under scrutiny. Gunther was glad for Rockwell that no one else was present.

"Yes, sir," Rockwell said. His voice had lost its fullness.

Now Mackensen turned to Gunther. "Alec, sometimes you can be an uncompromising bastard. There is a place for your belligerent manner, but it isn't now. Taking cheap shots at the uninitiated—it's disgusting." Mackensen was sizing him with a hard stare. There was no mistaking who the boss was here. "You've had your little digs in. Now let's get to business. And for your information, Alec, Peter is here because he's developed into a crack interrogator. He's suspicious of what people tell him and, you may have noticed, a bit cynical. If you'd try, you might see that the two of you could work together. One complementing the other." Gunther doubted it. He was beginning to change his mind about feeling sorry for Rockwell.

"Peter has been assigned by me to look into this Simon Pelado thing. But Pelado is a sly little sneak, and it will take someone who knows him, knows his type, to decide if what he's peddling has any truth to it. If so—and Peter here thinks there just might be—then we are in a very uncomfortable position."

"We?" Gunther said.

"The agency." Mackensen produced a file folder from the table beside his chair that Gunther hadn't noticed. "Someone's hitting our people. Killing them, I mean. It's a one-man operation, by the looks of it, and he knows exactly what he's doing."

"Representing who?" Gunther said.

"No one," Mackensen replied quickly. "That is, it isn't the Russians or Chinese or any one of the several extremist groups, domestic, or otherwise. No, this is a loner." Mackensen seemed to be sure of that. "He has his own reasons, apparently. It's a personal vendetta against us and he's goddamn good. If not for Simon Pelado, we might not have discovered that the deaths were anything but accidents."

"You forgot about the piece," Rockwell interrupted. "Tell him about the knights."

Mackensen poured himself another cup of coffee, leaning awkwardly out of his chair to reach the pot. "Ah, yes, the knights," he said, nodding to himself. He almost smiled. "A chess piece, Alec. He leaves one with each of his victims. It's his calling card."

"Interesting twist," Gunther said. A nagging thought begging to wake inside him. This was all sounding too familiar.

The file was open on Mackensen's lap and he was looking into it. "José Fanzone two months ago. He was the first. He drowned in a boating accident in Sixmile Lake." Mackensen glanced up. "Louisiana. Near the Gulf. That was about ten days before Albert Peloquin suffocated in a fire at Big Spring, Texas. There have been five since then. Harry was the last. That was two weeks ago, more or less." He ran his hand over his head like he used to do when he wore a crew cut. "Seven deaths so far and there's no reason to expect it to stop anytime soon. We just don't know what he's after, or we didn't until Simon stumbled on the scene." Mackensen was watching him, as he had watched Rockwell a few minutes ago.

"I think I know where you're leading," Gunther said.

"Do you?"

"It's Vargas, isn't it?" Gunther needn't have asked. He knew now. "Ollie Vargas."

"Oliva Raul Vargas," Rockwell began, like a dull boy. "Forty-three years old, native Cuban—"

"Oh, shut up, Rockwell," Gunther said hotly. "I know exactly who Vargas is."

"That's what Simon says." Mackensen was still staring as if he weren't sure what Pelado had to do with it.

"The chess piece—do you know the significance of it?" Gunther asked.

"Something to do with his radio call sign during the invasion,"

Mackensen said. Mackensen had a curious way of pretending not to be sure of something when, in fact, he knew everything. It was a trait of Mackensen's that Gunther admired.

"Yes. I suppose you know I went ashore with him and his troops. At least the ones that made it to shore."

Mackensen nodded, so did Rockwell.

"The beaches were designated Red, Blue and Green. They also had call signs. Green beach was Clover. Blue beach was Starlight and Red beach—Vargas's beach—was Taskmaster. In the months of training before the invasion, I got to know him well." Gunther glanced over to Rockwell, then back to Mackensen. "We were friends. Anyway, the night before the invasion I gave him a good-luck piece. He was known by a lot of his people as *El Caballo,* The Horse. Since his code name was Taskmaster"—Gunther shrugged—"I gave him a black chess piece for good luck."

"A black knight," Rockwell corrected.

Gunther ignored him. "So," he sighed, watching Mackensen, "Vargas is after us. He's good, we trained him."

"You trained him," Rockwell said.

Gunther was getting very tired of hearing Rockwell's loud voice booming in the night. "So shoot me, Peter."

"Not that," Mackensen said. "I think you have an idea of what this project is all about. It's yours now. I think you know what we want done."

Gunther nodded grimly. "You want me to find Vargas."

"Yes," Mackensen said. "We want to find him." He closed the folder and placed it back on the table. "And stop him."

Gunther was still nodding his head. There would be only one way to stop Ollie Vargas if he'd already killed seven people. He'd set his own rules. Gunther sighed. "It's time to talk to Simon," he said. "We can't afford to waste time."

5

Except for the worst enemy criminals, the guerrilla disarms his prisoners, gives them a scolding and lets them go.

Simon Pelado was dressed in a ghastly cotton print shirt, which hung outside his light brown trousers. It was a brilliant yellow with large swirling orange flowers and no pockets. He was what most people envision a south-of-the-border Latin to be except that he was not fat, or even pudgy, and thus appeared taller than he actually was.

Rockwell greeted him first, but Pelado immediately recognized Gunther and went to him like an old friend. They shook hands, Pelado smiling a gold-toothed smile and forever licking his lips, and Gunther nodding pleasantly, as if he'd run into a distant relative at the airport after trying unsuccessfully to avoid contact. Mackensen and Rockwell stood about like a pair of expectant fathers.

"Señor Alex Sheldon, it is so good to see you again," Pelado said, pumping Gunther's arm. "It has been so many years. You are not so lean as you were in the *montañas* of Camp Trax, *sí?*"

By the subdued light in the room, Gunther saw only a portion of Pelado's facial features. Half the smile was illuminated, with the effect that his gold tooth sparkled, making all his teeth look gold. The Cheshire-cat image seemed to fit Pelado rather well, Gunther thought.

"It's Alec," Gunther said. "Alec, no *x* in it." The Argentine was still shaking his hand furiously. The man was nodding his head excessively, smiling all the while, his tongue darting out and wetting his lips as if he were thirsty. Gunther supposed it was fear. "Why don't we sit down, Simon." He motioned Pelado to the chair he was to take. "Over there." They all sat at once, as if on cue, which made it seem comical to Gunther, like the beginning of some absurd parlor game.

"These gentlemen tell me you have something interesting to say, Simon." It was difficult to concentrate on Pelado, with the idiotic shirt distracting him.

"Yes, señor Sheldon." The smile was fading now. "You are the boss here?" Pelado apparently had told his story several times. He regarded Rockwell, the interrogator, with fear, as if Peter might strike him, and Mackensen, the stranger, with suspicion. Only Gunther was a friend.

"Just call me Alec. Like you used to, Simon." Gunther was not about to correct this desperate little man on his old workname. Back in the fifties Gunther had been allowed to choose his own workname, something he would be comfortable with, they had told him. He had chosen Sheldon, after an uncle in Michigan. Computers selected them these days, favorite uncles notwithstanding.

"Yes, I am the boss," Gunther nodded, glancing at Rockwell. "Just like old times."

It seemed to revitalize Pelado's golden smile. "That is good, Alec." He leaned forward slightly, toward Gunther. "I have a new name now. Max. It is an abbreviation for Maximilian. Max Koenig." He was proud of it, like he would be proud of a new car. "Do you like it, señor Alec?"

Gunther gave a faint shrug. "You'll always be Simple Simon to me."

Pelado laughed, more to vent his nervousness than for any other reason. Rockwell simply looked wearily at the ceiling.

"That is good, Alec. Very funny." Pelado glanced to either side at Mackensen and Rockwell, like a prisoner looking at his guards. The smile returned. The tongue flicked at the corners of his mouth.

"Suppose you tell me about Vargas," Gunther said casually. He bent forward to pour himself another cup of coffee. "Would you like some coffee?"

"Yes, *gracias*," Pelado said eagerly. At least, Gunther thought, the cup would keep his hands busy. Simple Simon kept twitching them in his lap. Gunther watched as he plopped two, three, spoonfuls of sugar into the small cup. Mackensen should be pleased at that.

Gunther waited until Pelado was situated back in his chair, "Now, Simon, tell me about Vargas."

"What part, señor Alec?"

"Everything, Simon. I want you to tell me everything you know about him."

Pelado's little head bobbed affirmatively. As prelude to speech, a flash of tongue darted out from between his lips. Simon Pelado had played this role of informant before.

"I saw him last a few weeks ago. I was—"

"Twelve days," Rockwell snapped. "Let's just keep it accurate for the record."

Pelado nearly dropped his coffee cup. Rockwell's interruption was like an attack from the flank. "*Sí, perdone Usted!*" Simon turned to Gunther, like a frightened child. "It was twelve days ago, señor Alec. It is true."

Gunther nodded protectively. "And before that?"

"Señor?"

"When did you see him before the last time?"

"Before the last time?" Pelado scratched at his temple to help him think. "It was, I think, in Turkey, señor Alec." He scratched again at the magic temple. "Yes, it was in Turkey. Istanbul. Three years ago." This was something he hadn't been asked before. Pelado smiled like he expected a reward. Gunther didn't bother to look at Rockwell's expression. So much for the crack interrogator.

"Tell me about it, Simon."

"I was Gabi Kalkavan in Istanbul," he offered brightly.

"Good for you. Tell me about Vargas."

"It was an accident," Simple Simon began. "I was doing some work in . . . ah, in *kara borsa*. With cattle."

"In what?" Rockwell demanded.

"*Kara borsa* . . ." Pelado was at a loss for words.

"Black market," Mackensen said with a sigh. "Do let Alec continue, Peter."

Gunther smiled winsomely in Peter's direction.

"All right, Simon. You were trafficking in cattle in Istanbul. Where to? Syria?"

"*Sí*. There was a shortage of meat in Syria."

"Naturally you wanted to help them out." Pelado showed all his teeth this time. Gunther wasn't sure which was more disgusting, the smile, or the shirt. "I expect the price of beef went up in Istanbul."

"Sixty percent," Pelado answered greedily.

"So, you met Vargas by accident. What was he doing there?"

"Smuggling, of course. What else can you do there?"

"What was he into, Simon?"

Pelado's finger went to the temple again. "It was opium, I think, señor Alec. I heard he had a small poppy field under contract near Afyon. I also heard he was using the profits for some other purpose."

"And what was that?"

"Señor?"

"What was Vargas using the profits for?"

Simple Simon's shoulders rose and dropped in a long exaggerated gesture of ignorance. "I truly do not know, señor Alec. It is not wise to ask many questions in that country. One could wake up one morning and find he had no heartbeat by asking too many questions. Besides, señor Alec, I did not know you would be interested to know these things from three years ago."

Gunther remained silent for several seconds, watching Pelado, but thinking about Ollie Vargas trading in drugs. It didn't seem like him. Outside, there was an orchestra of crickets scratching a midnight lullaby. A quiet breeze entered the room, disturbing the flimsy, delicate curtains. Gunther suddenly realized he'd been in the city too long.

"What did you and Vargas talk about?" Gunther finally said.

"In Istanbul?"

"Yes, Simon, in Istanbul. When you saw him at the airport."

Pelado shook his head. "We spoke of nothing. I mean, señor

Alec, we did not speak. I was too afraid to approach him. Maybe you do not remember, but he was a crazy man when I saw him before that . . . at Bahía de Cochinos . . . at the invasion. I do not forget. He would have shot me, señor. He was a crazy man then. The militia were upon us with tanks and heavy guns and many thousands of men. I am not so crazy. It was *estúpido* to stay there and be killed. I went—with others, señor Alec, with others—I went to the shore and found a small boat. We pushed the boat out and saved ourselves. Vargas was on the shore, shooting at us with his *pistola*. He was a crazy man. That was the last time I saw him until I saw him in Istanbul. Maybe he was still crazy then? I did not want to know."

Gunther remembered the incident, too. If Vargas's aim had been steadier, he might have killed them all in the boat. Gunther had nearly turned his own weapon to the sea and the men in that boat.

"So the only time you saw Vargas since the invasion was once briefly in Istanbul and once twelve days ago. Is that correct?'

Pelado nodded patiently. "Yes, señor Alec."

"I take it you did speak to him the second time you saw him."

"Very long time, *sí*."

"Where was this meeting?" Gunther leaned back slightly in the leather chair. "Tell me all about it."

Pelado drained the coffee that remained in his cup as if it were going to be a long story and he needed strength. He moistened his lips once more and began. "It was twelve days ago," he said, glancing quickly at Rockwell. "I was in Puerto Rico—"

"Puerto Rico! What in God's name were you doing in Puerto Rico?"

Pelado looked hurt. "Vacation," he stammered defensively. "I always go to Puerto Rico on vacation, señor Alec. San Juan." He looked at Gunther as if everyone went there.

Gunther turned sharply to Rockwell. "When was the last killing?"

"What?"

"The last one? Harry Phillips. When was that? How long ago?"

Rockwell flushed. "Look here, Gunther, if you want to discuss restricted information, I suggest you wait until your friend here is tucked away somewhere out of earshot.''

"Don't give me that bloody crap," Gunther said hotly. "When was it? Ten days, did you say?"

"Yes, dammit. Now everybody knows." Rockwell stared menacingly at Pelado. "You can just keep your runny little mouth shut.'' There didn't seem to be anything Rockwell could do but try to frighten him. Pelado's coffee cup clattered in the saucer.

"Lay off him," Gunther demanded. "What was Vargas doing in San Juan two days before Harry was murdered in Arizona?" It was the first time Gunther had put a descriptive verb to the killings, and when he realized it he became angrier. "It sounds to me as though he's getting some kind of inside help. A man just can't move that fast.''

"That's your problem now, isn't it?" Rockwell said.

Gunther looked to Mackensen for help. "I wish I knew," Mackensen said weakly. "I don't."

"Shit!" Gunther sat silently for several moments, staring at the floor. When he looked up at Pelado, the little man was sitting rigidly straight in his seat, hands balled together in his lap, feet together. He wasn't smiling. Fear had constrained his face to a solemn expression. The stark light by his side made hollow shadows where his eyes should be.

"All right, Simon," Gunther began, somewhat subdued. "Tell me how you happened to meet Vargas while you were vacationing in Puerto Rico."

"I—I—" Pelado couldn't get words out. Even his tongue failed him.

"It's all right, Simon. I'm not angry with you." Gunther looked at Rockwell. "No one is angry with you. Calm down."

Pelado took a deep breath. His darting tongue did its work and in a moment his lips glistened. "Vargas has killed someone?"

"It isn't your worry."

"Señor Alec, I didn't know he killed anyone when I was—" He stopped to look at his hands. "What if he learns I have talked to you?" Pelado, without looking up, gestured at Rockwell. "And him?"

"He won't, Simon."

"But señor Vargas is a very unusual man. He can do things other men cannot. He is crazy, but he is also smart, señor Alec." Pelado was staring pleadingly at Gunther now.

"He isn't crazy, Simon."

"But he is a very ferocious man, I think," Pelado said. "I think it is why he hunts these men. These men who were with us at the invasion. The Americans. Like you, señor Alec. I did not know he was going to kill them. He did not tell me that, I swear."

"What happened at San Juan?"

"Do you think no harm will come to me, señor?"

Gunther breathed a low, uncomfortable sigh. "No, I don't think you are in any danger. Now, tell me about San Juan. Did Vargas come to you?"

"Yes." Pelado seemed reassured. "He came to my room at the Cerromer Beach Hotel."

Gunther nodded approvingly. "Cerromer? Expensive. You must have done well selling cows to the Syrians."

"And other things besides," Rockwell interjected.

Pelado shrugged. "I am a capitalist."

"Opportunist is more the word," Rockwell said. Not one to mask his feelings, that one, Gunther thought. How did Mackensen stand him?

"All right, Vargas came to your room. Then what?"

"I was frightened, señor Alec. From the time on the beach, I was fright—"

"Yes, yes. You told me that. What did he want?"

"He wanted to talk. He was very friendly. He told me he had heard I was in San Juan and came to see me."

"Where was he before?"

"I was too afraid to ask. He is a very big man, you know. Brown, not black like many of his people are."

Gunther made a wave of his hand. "I know. Go on."

"Well, I was very upset for a while. I didn't know what he wanted. He just talked about things I had done. He knew all about me." Here Pelado lowered his voice slightly, as if he were afraid to admit it. "I have had some hard times these last few years. But Vargas knew all about that. He just talked and talked about the things I had been doing, like he was me. He knew everything about me. It was scary, señor Alec. But he was very friendly, like I said. We drank rum together. He was very jovial. We talked about the places I had been and some people I sometimes worked with. He knew them too, I think. Then we talked about the invasion, like it was a long time ago. I was afraid he would remember about the boat, but he never said anything about it. We talked a long time about the invasion. He asked me if I remember this person and that person and if I ever heard from them again. Sometimes I did, sometimes not. He was most interested in the Americans. He even asked about you."

Gunther's glance touched Mackensen. "And what did you say?"

"I said I had not seen you since the attack at Playa Larga." Pelado frowned, wetting the corners of his small mouth. "He said something curious then. He said you were working for the government as a clerk, because he saw you. He said you had some troubles and that it was too bad. He also said your name was not Sheldon."

Gunther laughed. He tried not to, but it couldn't be helped. Vargas, the poor Cuban black boy, was making him and the intelligence service he worked for look like fools. No one had a shred of data on Vargas or knew where he was or where he'd been since the fiasco at the Bay of Pigs sixteen years ago. Such a man is unusual, Gunther thought, and he couldn't help but feel a new respect for his former ally.

"Did he say anything else?"

"Sí, señor Alec. He told me to tell you hello for him when we met." Pelado raised his hands, palms up, in a gesture of surprise. "I did not ever expect to see you."

Gunther smiled. "But now you have."

"Sí."

"Isn't it amazing?" Alec Gunther shook his head almost imperceptibly and gave a short sigh. Outside, the crickets were in full symphony. The summer breeze from the windows was rich with the smell of the country.

6

Terrorism is an important revolutionary means. To repay the cruelty of a key individual in the oppressor hierarchy is justifiable. But it must never be used to eliminate unimportant individuals whose deaths would accomplish nothing. The use of terrorism comes down to a calculated risk.

The interrogation continued until Gunther felt a need to take a break. Pelado and Rockwell were both alert, taking the time to roam the confines of the room and surreptitiously eyeing one another like prizefighters before the first bout; Mackensen remained seated, glancing sleepily through his file. Michael was called and instructed to brew more coffee. Everyone visited the first-floor rest room.

Gunther took time to reexamine the books in the recessed shelves, righting one that had been inserted upside down. He thumbed through one large volume of photographs of works by Michelangelo and was struck by the amazing likeness that Mackensen shared with Lorenzo de' Medici's marble facsimile in the chapel in Florence. Mostly, Gunther supposed, he was reminded of Mackensen in the way The Magnificent was posed with an index finger resting crookedly against his upper lip as if he were contemplating someone's execution. That was Mackensen for you, always thinking. Somewhere else, further back in the book, he thought he saw the likeness of Judith, but he didn't linger on the page.

"All right now, Simon, I want you to tell me what you remember about specific individuals Vargas discussed when he was in your hotel room."

Everyone had taken seats again, each in his proper place and each with a full coffee cup, thanks to Michael. But Michael was no cook, Gunther suddenly realized, and the proof of that was in his cup. No amount of Mackensen's sugar could hide it, though everyone except Gunther tried.

"I cannot remember them all, señor Alec. He came in the afternoon . . . to my room. We talked almost all night."

"Not everyone, Simon. The Americans. Just the Americans."

Pelado nodded agreeably. "I will try."

Gunther glanced at Mackensen, who was looking over the open fire. "Check Phillips. What was his workname?"

"Must you let Pelado in on everything?" It was Rockwell again. He was scrupulously concerned that this little Argentine might some day tell the Russians or the Chinese or God knows who that Harry Phillips, former agent, now deceased, once was involved with the abortive Cuban invasion of sixteen years ago. Prime data, that.

"He's permanently retired now, Peter. There's no harm in it," Gunther said.

Rockwell persisted. "But it is restricted information."

"Look, Peter," Gunther said, trying to be pleasant. "Unless his family is suddenly whisked away in the dead of night by a Communist squad of terrorists from their home in Mesa, Arizona, I really don't thing anyone will be tortured behind the iron curtain for information about Harry Phillips."

"This is hardly a subject to be flippant about."

"Drink your coffee like a good lad and don't interrupt me again," Gunther said at the end of his patience. "Otherwise I'll call for Michael and have him put you to bed." Gunther turned to Mackensen, who looked to be embarrassed that he had brought Rockwell along. "Workname?"

"Reeves," Mackensen said. "Phil Reeves."

"All right, Simon. Do you remember talking about a man called Reeves?"

Pelado rubbed his hands, palms together. He was less nervous now than before. He seemed to sense that Rockwell was not a threat to him as long as Gunther was still his friend, and he obviously wanted to maintain that friendship. As long as Gunther was looking at him, he was smiling. He smiled now, wetting his lips first.

"Yes, we talked about señor Reeves, but I was not much help. The last time I saw him was in Puerto Cabezas."

"When was that?"

"Two days before we boarded ship for the invasion. The Nicaraguan port was known also by another name. I forgot, señor."

"Trampoline," Gunther said.

"*Sí*, that was it," Pelado offered brightly. "Trampoline. There were so many names of code. It is hard to remember."

"Do you remember the code name of your invasion force? The one that landed at Playa Larga?"

"I will always remember that name, señor Alec." Simon's smile faltered for an instant. "It was called Taskmaster."

"What were the others called, do you recall?"

"One was Clover. I forget the other."

"Starlight."

"*Sí*," Pelado nodded. "Starlight, Taskmaster and Clover. I remember now. It is an *ironía* too, señor Alec. These names, they were not so lucky."

"What did Vargas say about Reeves?"

"Not very much," Pelado said with a shrug. "He asked me what I thought about him and if I ever saw him again. I said no."

"Did he ever say why he was interested?"

"He told me he might visit the United States soon. He said he would like to see some of the Americans that he knew from the days in Guatemala when we were training." Pelado sighed as if he wished he could be of more help. "That's all he said, señor Alec."

"He never indicated where in the United States he might go?"

Pelado shook his head apologetically.

"Never mentioned Arizona?"

"No."

"Louisiana or Texas?"

"I am sorry, señor."

Gunther turned to Mackensen. "More worknames."

Rockwell started to object, but decided against it.

"Señor, these names, I do not think I can help very much with these names. I remember them, *sí*, but señor Vargas always asked

the same questions about them—if I ever saw them since Cuba—
and always I answered the same. I have never met any of them since
that time.''

Gunther leaned back tiredly into the leather chair. He waved off
Mackensen and his file and sat staring at Pelado, polishing his
glasses with a napkin from the trestle table. Finally he said, ''Was
Vargas angry that you hadn't met up with any of us?''

''No, señor. He was never angry. He was always very friendly
toward me. He never mentioned the boat.''

''Why was he in San Juan?''

''I do not know. He did not say and I did not ask him.''

''But you always go to San Juan, right? For vacation?''

''Every year since 1965. It is very pleasant there. I was doing
very well in those years.''

''And Vargas knew about you, all about you. So he must have
known you would be there this time of year.'' Gunther wasn't looking for a reply. Something about Pelado interested Vargas and it
wasn't information. So, what was it? ''Simon, you say you haven't
been doing well these last few years?''

''I am very healthy, señor Alec.''

''I'm talking about money.''

''Oh, sí, It has been very slow for me.''

''How do you afford to keep going to San Juan if you're not doing
so well financially?''

''That is from my investments, señor,'' Pelado said, revitalizing
his golden smile. ''I have certain investments. Reserve, I think it is
called. It is the active account that suffers. My business is mostly in
trade—like the *kara borsa*—and business is slow for me. I have had
difficulty finding a patron these years.''

''What kind of investments?''

Pelado smiled even more graciously. ''I do not discuss them, señor Alec. I am sorry.''

''You are mistaken.'' Gunther, for the first time, was angry with
Pelado and he meant for it to show; his eyes bore into Simon's.
''You will discuss it with me,'' he said ''Right now.''

''But, señor—''

''Now, Pelado, goddammit! Right now! If you think Vargas is a
mean bastard, wait until I'm through with you. I can be crazy too.''

Pelado was suddenly stunned. And from the look on his face, so was Rockwell.

"What about these investments?" Gunther demanded.

"They are nothing, señor . . . an account . . ."

"Where?"

Pelado jumped.

"Where, I said!"

"Zurich . . . on Bahnhofstrasse," the little Argentine answered fearfully. "Union Bank . . ."

"Private numbered, I suppose."

"*Sí.*"

Gunther leaned forward. "Why would you need a Swiss account like that, Simon?"

Pelado shrugged gracelessly. "Business investments. It is—"

"Oh, shit!"

"But it is true, señor Alec."

"How much? I want it exactly, Simon."

"Five hundred seventy thousand francs, Swiss," he said vapidly.

"Jesus!" Rockwell was shocked. "That's . . . that's over two hundred and twenty thousand dollars! Where'd a little runty twirp like you get that kind of money?"

"Yes, Simon, where?" Gunther pressed. "It wasn't selling cows."

"A long time ago," Pelado said, his tongue darting rapid-fire out over his lips. "A long time ago I did some work for the French—the SDECE."

"When?"

"About 1963, I think it was. Maybe before."

"What about it?"

"A man named Attia hired me to work with some *barbouzes* who used to be in Algeria. We were to do some . . . some work in Katanga and Abidjan." Pelado was visibly upset at the memory: his hands were fidgety and he kept looking around the room as if someone else might be listening. "I was told it was for France, señor Alec."

"You fought the OAS?"

"There was much killing. I was afraid not to be with them. They would have killed me, too. We had many assignments, some in

Algeria, but mostly in Katanga. We usually traveled together, three of us. That is why I was so afraid; they were assassins, señor Alec. They would have killed me, too, if I tried to leave. Then we were summoned to go to Algiers. It was very important and very secret and we were to go there quickly. We were to drive to a location near the citadel and—and kill a man. He was very important.''

"Who was the man, Simon?"

"I do not know his name, señor Alec. I swear. I never knew who he was, except he was very important." Pelado was nearly pleading for Gunther to believe him. He was trembling, rocking back and forth in his seat. "We got there—at the place—we arrived late and this man was not there. Our superiors were very angry. Then they decided on a new plan. I was to drive a taxi they had stolen and wait outside a hotel. This man would take my taxi and I was to drive him to another spot where we would do the job. At first, I did not think this was a good plan because there are many taxis, but I said nothing. I waited. Then a man I did not know came out of the hotel and came to me and told me the man who came out next was who I should pick up. I drove to the front and a dark man wearing a hat came out and got in and told me to take him to . . . somewhere, I forget. I could not see his face very well, but it must have been the right one. He was holding a small case.

"I started off, following the directions I was given, but this man, he knew something was wrong. He told me we were going the wrong way. I was very frightened, señor Alec. I thought maybe he had a *pistola* too. He became very insistent, then he started to cry. I stopped the car and told him to be quiet or I would shoot him. He begged me not to take him to his death. He said he had two daughters. He would not stop crying. Then he gave me the case. It was full of money, señor Alec. It was more than a million French francs. He said I could have it if I let him go. I was afraid, but it was so much money.''

Gunther nodded with a long sigh. "You let him go."

"I did, yes," Pelado said.

"And the two others? Your friends?"

"They were not my friends, señor Alec. They were killers, very bad men."

"So what happened when you didn't show up with the mark?"

"I came to them and told them that he escaped. They were very angry. Pepe, he beat me. I could not drive because I was bleeding, so I got in the back. That's where I hid the money, under the seat. They didn't know about the money."

"And?"

Pelado took a deep breath. "I shot them," he said, keeping his glance away from Gunther. "Pepe first because he beat me and because he was not driving. Then Gabriel. They were cruel men, señor Alec. They deserved to die."

Gunther was polishing his glasses with the napkin, watching Pelado. There didn't seem to be anything to say.

"They *were* very bad and cruel men, señor Alec," Pelado repeated.

"Yes," Gunther said, not looking at the little man across from him. "Do you know who that man was? The one in the taxi?"

"I said I did not, señor Alec."

"His name was Abdel el Madsoud, but that isn't important because he is dead now." Gunther wiped a hand across his forehead as if batting away a fly. "He was an Egyptian courier for the KGB. The money was installment on a payment to a double in the OAS who was recruited by the Russians. They thought he kept the money and lied about the kidnapping." He shrugged. "So did we, for that matter. But it was you, eh, Simon?"

"*Sí.* I was very careful."

"Did Vargas know about all this?"

"Vargas? No, I have told no one. No one knows about it, señor Alec. Until now."

"You said he knew about your background. How would he know so much and not know that you stole a million francs?"

Pelado shook his head solemnly. "It is not possible—about the money. I have told no one. It could be very dangerous for me."

"So . . ." Gunther glanced up at the ceiling. "You and Vargas had a pleasant little chat for several hours in your expensive hotel room in San Juan. Then you parted, the best of friends, and you haven't heard from him since. That about sum it up, Simon?"

"Exactly so, señor Alec."

"Bullshit!" Gunther exploded. "That's utter bullshit! You expect me to believe that Ollie Vargas just dropped in on you casually one day to reminisce about old times? He was after something, or he wouldn't have wasted his time. You had nothing to offer him, you didn't know anyone from the brigade, you had no contacts, you offered him nothing in the way of information, but still he came to see you. Why, Simon? What did he really want? You'd better start talking to me." Gunther looked away in disgust and noticed Mackensen had moved forward in his seat as if he were very interested in Simon's response.

"Señor Alec, there was nothing—"

Gunther slapped his palm hard against the leather arm of his chair, causing a loud report like that of a rifle shot. He turned angrily to Rockwell. "What kind of deal has this black-eyed little bastard put to you?"

Rockwell sat up attentively. "Information for protection," he said, raising his eyebrows. "As you can guess, he hasn't been quite the apple of anyone's eye for some time. Lots of people would like to meet with him. The word is he probably won't survive the meeting. He's not well liked, you know."

"And how long has the word been out?"

"Not long, if I'm any judge," Rockwell said.

"Our friends from Dzerzhinsky Square?"

Rockwell offered a slight smile. "You have been away, Alec. The Russians have moved most of their foreign operations out of that office. But, yes, the KGB. Also, the French, Egypt, Turkey, Israel . . ." He raised his coffee cup to indicate in the air. "Others, too. Very popular, your friend."

"Why us?"

"I suppose he thought he'd be safe with us." Rockwell sneaked a sideward glance at Pelado. "He's demonstrated an acute desire not to speak with anyone but us."

"Has he?" Gunther turned to Pelado. "Do you know what I think, Simon?"

The little Argentine said nothing. He was fidgety again.

"I think you haven't given me any information, that's what I think. I think perhaps we're too polite to you. Maybe we should just turn you over—"

"Señor Alec, no!"

"Maybe we *will* turn you over to someone who isn't as tolerant as we are. You're not being very informative with me. The deal is information for protection. No information, then . . ." Gunther paused. "Are you getting my drift, Simon?"

"They would kill me," Pelado blurted. His mouth looked dry for the first time. Despite the cool breeze from the windows, he was perspiring; beads of sweat collected at his temples. "Please, señor Alec. They would kill me because of the money." He began to cry. "Some other things too. I have done other things . . . I am ashamed . . ."

"Like in Algiers?"

Pelado's whimpers mounted to sobs.

"Slaughtering cows isn't your only trade," Gunther observed tersely. "So Vargas knew about you, after all."

"I don't know how it was possible," Pelado blubbered through his tears. "I was very careful. But he knew many things. He told me I must go to the Americans and tell them he would be visiting some of their friends. He said, 'Tell Alec the cast of a die puts us in opposite corners.' That was his words. He said I must contact a certain party in—in Mayagüez and deliver the message that Taskmaster—he made me repeat it several times, Taskmaster, Taskmaster, Taskmaster. He said that Taskmaster returns like the phoenix. I thought it was a joke. I did nothing, but the next day he called me on the telephone and was very angry that I had not gone to Mayagüez."

"John Kersey," Mackensen said, filling in. "He's one of the old hands, been out for years. Lives in Mayagüez. We don't know how the devil Vargas knew he was down there. John cabled us the minute Pelado finished his story. Seems Vargas put the word out on Simon here right away. I guess he figured Simon would deliver the message, then someone, probably KGB, since they're closer, would take care of Simon once and for all."

"Then Simon is only a delivery boy?" Gunther said. "He really wasn't meant for anything else."

"Apparently not, Alec. He knows nothing about Vargas, except the chance sighting in Istanbul, which may be lucky for us. Otherwise, we have nothing on Vargas. Nothing at all."

Gunther sighed. He was quietly aware that the black of night was slowly fading to gray, a first sign of dawn's coming. There were fewer crickets now, but more birds. The breeze had lost its cool edge, turning chilly. He hadn't seen a country dawn, really seen one, since he and Judith made that trip to Pennsylvania. Somewhere near Lancaster, at her uncle's farm. For a moment he wondered why he was thinking so much about Judith lately, then turned his mind back to the living room and the large Persian rug and the object in the orange-and-yellow shirt, sitting across from him, behind the trestle table. Judith, after all, had initiated the divorce.

Gunther cleared his throat absently. "It looks to me like we can solve our problem fairly simply," he said, eyeing Pelado for no particular reason. "Vargas is after those of us who worked the invasion. The ones directly involved, I mean. That can't be more than forty, maybe fifty. A few have died, several have retired; they shouldn't be hard to locate. We'll just take them out of circulation. Replant them."

"That wouldn't do, Alec." Mackensen was in his Lorenzo de' Medici pose, finger across the lip.

"Why not? It wouldn't be difficult."

"It's admitting defeat for one thing. Besides, there's no guarantee Vargas wouldn't find them again, just as he's found seven already."

"But we've had similar threats like this before."

"Never so successful, I'm afraid. No, Alec, Vargas has to be found. You know him best. You find him." Mackensen nodded slightly in the direction of Pelado, who had calmed himself. "Besides, he seems to expect you."

"He may go anywhere."

"Then you follow. You won't be using cover, since he knows who you are, so there's no worry there. Just find him, Alec, and do what is necessary."

"Kill him, you mean."

Mackensen nodded as if giving permission. "Vargas must be stopped."

"Yes, I suppose so," Gunther said, staring out the window. "Of course." The sky was just taking on a bit of pink. He thought of Judith again and wondered how she could divorce such a wonderful fellow.

7

The individual guerrilla warrior must have the right physical, mental and moral attributes to do his job.

"I believed what I said back there, Alec, about you being one of the best."

Not the best, Gunther noted silently. Just one of.

They were outside, just the two of them, walking quietly along the winding path that surrounded the house, inside the fence. Mackensen had suggested it when Gunther indicated the session with Pelado was finished. An unseen sun cast long patches of shadows over them as they made their way past shrubs and small fruit trees. Twenty-five yards away, across the lawn studded with shade trees, the second floor of the house was sprayed with sunlight, making the building appear two-tone white. Near the path at the rear of the property was a small garden of tomatoes, radishes, lettuce, carrots and watermelons. Mackensen had stopped to pick two carrots, dusted them and offered one to Gunther. Somewhere—Gunther thought it must have been the road at the front of the house—a car passed. He wondered who was taking care of the place.

"What do you think, Alec? About Vargas, I mean. Why do you think he's doing this?" Mackensen had a way of talking to you without looking at you, not uncommon, except he seldom used any hand gestures. He walked slowly, at Gunther's left, one hand thrust in the pocket of his jacket, the other holding the carrot across his chest. He was a very neat man, Gunther thought.

"I don't know why. Revenge, I suppose. He thinks we deserted him and his people in Cuba."

"That was sixteen years ago." Mackensen bit into his carrot. "And we *didn't* desert him, you know. That was Kennedy's doing. He and the others were responsible. *We* did everything we could do."

He sounded as if he were talking about an enemy.

"Still, to him—Vargas—we all look alike," Gunther observed drily.

"But it was all so long ago. What are your feelings on that, Alec. Why is he making his move now? Why not before?" Mackensen was shaking his head sadly, as if this all would be behind them now if Vargas had cooperated.

"Maybe this is his first opportunity," Gunther offered lamely. "We don't know where he's been since Cuba." He wished he could stop saying that.

"I have his file, such as it is. It was the information he gave us in sixty-one." Mackensen stopped and looked back at the house as if it were important that he keep his bearings straight. "There isn't much, but you'd better have it to look over." He glanced at Gunther and gave a short, helpless sigh and moved on down the path, slightly ahead. "You probably know most of what's in it, since you two were friends, but, still, it may help. He took English and languages at Michigan. Studied, I mean. Army ROTC, as well. You know, I suppose?"

"Yes," Gunther said. "French and German. He was a very good student." He skipped a step to catch up. "He was quick to learn tactics when I knew him. Very earnest." Gunther needn't have added it, but he sensed Mackensen was interested.

"Tehnically, this is a matter for the bureau," Mackensen said, ducking under a pear-tree branch. "Domestic soil and all that. We've had to be careful lately about operations in the country." Then, as an afterthought, he said, "Don't ever get involved in politics when you're out, Alec. We've had enough trouble with company people getting involved in political operations when they had no business. It reflects on the company and makes us look bad. And don't write any damn books.''

Gunther smiled to himself. "I won't. Can't spell.''

"What's that?''

"I say I can't spell,'' Gunther said, sorry he'd mentioned it. "I couldn't write a book.''

"See that you don't.'' It was Mackensen's final word. "As for the domestic thing, I don't want to bring anyone else into this. This is an internal problem of ours and we'll take care of it. We can't have the bureau stumbling around trying to clean up our messes. It wouldn't do. In the same manner, I don't want you involving any police. If you need anything, anything at all, you are to contact me''—he paused a moment—"or Rockwell. I'm putting Peter on this, as coordinator in Virginia. You'll have a number where you can reach one of us day or night. And so there is no mistake, I'm putting it in the form of an unofficial operation under Special Ops. My authority.''

"Unofficial?''

"Of course,'' Mackensen said shortly. "The situation demands that.''

"What type of coordinating will Peter do?'' The thought of Rockwell participating with this in any way brought back the memory of Miller Beadle muddling in the Hamburg operation. Gunther thought he'd proved Rockwell's ineffectiveness, during the session with Pelado. "I don't think this operation can stand much coordination. Peter's, that is.''

"Strictly administrative. Peter will be responsible for seeing to it that you have whatever you need. I told you the bureau was not to be involved—or the police. You're going to need help, Alec. Running down leads, checking information, whatever it is. Nothing more than that. This is your assignment, and so there won't be duplication, no one else will be involved. Peter will see to your needs and report to me. I said it was to be unofficial; only a minimum of people will be advised of its details. We don't want everyone in the Clandestine Service looking over their shoulder.''

"I see,'' Gunther said. "Covert, but still all proper.''

"And, please, don't be so damned snippy with Peter. There are worse, you know."

Gunther was pleased to see that Mackensen at least shared some of his disgust for Rockwell, though Mackensen would never say so outright.

They walked a bit further in silence. The sun was up now; Gunther could feel its warmness when they walked between the shadows of the trees. He heard another car pass and realized they had walked almost full circle around the path. There was a small patio at the front of the house, protected from the road by a high untrimmed hedge, and Mackensen headed for it. The metal chairs and table were slightly rusted and wet from the previous night's rain. He found a dry spot on the table's edge and hoisted himself up on it so that his short legs dangled below him awkwardly. Gunther leaned against a tree.

"Alec, I want you to tell me if you have any reservations about this," Mackensen said. He was looking at the pattern of the patio stones before him, swinging his feet lazily, like a listless schoolboy. In the sunlight he looked pale and almost weary, and the growth of stubble along his chin sparkled.

Gunther said nothing. He shook his head.

"It must be done, you know."

"Yes, I know," Gunther said. "What about Pelado? What will you do with him?"

Mackensen shrugged with an unconcerned grunt. "You came up with a good suggestion there, Alec. Turn him over to the Russians. I might have—" He glanced at Gunther, then looked back to the patio design. "Mideast section will want to talk to him, no doubt. Otherwise he's not much good to us. I'm not sure what procedure is." A sigh. "I suppose he'll be taken care of. California, I would think. Somewhere near the border. They'll want the money, of course. Most of it, anyway. Sneaky little bastard, salting it away like that. Wonder why he didn't spend it all by now."

"Fear of being discovered would be my guess." Gunther made designs in the moist dirt with the toe of his shoe. He was waiting for Mackensen to tell him to get started.

"Oh, yes. Being very careful, I think he said. Strange, I didn't take him to be a very courageous type—shooting those two, I mean."

"Three hundred thousand can be a great incentive, even for that."

Mackensen nodded as if he were all too familiar with such things. "We'll contact everyone Vargas may have known who was involved with Operation Jupiter. I'll have a list to you as soon as possible—this evening—where they are, what they're doing, all that. We'll tell them something is up, but no more. Just enough that they will take precautions."

Gunther removed his glasses and rubbed his eyes. He was just realizing he hadn't slept all night. "I'd rather we told them everything or nothing. People act awfully stupid when they don't know details." He meant agents. "Also jumpy. We like to know what's going on. I would."

"You recommend telling them, then?"

"I do."

"Even those retired?"

"Harry Phillips was retired," Gunther said.

Mackensen nodded again. "All right, it'll be done."

"I may want to contact some of them if we can settle on some kind of pattern Vargas is using. Have them stay close to home or whatever. Anyone in the field we won't bother with at the moment. Vargas seems to be concentrating on those in the states." He wiped the glasses with his shirttail. "I'll need a list of phone numbers, too."

"Done."

Gunther put his glasses back on. He was extremely tired. "I'd like to get started as soon as I have some sleep. Do I stay here?"

"Yes, the place is yours. There is an extra phone in the main upstairs bedroom. I'll be leaving shortly with Peter and the others. We'll leave you the Volvo. I'll have this information sent back right away. Probably get it to you by late this afternoon—courier. I'd rather not use the phone except when we have to." Mackensen hopped down from the table. "The phone you'll be calling me at is a secure line. When you use it, do be sure to call from a pay station."

"I haven't been away all that long," Gunther said sourly.

"You're sure it doesn't bother you," Mackensen said again. "Vargas? Finding him? Tell me if you have the slightest hesitancy. It's important that you have no qualms about the job—what it means."

"I've always understood the rules," Gunther said. He was anxious to shower and find a bed.

"Sure?"

"For Chrissakes, yes!"

Mackensen frowned at that, but made no comment. "If you come off this well, Alec, I think you can look forward to a brighter future than sorting paychecks." He was standing with both hands in his pockets, his back to the house, so if anyone was listening, they would not hear. "Probably not something in the field right away—if ever—but a step up. I need responsible people, people who know the territory back home. I could use a good man like you."

Mackensen was trying to be conciliatory, Gunther thought. It wasn't something he was good at and it wasn't what Gunther needed. He nodded as if he would think about it.

"Oh, yes, Alec, about your calling me. We'll need something as a signal that it's you calling. I would prefer that not everyone know who it is. Not a cover name or anything like that, since you won't be using one anyway, but something I can recognize right off."

"Not my own name?"

"I told you before that you were not one of the fair-haired boys around the place anymore. There aren't too many who know I've put you on this." Mackensen shaded his eyes from the sun with one hand. "I would rather the word not get around just yet."

Gunther thought a moment. "There's Sheldon, my old workname."

"I already have a Sheldon on my staff. Richard. That would be too confusing."

Gunther pivoted slightly as he heard another car passing. Somewhere in the house a radio was playing. He could hear the tune, but not the words, of a popular song. "How about Taskmaster?" he said finally. "Taskmaster calling. That's not something you'll mistake for anything else."

"We already have one Taskmaster," Mackensen replied curtly.

"Yes, but he's not likely to call you up."

Mackensen took a deep breath. "All right, then. Taskmaster. We'd best get started." He started toward the house and Gunther fell into step beside him. "I want to leave as soon as Peter and the others have had something to eat. It's been a long night for us all."

"I'll just go upstairs and find the shower. I can find something to eat, after I've slept."

"Fine, do that," Mackensen said absently. "This is very important, Alec. You understand that?"

"Yes," he said, wishing Mackensen would drop it. "It's all very clear to me."

They reached the house. Before they went in, Mackensen said, "I hope you're . . . I mean I wish you good luck, Alec. You're *my* good-luck piece now. The white Taskmaster, as it were. Do this well and you can look forward to better times."

"I'll do my best."

"Yes, yes, I know you will," Mackensen said. He was in the shadow of the house now and he looked healthier than he had in the sun, Gunther thought. He always looked healthier indoors.

8

When ready, the guerrilla comes out via a safe route to strike the enemy by surprise, destroying, killing and sowing panic.

He paid the cab at the curb and told him not to wait. The house was white stucco with a rust slate roof. Two small palm trees guarded the arched front porch entryway, which was shaded by a lattice grill and heavy stone walls painted white. It was a fairly typical Santa Monica beach residence, with a wide expanse of sand and trees separating it from neighboring houses on either side. A cool breeze was coming from the sea. A lovely day.

He rang the doorbell and heard chimes echo inside. In a moment a teenage girl opened the door. She was dressed in faded jean cutoffs and a light gray T-shirt identifying itself as the property of the UCLA Athletic Department.

"Hello," she said. Her long blonde hair, bleached by the sun, was done up and held with a rubber band at the back. The man guessed she must be about fourteen. Her face and arms were tanned a golden brown.

"Good morning. Is Mr. Tripp home? I tried to call earlier, but the line was busy. I'm from the office." He shifted the briefcase to his other hand.

"Daddy's still asleep, I think," she said with a small frown. "Something's wrong with the phone. It was just dead this morning." She said it with irritation, as if she were expecting several important calls. "Come on in. I'll get my dad." A smile. "It's time he got up anyway. He's on vacation," she added as if to explain.

He nodded his understanding and stepped inside, closing the door quietly behind him. He followed the girl into a large living room that had a view of the beach through wide sliding-glass doors.

"I guess you can just sit down in here while I get Dad," she said. "Mom's gone to take Kenny to the dentist." She started away, then turned back. "What's your name?" She seemed a little embarrassed to ask.

"Vi—Ollie," the man said.

"Okay. Mine's Jenny. Be back in a minute."

She gave a little wave and skipped down a corridor that led to the back of the house. He found a seat and placed the briefcase across his knees. The living room was decorated with wood paneling on three sides. The wall facing the beach was glass except for a large fireplace made of stone. On the mantel were three pictures: one of Jenny, one of a younger boy whose smile exposed a missing front tooth and the last of Tripp and his wife, in bathing suits, standing to the side of a volleyball net. In the background was the house. The man watched the sea through the glass doors for some minutes. Far out he could see a cabin cruiser slapping small swells as it headed south. It was a white boat with a red cabin. It looked to be going too fast for its size, he thought.

When Jenny returned she was wearing a bikini bathing suit, the top of which hung loosely over her small breasts. The man didn't get up.

"Dad's coming," she said brightly. "I'm going down to Jimmy's beach, if Dad asks." She grabbed a towel that was draped over the back of the sofa near the window. At the sliding door she paused and turned back quickly to wave. "See ya." He watched her as she skipped down the beach, past the volleyball net to the surf, and disappeared from view.

Tripp was wearing light green Bermuda shorts and striped shirt when he entered the room. He was a square man, tall with broad shoulders and a wide, but trim, waist. His face was tan like his daughter's, but not as deeply, because of the creases and lines around his nose and eyes. He had the discipline about him of a man who walked to the center of things and took charge. He was pulling at the hair on the side of his head that stuck up awkwardly where he'd slept on it. The man remained seated.

"What's going now?" Tripp said impatiently, slurring his words as if he weren't fully awake. "I'm on leave time. Champion send you?"

"No," the man said. "From Center."

Tripp yawned and looked for a place to sit. "All the way out here? Look, ah . . ." He glanced at Vargas for help.

"Ollie."

"Ollie. I'm due my leave time and I intend to take it without interruption. I'm due it, you know. It took me months to find this place to lease. Months. And I intend to enjoy it with my family." Tripp settled in the same sofa from which the girl had taken the towel.

"This won't take long." He unsnapped his briefcase.

"Who you running for at Center?" Tripp asked.

The man smiled as he pulled out a folder from the case. "Gunther. Alec Gunther."

"Gunther!" Tripp grunted to himself. "I thought he was out. When he'd start back active? I thought they canned him after that mess."

"He's back. Something special."

Tripp shook his head. "You never know, I guess. I worked with Alec once. Knows his job, Alec does." He glanced up. "What's this about?"

"I've brought something you're to read." He handed the folder over to Tripp. "It's important."

"The man rested one hand gently on top of the case, the other he held inside the partially closed lid.

"What is it? A report?" Tripp glared at the folder without opening it. "I'm on leave. I keep telling you that. Doesn't anyone care?"

"I think the material there will be self-explanatory," the man said, indicating the folder with a nod. He looked toward the beach. "I have to catch a plane this afternoon."

Tripp reddened. "Ho, *you* do!"

"Yes." He was watching the sea; he hadn't bothered to look at Tripp. The red-and-white cruiser was moving back to the north. It seemed to be having a tougher time than before.

"Listen, ah—whatever your name is, I don't take orders from—"

"A nigger?"

"Now just a goddamn—" Tripp stopped short when he saw the gun. It was a French Star automatic of Spanish manufacture. The man had drawn it slowly from inside the slender case. "What is that?" Tripp said stupidly.

"An inferior imitation of the standard Colt," the man replied drily. "It isn't an effective military weapon, but it will do." He rested the muzzle on the edge of the case, pointing at Tripp's midsection. "I asked you to read."

Tripp froze in his chair. "Who are you?"

"I've been called a Taskmaster."

Tripp's eyes flickered with faint recognition. "Taskmaster! That was . . . Cuba!"

He said nothing. His glance went to the folder. "Read."

"What is it? You could tell me that."

"The reason for my visit." he said. "I prefer that you know why I'm here. It concerns something you participated in, Kenneth Tripp." His voice was hard and he kept his eyes on Tripp's.

If Tripp was contemplating rushing him or making some desperate move, his face didn't show it. He watched the man's black eyes, dividing his glance between them and the muzzle of the gun.

"What do you intend to do?"

"First, I want you to read the contents of that folder."

"Then?" Tripp's neck muscle tightened.

"Then I'm going to shoot you," he said, indicating the gun. "With this." He cocked the hammer back with his thumb. "You shouldn't ask so many questions."

9

Nothing helps the combat forces more than accurate intelligence.

Gunther slept until shortly after noon. The main bedroom was on the west side of the house, where it was cool and protected from the afternoon sun by the shade of a large elm. The house was quiet, the only sounds being an occasional automobile passing by outside.

He showered again and found a terry-cloth bathrobe in the closet. The robe was too long, of course, cut for a man well over six feet, but Gunther wasn't expecting anyone soon so it didn't matter how ridiculous it made him look. He went downstairs and cooked himself a large breakfast of eggs and ham and drank water because there was no milk. He brewed a fresh pot of coffee and, holding his cup, explored the rest of the house, padding around in another man's slippers.

The writing den was a converted attic above the garage. The room had a single window facing the drive. It was furnished with a sprawling U-shaped desk at one end and a threadbare sofa at the other. Everywhere were books in shelves or piled on tables. Gunther poked around nosily until he found a stack of stationery boxes filled with carbon copies of manuscripts. He chose one, *The Death of Roman Westlake,* and settled in a corner of the sofa to read.

By the time the courier arrived with the Mackensen papers,

Gunther had read little—about eighty pages—but thought a lot about Vargas and the days and nights of training in the mountain jungle of Nicaragua, about Cuba, the invasion, Berlin and, oddly enough, about Judith and her new life. And like an old master reminiscing about lost matches, with no one to make excuses to, he wondered about the role he'd played in his own life, something he hadn't done since Berlin.

"I was told to instruct you that the material stamped with a registry number was to be destroyed after you'd finished it," the courier said. He was young, probably not long recruited out of college, Gunther imagined. He had a new man's compulsion for relaying messages precisely.

"I also have a book of five thousand dollars in traveler's cheques. Five books, I mean. A thousand each. You're to sign each one, then sign this expense voucher."

Evidently, Gunther was to sign them in this fellow's presence. As he did so, he was reminded of the Gibralter Service Company. He wondered who would be coming in now on Tuesdays and Thursdays.

Gunther handed the signed receipt back to the courier.

"Thank you, sir," he said, taking the paper and putting it carefully inside his coat pocket. "Mr. Gunther, Mr. Mackensen said that if there was anything I could be of use for, I was to give you a hand. Reading or sorting, that is."

They were in the kitchen, sitting at the cutting-board table. Gunther felt a bit silly, being spoken to with such dignity as he sat in someone else's slippers and robe with the sleeves rolled up. People didn't usually call him sir.

"No. I'll manage, but thanks all the same."

"Yes, sir." He got up. "I guess that's it, sir."

"I guess so," Gunther said.

The young man started to leave, then turned back at the door. "Sir? I—I just wanted to say, well, good luck, Mr. Gunther."

"Good luck?" Gunther was startled. "What for? Do you know what this is all about?"

"Oh, no, sir. I don't have any idea. It's just that, well, you've been put on ice since that, ah, since you came back from Germany.

We all know about it. I mean, that you had a rough time. I'm glad you're finally going back to fieldwork. When we were at the Farm—in school—we studied some different operatives and how they worked and what they'd done. They didn't tell us outright, but we learned who most of them were. We studied a lot of your work and''—he coughed, straightening up with some embarrassment—''and I just want to say I admired what you've done for the country.'' He glanced past Gunther, avoiding his eyes. ''I just wanted to say good luck to you, sir.''

Gunther sat rock-still. He'd never heard such drivel. One didn't *admire* work like his in the Clandestine Service, he thought, particularly if it had anything to do with Special Operations, the acknowledged orchestrators of violence. He remembered his days at Camp Peary—he had been a year out of Princeton—when it was a squalid, cramped little place, secret, where they were interested in tradecraft and espionage in the classical meaning of the word. Gunther never had been taught to admire anyone, which he didn't. He realized, quite abruptly, that he was facing his legacy, though he had had no part in forming it, no active voice. It was as if the man before him had sprouted full-grown from a mysterious generation between them, and he felt suddenly square-toed and tired at the revelation.

''It isn't what you think,'' Gunther found himself saying with a bitterness that seemed to startle the boy. He didn't need anyone to remind him of what he was. ''One day you'll see that. Now get out.''

He listened to the car start and crunch noisily out of the gravel drive until the sound faded into the afternoon quiet of the gabbling birds and the light rustle of leaves. He sat at the table for a long time and smoked a cigarette from a pack Michael had left. Gunther was not a philosophical man and never had been, but his inclination of late to be reflective annoyed him. There was no profit in it. He supposed it was age.

The file dispatched from Mackensen was of little value for the most part. There was the dossier on Vargas, which Gunther was already familiar with—born in Havana, schooled there, accepted on a scholarship in the United States, his father dying of tuberculosis while he was away, his mother now dead also after fleeing to Miami from Cuba, Vargas recruited into the brigade. Attached as well was a copy of Vargas's security-clearance investigation. There was nothing more. After the invasion he'd been caught in the swamps with some others trying to get to the mountains. When the brigade was released December 23, 1962, Vargas was not among them. No one knew what had happened to him, since the commanders had been isolated from the others in solitary confinement. The last page of Vargas's file was stamped MISSING (PRESUMED EXPIRED IN CAPTIVITY). Gunther had never seen words used so without pity, as if a stupid Arctic Hare had wandered off into the lion's den at a zoo.

The other pages in the file were registry copies of agent histories that included all forty-six company men who'd been directly involved in Operation Jupiter. Each individual's history was like a financial ledger sheet that described where he had been assigned and gave a brief description of his duties since the Bay of Pigs, though the Bay of Pigs was never specifically mentioned and only the operational code name was used. The final page was a folded computer printout headed OPERATIVE STATUS (OP JUPITER) that listed by name and workname every agent who had participated in Operation Jupiter. Of forty-six who had been operational, eight had died (NATURAL CAUSES), fourteen were KILLED OR MISSING, eight were retired, four were active but on leave, five were active (Gunther listed among them), and seven—the ones eliminated by Vargas—were listed simply under the heading RECENTLY DECEASED.

Gunther was struck by the sterility with which a man's life and death could be so clinically arranged on paper. Under KILLED OR MISSING were two listings, ledger items catalogued conveniently by date, that caught his eye:

DATE OF ACTION	NAME (WORK)	PREVIOUS STATION	STATUS
SEPT. 29, 1974	JOHN MILES (ULBRICHT)	GDR (BERLIN)	KILLED (SHOT)
SEPT. 29, 1974	JAMES ROBERTS (KOLBE)	GDR (BERLIN)	KILLED (SHOT)

Miles and Roberts or, technically, Ulbricht and Kolbe, had died the night Gunther was caught. It was the night his network had ceased to exist. It was a night Gunther had tried to forget—with the soaking rain they were all caught in and the death measured out in short, choppy bursts from Soviet-made machine guns in East German hands. His name easily could be there, Alec thought; it probably should be. They told him he was lucky.

When the phone rang, about eight-fifteen, it was almost dark. Gunther had gone over the file carefully and come up with a definite pattern. Vargas had struck first in Louisiana. There was a possibility he'd come into the country somewhere along the Texas border, or perhaps he'd slipped in by ship to New Orleans. But more importantly, he was trailing a pattern. Franzone was first in Morgan City. The next hits went from Big Springs, Texas, to Dodge City, Kansas, to Boulder, Colorado, to Denver, to Albuquerque and to the last, Phillips in Arizona. It was like a road map. Vargas was headed west. His next stop would be California.

"Hello."

"Alec?"

"Mackensen," the voice said. "Bad news, Alec. He's hit again."

"Shit!" Gunther slapped his hand hard against the wall beside the kitchen telephone.

"California," Mackensen continued. "Santa Monica. Kenneth Tripp, chief of station at Veracruz. He was on leave."

"I knew it would be California," Gunther said bitterly. "He's established a pattern: moving west." He reached to the table for his notes. "There are only two in California. Tripp in L.A. and"— Gunther ran his finger quickly down the list—"and Hix . . . Richard Hix in Sacramento." He noticed Hix also was on leave. "That's where Vargas is heading. I'll catch the next flight out of here. You give Hix a call."

"He isn't being subtle anymore, Alec."

"What do you mean?"

"Tripp was shot to death in his own place. Close range, they tell me. He isn't rigging up any more accidents, Alec. He knows we're chasing him."

"Me," Gunther corrected. "He knows I'm after him. He seems to want that."

"He left the piece on the mantel," Mackensen said almost admiringly. "The chess piece, black." There was a pause. "I want you to get the first plane out, Alec. Be in Sacramento by morning."

"I will." Gunther was alive again. He could feel something stir inside him—frustration, excitement, fear—things he had forgotten now came back. He would find Vargas. Stop him. Kill him. This time he had an enemy he could identify.

II. SEEK

One does not have to wait for a revolutionary situation to arise; it can be created. Above all, do not wait for opportunities once the initial contact has been made; be the aggressor always; seek the enemy, for it keeps him off balance.

Fundamental Two, Che Guevara

10

It must always be remembered that the guerrilla's most important source of supply is the enemy himself.

He was met at the airport by a man named Fleming who'd been sent from San Francisco. Reservations had been made at the Senator Hotel in Sacramento, downtown near the convention center.

"Don't you people ever carry luggage?" Fleming said, looking sideways at Gunther. They were in his car, a tiny Honda, and Gunther was cramped in the passenger seat. He was wearing the same suit he'd worn for Pelado's interrogation. Beside him was the small flight bag he always checked through at the ticket counter. Airlines take a dim view of passengers who carry on weapons, even small ones.

"Sometimes."

"Staying long?"

"I don't know yet." Gunther glanced out the window as they passed a vacation-Bible-school bus loaded with children. "Probably not."

"Sacramento's a great city, I hear. Don't get over much, though. My sister-in-law lives here. Married a divorced captain from McClellan." He gunned past a large truck and settled back into the right lane. "Frisco's my town. Love it."

"Mackensen call you?"

75

"Me?" Fleming shook his head. "No way. Barton, my section chief, got the call. Guy named Rockwell. That's who gave me the dope. Says come pick you up and set you in the Senator." He glanced at Gunther. "No questions, he says. Just leave you alone."

"What section is that?"

"Say again?"

"What department are you in?"

"Personnel," Fleming said. "Applicant screening, mostly."

"Like it?"

"Sure," he said, slightly surprised. "Why not?"

Gunther didn't answer. He looked away at the subdivision they were passing, with its hundreds of houses jammed together on perfect rectangular blocks and separated from the highway by a Cyclone fence. The rear of the houses faced the interstate; their glass patio doors were unprotected from the curiosity of passing motorists, except by an occasional strategically placed poplar or a clothesline sagging with linen. It was a different life out here, Gunther thought, and the automobile was responsible for it.

"Have you contacted Hix?"

Fleming shook his head. "No, I don't think so. We've called at the number he left us, but he hasn't been around to answer it. Bachelor, you know," he offered quickly. "Probably out and about. He's on leave."

"But you've been to his house, haven't you?"

"Why no," Fleming said. "Actually, it isn't his house. He's staying with his brother James, I think—"

"Goddammit, someone was supposed to go to his house!" Gunther said hotly. "He was supposed to be contacted personally."

"Well, you don't have to snap my head off. We don't have anyone in Sacramento anyway. I was told—"

"By who?"

Fleming faltered. "By, ah, that guy Rockwell. He told me to get hold of Hix and bring him to meet you, if possible. Otherwise, just tell him to wait for us." Fleming shrugged defensively. "That's all he said. There wasn't anything about actually going there."

"Where does he live?"

"Hix?"

"Of course, Hix. What's his address?"

"Somewhere in South Terrace, I think. I have the number."

"Can you find it? Right now?"

"Yeah, I guess so." Fleming nodded at the glove compartment. "I have a street map in there. You want to go there now?"

"Yes," Gunther said. "Right now."

Fleming nodded again. "Okay. They didn't say this was an emergency, you know. Nobody said anything like that. It isn't my fault if no one tells us anything. I'm in personnel, I told you. We don't live in your secret little world—you're Special Ops, aren't you? Clandestine Service?"

"Something like that."

"Not that I care what you're up to," Fleming continued. "But you people *could* get better organized. Let us know what you want. Outside your world, we *are* responsible, you know."

Gunther was losing his patience, but blowing up now would accomplish nothing. Besides, Fleming was right, it wasn't his fault. "Just drive," he finally said. "Just take me to Hix. You're doing a wonderful job, you people in personnel."

The house was in an old established neighborhood with trees and long driveways to separate garages behind the houses. Almost all the houses on the block had screened-in front porches in the tradition of the 1940s. The sidewalks were clean and cracked with only about two feet separating them from the curb, a fairly recent concession to the widening of residential streets. James Hix lived next to the last house on Woodstock Street in a neat two-story yellow frame building. While Fleming waited in the car, Gunther rang the doorbell. There were two morning newspapers on the front step. Either Hix hadn't wanted to read his morning newspaper for two days or he couldn't. The longer he stood there ringing the doorbell, the more Gunther feared it was the second alternative.

He was turning to go to the back door when a plump middle-aged woman waved at him from the door of the house next to Hix's.

"Young man, oh young man." Gunther could hear a television from inside as he approached the woman.

"I'm looking for the Hixes," Gunther said, coming up the slope of her lawn.

"No one's home," she said with a pleasant smile from behind the screen door. "They've gone to see James's mother in Bakersfield."

"Today?"

"Oh, no. Tuesday. I'm watching the house for James." Gunther noticed a pair of cats sleeping at opposite ends of a worn davenport inside the porch. He guessed she was a widow; elderly men seldom have patience with cats. "Have you been calling James? His telephone has been ringing all day."

"I'm really looking for his brother, Richard. He's supposed to be staying here."

"Richard, yes, Richard was here too. Such a friendly man. He fixed my disposal. Works for the embassy in South America. Oh, I guess you know that. They went to see Ida—that's their mother. Bakersfield. Richard's home for a few days." She felt in the pocket of her housecoat. "I have the address here somewhere. I'm always misplacing things. Dear, now where did I put that." She patted her pockets, then went to the telephone stand just inside the door to the living room. "Here it is." One of the cats hopped down from the sofa and disappeared into the house. Someone had just won a roomful of carpet and furniture, according to the television Gunther could only hear. "Jefferson Drive, 6914 Jefferson Drive," she said, returning to the screen. "In Bakersfield. Are you from Washington, too?"

Gunther was silent a moment. "No," he said. "Why do you say that?"

"Oh, that other man had some papers for Richard. But he said it wasn't important. Just signing, he said. Everyone wants us to sign things when they work for the government."

"Did he say who he was, this other man."

She cocked her head. "You know, he did, but I don't remember. I've never been very good at remembering names. But he was a very nice young man. Very polite. A Negro, I think."

"When was he here?" Gunther forced a patient smile.

"Oh, I guess it was about six o'clock yesterday. Early in the evening. Did you say you were from Washington?"

"How did he get here?" Gunther asked politely. "I mean, was he driving? Did you see a car?"

She touched a delicate hand to her white hair. "Oh, my, I really don't remember. He did ask me how far it was to Bakersfield. And he made a telephone call. I thought it was all right, since he was a friend of Richard's.''

"Did he call Hix?''

She shook her head apologetically. "I'm sorry. I really don't know, but it was just a short call. He said another man from Washington would probably come by today. I remember it was sort of funny the way he said it—something like everyone having to sign the same papers. But he said that if someone comes, I should tell him, I mean, give him a message.'' She patted her pocket again. "Oh, let me think, what was that now. Oh, yes, he said a man named—named—oh, yes, a man named Gunter would be by. He said it was easy to remember because it rhymed with 'hunter.' ''

Gunther sighed despondently. "I'm Gunther,'' he said.

"From Washington?''

"San Francisco. The papers we have to have signed are from Washington.''

She nodded as if she understood. "Oh, yes.''

"What did he say? What was the message?''

"Just not to worry about Richard. He said he'd catch him later.''

"I see.''

"And he said he was sorry to disappoint you, but he would make it up in Montana.'' She stopped to think a moment. "I think it was Montana he said, or was it . . . Yes, yes, it was Montana. He said he was looking forward to getting back to the mountains.''

When Gunther was back in Fleming's Honda, he told him to take him directly to the airport.

"But what about the Senator Hotel? Aren't you staying?''

"No.''

Fleming pulled away from the curb and headed for the interstate. "What did that old lady have to say? Where is Hix?'' he asked.

"Hix is alive and well and visiting his mother,'' Gunther said, staring out the window. "I'm only a few hours behind him.''

"Who, Hix?''

"Someone else.''

"Where are you going?''

"To the Rocky Mountains.'' Gunther checked a slip of paper

from his coat pocket. "Victor Quill. Butte, Montana. Retired."

"You mean I came all the way over here from San Francisco just to drive you back and forth to the airport?"

Gunther smiled. "Don't think I'll forget. You're a very good driver."

11

One should not engage in any clash that does not produce victory, as long as one can choose the "how" and the "when."

The best connection he could get was a United flight to Salt Lake City, where he could change to Western, arriving Silver Bow County Airport in Butte about 7:00 P.M. Gunther had just time enough to call Mackensen.

"This is 555-2028," the southern voice said. "May I help you?"

"This is Taskmaster calling. Put me through to Mackensen."

"Taskmaster calling Mackensen," the voice repeated. "One moment, please."

Gunther had cashed three more $100.00 traveler's cheques for the plane fare and asked for $5.00 in quarters. He'd probably chosen the only pay phone in the state without a light, he thought. And now he couldn't remember how many quarters he'd deposited in the slot. The operator had said $2.10 for three minutes. He put four quarters in his pocket and deposited the rest. He was glad he didn't have to account for all his expenses.

"Hello? Gunther?" It wasn't Mackensen. "Hello?" Rockwell said again.

"I'm in a hurry, Rockwell. Where is Mackensen?"

"He's out. Where are you? Did you find Hix?"

"Hix is in Bakersfield. He's okay, as far as I know. Look, I'm at

81

Sacramento airport. Vargas is on his way to Butte, Montana, and that's where I'm going—"

"Wait a minute, Gunther," Rockwell said. "What's Hix doing in Bakersfield? Mackensen will want to know."

"Visiting his mother."

"I'll have to report this to Mr.—"

"Dammit, I haven't got time. My plane is boarding now. Hix wasn't here when Vargas came looking. He went with a brother to visit his mother. Her name is Ida Hix. Lives at 6914 Jefferson Drive. Call there and tell Hix what's up, but I don't think he has to worry. Vargas is moving on to the next name on his list. Victor Quill in Montana. I'm leaving for there now. Got that?"

"I think you'd better wait for instructions. Mr. Mackensen will want to know about this."

"Goddammit, Rockwell. Shut up and listen!"

"I'm your control, Gunther," the voice said angrily. "Remember that."

Gunther closed his eyes a moment to contain his temper. "Do you have that information down about Hix—where to find him?"

"Of course I do. This is being taped."

Of course, Gunther thought. He'd almost forgot who he was dealing with—Peter Rockwell, crack interrogator and agent controller extraordinaire. "There's something else. Vargas has to be getting from one point to another somehow. There are only two flights a day leaving Sacramento for Salt Lake City, and only one from there to Butte. Vargas must be flying. Have the passenger lists for all passengers changing from a Sacramento flight to Montana—I mean to Butte. There can't be that many. Check them out. See who they are. He probably isn't using his own name, but then he's an arrogant bastard, so maybe he is. Just find out who they are and where they are. Can you do that?"

"Yes, Gunther, I can do that," Rockwell said. "Why are you so sure Vargas is going to Montana?"

"He left me a message."

"Oh." Rockwell paused a moment. Gunther checked his watch. "You're sure it was Vargas?"

"For Chrissakes, Rockwell, who else would it be!" Gunther

shouted. I'll be landing in Salt Lake City in about two hours. Can you get that passenger information in that time? I'll call again from there."

"In two hours?"

"Vargas has half a day's start on me already. He's bound to be there now. If you can't get the passenger stuff by the time I get to Salt Lake, then I'll call you when I get to Butte. But just get it! Make sure Quill has been contacted. Let him know I'm on my way." Gunther opened the door to the phone booth and heard the final call for his flight. A man in a short-sleeved shirt who was standing nearby, apparently waiting his turn for the telephone, smiled pleasantly and nodded at Gunther. "I've got to go, Rockwell."

"One question," the voice said. "I'm looking at a map with little pins in the cities where all the rest of these agents are—the ones connected with Operation Jupiter. The ones Vargas is supposedly after."

"What about them?" Gunther saw the ticket agent at his gate look around for any other passengers. The waiting area was empty.

"Well, something occurred to me about this idea of yours that Vargas is on some kind of schedule—you know, moving west, now evidently east."

"Hurry up "

"What I was thinking is, if somehow he gets by you in Montana, how will you know who's next? The rest of the agents are scattered all across the East Coast." Rockwell paused. "If you miss him, where will you go next?"

"Don't worry about it," Gunther said. "Vargas isn't getting out of Montana." After he'd hung up, Gunther wished he hadn't promised anything. Promises in this business meant nothing.

As he slipped into the boarding tunnel after getting his seat assignment from the flight attendant, Gunther noticed that the telephone booth was empty and that the man in the short-sleeved shirt was gone.

12

The one thing history does not tolerate is errors on the part of analysts and executives of the master plan. No one can seek command of the vanguard force who is not fit to assume the responsibilities of leadership.

He had four whiskeys over ice shortly after the plane took off, and he might have had more if he hadn't fallen asleep.

In his dream, sprinkled with flashes of his other two failures, Berlin and Judith, Gunther relived the landing at Red Beach. He sloshed ashore, stumbling over coral, falling a dozen times in the briny water, until finally he reached a small grove of pine trees. The shoreline was lit by two rows of smudge pots, and he could hear voices behind him cursing in the dark as more members of the battalion made their way inland. Ollie was ahead with his radio operator, pointing to some shacks along the waterfront.

"Who is that?" the radioman said, twisting around wide-eyed with his .45 pointed in Gunther's direction.

"I'm a Taskmaster for Chrissakes! Point that somewhere else!"

Ollie Vargas patted his frightened young communicator on the shoulder. "Felipe, you must not shoot Alec," he said coolly. "He owes me money." It was amazing how calm the man could be, Gunther thought. This was his first combat experience and yet he was unruffled as a veteran.

It turned out that one of the shacks was occupied by three militiamen with a microwave radio. They'd been transmitting frantic calls to Cayo Romando, a small militia outpost north of Girón. By the time the radio was silenced, it was too late: Castro knew of the invasion before a hundred men had been off-loaded from the ships. The element of surprise was lost.

Confusion and sporadic fighting meandered languidly through Gunther's mind in obscure images like frames from a broken kinescope. He directed men in shadowy firefights; he fought against tanks and blew up trucks loaded with troops. There was the stench of cordite mixed with that of scorched and burning flesh. There were the cries in the night of wounded and dying men.

Suddenly the dream changed focus and he wasn't on a battlefield of sand and broken mangroves; he was crouched behind a crumbled wall that had once been part of a courtyard. He was between two buildings and exposed to a fierce rain, and John Miles and James Roberts were with him.

It was to have been a simple escape. Gunther had the papers for them and they were to wait for the driver at the Brandenburg Gate late in the afternoon, but the driver never showed. After dark the plan was blown and they had nowhere to go. Roberts had acted stupidly when they were stopped by the Vopo for a routine identification check on Greifswaler Strasse. When the East German had pressed for more information, Roberts had killed him by breaking the man's back with his knee. They had hidden the body as best they could and taken his gun.

The only way out now was the Wall. Miles knew of a place in the Pankow district, near the old railroad crossing from Wedding on the West German side, where escapes had been successful. "But it is dangerous," he said, "because since the last crossing the Vopos have increased patrols with unscheduled outings."

"Is there any other way now?" Alec asked.

"No," Miles replied bitterly, pitifully, as a man betrayed. Gunther sensed Miles had more to say, but there wasn't time. Roberts was convinced they'd be caught. He was going to kill an East German first. He had the gun.

They hid in the courtyard until after midnight. There was no light except from Bernauerstrasse in the distance, until the lightning began. In the brilliant flashes Gunther could see the rubble of stones and bricks around him and the hollow buildings with their boarded windows and empty doorways. It would be an irony, Gunther thought, to die in such a place, amidst the decay and shooting of a war he'd only read about.

When Miles decided the time was right, they ran through the shadows down a narrow alleyway that led to the Wall. The line of the Wall was broken and uneven where it followed a road on the East German side. The nearest tower was about fifty yards away, searching with its beam the open strip of ground between the buildings and the Wall. It was a good sign that the rain was forcing the Vopo sentries to steer the light slowly over the ground.

Miles went first because he knew the exact spot on the Wall where they would cross. The other side was the British sector, and Gunther wondered briefly how they would react when they found out that three Americans who'd killed one Vopo already were sharing their blankets and coffee. The British were very stuffy about killing East Germans.

Roberts, with the dead Vopo's gun, went next. Gunther waited about thirty seconds after he disappeared into the rain, then he started running. He kept his eyes on the Wall, oblivious to the rain that matted his hair and ran in streams down his face. He ran straight for the Wall, his pulse pumping wildly in his head, but his dream would not allow him to gain any ground. He ran and ran, but the Wall never got any larger: it just flickered in the rain like a ship on a mirage. When he thought he would collapse, still staggering forward, a huge bolt of lightning shattered the darkness. Miles was at the Wall, reaching for a metal piton. Roberts was twenty yards away, stopped, pointing the Vopo's gun around crazily, challengingly.

They shot him first, probably because he had the gun. The lightning had illuminated the open strip at the right time, for a Vopo yelled to his comrades in the tower. Immediately, the beam was on them. There was a short burst from a machine gun to find the range, then another burst that caught Roberts in the midsection, tossing him backwards on his side. He held the gun up, pointing it in the direction of the beam, the right side of his face in the mud, and they shot him again, knocking the gun away.

Gunther had his hands up. He was yelling against the rain for

Miles to stop, but Miles was halfway up the Wall. Then they killed him with several shots from rifles and small arms. Miles had grabbed for the strand of barbed wire before he fell. Gunther stood frozen in the rain with his hands raised high, screaming in German for them to stop shooting. When they did, there was much shouting until a Russian vehicle pulled up behind Gunther with its headlights silhouetting him against the rain. A figure got out and slapped Gunther to his knees. Even now Gunther knew it was only a dream, but the nightmare always ended differently from the real experience, as if the proper conclusion to the Berlin incident was somehow mishandled and only Gunther could set it straight. Instead of allowing himself to be led away, Gunther, with the poetic license of his subconscious, produced a pistol magically from his coat and shot the East German captain carefully, neatly in the heart, just beside his left breast pocket near the rows of ribbons. It didn't happen, but Gunther willed it to be true in his dream because then they killed *him,* all of them shooting at once, and the last thing he saw was the mud and the polished tip of a Vopo's boot.

Gunther came awake in a drenching sweat.

He made his way to the plane's lavatory and soaked his face with water and sat on the lid of the stool for several minutes. He held his hands out before him, palms down, and willed them to stop trembling until they did. It was the drinking and the nightmares that finally had forced Judith to leave, he remembered, and Berlin was the cause. She had not once questioned him about his work, not once asked why he took to coming home at odd hours of the night and day. She wasn't like other wives Gunther had known who harped at their husbands. She was the wife of a state department political officer, for all she knew. Judith never knew the truth until he was arrested in Berlin, and even then she didn't know much. She'd been taken once by the company to a place in Connecticut. Everything from their Berlin flat had been packed and sent there. When he was finally released, there was no explanation of what he'd been arrested for. She was forced into reclusion during those months of debriefing when she let strangers into their Connecticut house who kept her out of their meetings with Gunther. She didn't go out, but waited for the time when "those men" would leave and she could have him back. Gunther remembered it now.

It was a spacious two-story frame house there in East Haven on an uncluttered plot of land not far from the municipal golf course. (Gunther detested the game and the one time he had been forced to prance around those manicured greens, when he was wheedling a GDR military courier to the role of informant, he had managed to lose all his Spauldings in a dogleg pond at the seventh tee.) The house was one of several such places owned by a Delaware front corporation and used by the agency as a safe house or, in this case, as an airing-out retreat. Judith loved it and called it their New England country mansion, though she never knew Gunther paid no bills toward it. Remembering it, Gunther was reminded of the New Jersey house where he'd met with Pelado. The air was the same or seemed to be.

"Do you still love me, Alec?"

They'd been walking in a meadow after a picnic Judith had fixed. She'd persuaded him finally to get out of the house and the room tainted with the stale scent of cigarette smoke. Gunther had been given to moods of silence after the interrogators finished, as if the men had made him use up all his words. He'd hesitated at first, but Judith gently insisted, so they went. They'd had their lunch of tuna sandwiches and baked beans under a tree where they also had a view of a long fairway and its groups of motorcarted players swinging in the distance like chain-gang laborers in a weed patch. Now they lay together under another tree not far from the house. Gunther had enjoyed the outing more than he'd imagined he would.

"Alex, are you asleep?"

"No, I'm trying to think of an answer."

"Well?"

"I forgot the question."

She bent down to look into his face. She was still the most beautiful woman he had ever known. "Talk to me, Alec. Please. I want to know about—about what you're doing. Those men who were here, I know it was to do with the trouble in Germany. You're not simply a political officer with the embassy, are you? It's something more—"

Gunther closed his eyes. "Yes, I still love you."

"The papers said they traded you for another espionage agent in

France. A man in prison for spying.'' He felt her lean back against the tree, felt her fingers touch his face, the line of his jaw. "Can you tell me, Alec? Can you talk about it? I won't press if you can't talk about it.''

Gunther took her hand, held it against his cheek, but said nothing.

"They've all been very polite to me. At first, in Berlin, they said you'd been called away for several days. Then a man from the embassy—the one who always seemed to need a shave—Swanson, I think, came to the flat. He said I'd need to be going home, to the states. He said I shouldn't worry, but that you'd been detained by the East Germans and I should pack some things and he would arrange transportation. It was a small matter, he said. It would be cleared up in a few days, and you would join me soon. There were people with me every minute until I came here.'' She paused a moment and took his hand in both of hers. "Oh, Alec, I'm not so naive. The work you did, I knew it was not ordinary, not what some of the others did. Important, I suppose, but not something so—so— Oh, Alec, please talk to me!''

Gunther stirred slightly, twisting to a more comfortable position. "An intelligence officer for the Department of State,'' he said. "That's all it was, my job. I read dispatches about how many people we had and how many people they had, how many planes, how many missiles, how many pilots, how many Band-Aids in the hospitals and the number of spare tires in the warehouse. Very important work. I had a desk in a large office and an adding machine and I counted things.''

"That isn't true.''

"Important work like that is kept secret, Judith. Our side doesn't want their side to know how much we really know about the warehouses and the spare tires. It's a very interesting game and everyone plays it.''

"Spying?''

"Intelligence is not spying. Spying is spying. James Bond does that sort of thing. I just count. I am a first-class counter.''

"And Berlin?''

Gunther said nothing.

"Why—what were you doing on the East side, then? If all you did was—"

"Don't ask me, Judith." Gunther sat up. Until today he'd never *had* to lie to her. She was the calm he could return to from the chaos outside where deception was reality, and security a commodity to bargain. "It—I just can't talk about it. All right?"

"I'm sorry, Alec. I didn't mean—"

"Yes, I know, I know." He pulled her to him and they fell in the grass. "Let's go somewhere," he said. He smiled his old Alec smile and she looked relieved that he wasn't angry. "I have some time off. We can drive anywhere you like."

"No more meetings?"

"No more meetings," Gunther said.

She kissed him lightly on the mouth and Gunther responded deeply with his own kisses, rolling over her and being careful not to press his weight too hard.

"I'm not a china doll, Alec. I won't break."

Gunther kissed her again. "I liked that," he said.

"I was hoping you hadn't forgotten. But it isn't the most fun. Next comes foreplay. And after that, well, I like that part best of all."

"Do you?" He unbuttoned her blouse and placed his hand over her breast. "It's been too long."

"Yes, too long," she said. "But now you're home."

"I do love you, Judith."

"I know," she said, and held him tight as if he were a little boy. "I know."

They made love like two first lovers, fumbling with garments and remaining silent in the shade of the tree when it was over. She lay in the crook of his arm, on her side, her head resting on his shoulder.

"I know where we can go, Alec." She propped herself up on one elbow, letting the blouse hang open in the afternoon breeze.

"Where can we go?"

"Staten Island. I want to go to Staten Island on the ferry. It isn't far to drive, Alec. We could be there tonight. It would be so nice to take the ferry tonight. A second honeymoon. We could stay at a ho-

tel, an expensive one—the Plaza! Oh, Alec, please, could we?"
Her eyes were bright with anticipation. She hadn't smiled like that
in weeks, if he could remember.

"Now?"

"Yes, Alec. Oh, please!"

Gunther shrugged, then smiled. "Only if you promise to dress
yourself properly. I refuse to be seen with a woman who's been fro-
licked under a Connecticut tree and who hasn't the decency to cover
her knockers."

"Boobs, Alec."

"Whatever, then."

Judith tucked the ends of the blouse into her pants. "Up, Alec,
up. We have to hurry. We have to leave now."

They left the tree and the spot where their impressions remained
in the grass, Gunther walking, Judith running ahead, begging him to
hurry. When she reached the house, Judith stopped short in the
doorway. Four men were waiting. Mackensen was one. He was
standing near a window examing a small porcelain figurine.

"Good afternoon, Alec." He nodded politely toward Judith. "I
hate to interrupt anything, but I'm afraid I have to take up a bit more
of your time. You don't mind, do you, Judith?" He paused to
glance casually out the window. There was a clear view of the place
they'd just left.

"Jenkins said I was finished," Gunther said coldly.

"You were . . . with Jenkins." Mackensen set the figurine
back in its place. "Now it's my turn."

Mackensen's debriefing lasted days. When it was finished,
Gunther was sent to Virginia, where he was assigned to a job he im-
mensely disliked. Judith never again mentioned the trip to Staten Island. It was as though they'd missed the last chance. Gunther began
to drink heavily. Then there were the nightmares, especially during
storms, when he would come awake screaming German names. He
drove Judith out, finally. He knew that. He'd exposed her to a part
of his life, and as he tried to hide it again, he only succeeded in
pushing her away. When she moved to her mother's in White
Plains, Gunther never called. He lived in cocktail lounges more than

in his hotel room. Slowly, over the months, with the whiskey to
help, Judith became a memory that he fought not to recall. Until recently. He didn't think he cared anymore.

There was a light tapping at the door. "Sir? Sir, are you all
right?"

Gunther realized he'd been in there too long. Time, lately, had a
way of getting away from him. He unlatched the door and opened it
to see the stewardess.

"Sir? You've been in there so long," she said, slightly embarrassed. "We wanted to be sure you were all right."

"I'm fine," Gunther said. "I was a little warm."

She nodded as if she'd dealt before with warm passengers. "Yes,
sir. There's an air vent over your seat. Can I get you some water?"

"Thank you, no. I'm fine now." Gunther started toward his seat.
He didn't like making a fuss; he didn't like strangers looking at him.
The stewardess followed him, and when he was seated she hovered
over him, fiddling with the air vent, directing it into his face. "I'm
fine I told you," he said a bit unpleasantly. "You needn't bother
with me."

But she wouldn't be put off. "We want you to be comfortable."
She was screwing the little air gadget for maximum flow.

"Just leave it!" Gunther said.

Startled, the stewardess jumped as if he'd bitten her. She started
to say something, but didn't. Gunther looked to be a man who might
make trouble. He didn't pretend to be a gentleman. For twenty minutes, until they landed, she didn't bother him again.

"What are you doing in Salt Lake? Why aren't you in California?" There was concern in Mackensen's voice; he sounded surprised.

Gunther glanced through the phone booth glass to the televised
schedule of departures. "Vargas isn't in California. He's in Montana or on his way there. Didn't Rockwell tell you I called?"

"Yes, yes," Mackensen said impatiently. There was a pause.
"What's he doing in Montana?"

"Quill," Gunther said. "Victor Quill. He's next, you know."

"And Hix? What about Richard Hix?"

"Rockwell was supposed to have explained this to you," Gunther said angrily. "Hix has gone to visit his mother. Vargas just missed him. He knows I'm close behind. He left a message for me in Sacramento. He's after Quill now."

"It isn't procedure." Mackensen sounded annoyed. "We're supposed to be informed where our people go on leave."

Gunther couldn't believe the pettiness. At least Hix was alive. "We've kept Vargas from making a hit. That's important. He's off-balance, I hope. He thinks this is a game."

"What makes you think Hix is not being tracked by Vargas right now? That this Montana thing isn't just a smoke screen?"

"Because it's like Vargas to play it this way," Gunther said. "It's the first thing he's done that looks like something he'd do. He liked to play games."

"I see." Another pause. "You may be right. Vargas probably is after Quill. I don't like it."

"Of course he's after Quill. That's what this is all about, isn't it?"

"What do you mean?" Mackensen replied sharply.

Gunther sighed heavily, but not so Mackensen could hear. "Vargas is sticking our nose in it. He's one step ahead of me and he wants to show us he can run rings around our dragnet, such as it is."

"He wasn't supposed to get out of California. I don't like this. I wanted to end it in California, Alec." He sounded as if Vargas was supposed to cooperate. "Do you know Quill? The kind of man he is?"

Gunther remembered him. Victor Quill was one of the strongest and cruelest men he'd ever met. He'd been useful in Nicaragua during training. Forced march was his thing in the jungle terrain, Gunther recalled. An ex-Marine, and dark-complexioned, almost Negro. Quill had no use for blacks and it helped matters little when he was sometimes mistaken for a black. The ironic thing was, back in those mountains of Latin America, that Ollie was the only man in the brigade who could keep up with Quill. That must have galled the hell out of him. Gunther wondered if he'd changed any.

"I knew him. He was very outdoorsy."

Mackensen grunted. "Still is. There was a time when he worked for me. Now he's officially out of the agency. He doesn't talk much. The last I heard, Quill had bought himself an interest in a ski lodge up there. He may be difficult to track down right away."

"Just as long as I find him before Vargas does," Gunther said. He remembered Rockwell. "Did your assistant get the flight information I asked about?"

"I have it here. Peter is sure Vargas did not fly into Butte by commercial airline. The only other place is a private airport and that isn't likely."

"No?"

"It belongs to Quill. A little grass runway with no lights, near the lodge. Probably no one outside the lodge even knows it's there."

"You're sure?"

"Alec, there are probably a lot of things Vargas can do, but there's one thing he can't. It's the most logical way we had of knowing positively he hadn't flown into Silver Bow airport. Besides, in the last two days there have only been fifty people fly in there."

"And how did you know positively he didn't fly in?"

"Because he's black, and there hasn't been one fly in there in almost a week." Mackensen said proudly. "Even Vargas can't change the color of his skin."

13

To wage guerrilla warfare in more or less open country, all the regular principles have to be followed with even more skill and intensity. The maximum possible mobility is required and preferably at night.

He watched the Silver Bow County Airport appear beneath him as Western Flight 73 banked to the southwest over Montana's snow-capped peaks. They'd flown almost directly north from Salt Lake City and Gunther was again reminded of his abiding respect for the power and majesty of the mountains. They were not kind or cruel, but, like the sea, could only be challenged by man on their own terms.

As the plane made its final approach, he could see the city clearly: set on a bare slope, slanting to the south, Butte was surrounded by gaunt mountains, and its center district seemed pitifully vulnerable with its grimy open-pit mines and countless piles of slag. It was a city that hadn't met the challenge, but that was fighting more against itself than the mountains for survival. Everywhere Gunther could see dilapidated buildings and empty weed-infested lots. The mountains were making this city pay for the billions in ore that had been given up. In ten thousand years, Gunther thought, this wound called Butte, with its white rock painted *M* for the state school of mines, would be swallowed up and healed, and not a trace left behind.

Gunther spent two hours in the city. He made some clothing purchases and rented a car. By ten o'clock he'd driven to the ski resort, and after finagling with the assistant hotel manager (because the ho-

95

tel was normally closed in the summer months), won himself a room, but at an exorbitant rate. He paid for two days in advance, then set out to find Quill.

"He's a big man," Gunther explained to the clearing-crew foreman, raising his hand a foot above his own head. "Name's Quill."

He was standing in the hall outside the first-floor room of John Stroup. Stroup was slightly taller than Gunther, barefoot and wearing a T-shirt and workpants. His face and neck were sunburned and grimy with sweat. Gunther could hear the shower running.

"Vic?" the foreman said. "The old leatherneck?" He had a westerner's accent.

"Yes. I'm trying to find him."

"Well, he's here. Just back from flying his little plane. We're clearing the west slope. Vic gives us a hand in the summers. Strong as a goddamn ox, that old man." Stroup paused to scratch at his belly and look Gunther over. "You a friend of Vic's?"

"I haven't seen him in fifteen years," Gunther said. "We worked together once."

"We got a little camp up on the run at the first lift station. Three other guys and Vic. He's up there."

"How do I get to the lift station?"

"Only got one lift, but it ain't working now—being overhauled. You can go with me and Jess in the morning. Five o'clock."

"What about tonight? I'd like to see him tonight."

"Tonight?" Stroup pulled a battered pocket watch from his pants. "You know it's after eleven o'clock. They're asleep if they're not horsing around. I should be asleep, too." His eyes narrowed as he peered at Gunther. "What's the problem? You a cop? I've had some rowdy heads working for me, but Vic ain't one. Straight, you know what I mean?" He gestured to the room behind him. "He even owns part of this. What's so important you gotta see Vic tonight?" Stroup opened the door to his room wide and leaned forward on the doorjamb.

"We worked together once," Gunther repeated patiently. "It's about a job we did. He knows me. I'm not from the police." Gunther watched Stroup's eyes and was conscious of his hands. Stroup looked like a man accustomed to violence: he was heavyset and thick in the chest. His face was crisscrossed by coarse lines that age and the sun had hardened. His graying hair was streaked and dirty and fell in undisciplined patches on his head. He seemed to be a man who'd avoided reckoning with society and all the debts that it incurred. He had very large hands.

"He ain't in any trouble, then?"

"No," Gunther lied. "But it is quite important. I need to talk to him as soon as possible."

"You want me to take you up there?"

"Just tell me how to get there."

"Couldn't find it alone," Stroup said. He let out a long sad sigh. "Okay, I might as well take you if you're determined to go. Rather that than spend tomorrow hunting you lost. Come in. I'm going to take a shower before I go running around up there again. Damn wood ticks drive me crazy."

"I appreciate it," Gunther said.

"Yeah, you'd better."

They drove up in Stroup's Land Rover. It was just after midnight, but Gunther saw the four-man wall tent on a slope past the log-cabin lift station. By the time Stroup cut the engine, a large man was standing in the tent's doorway sleepily shielding his eyes from the glare of the headlights.

"John, that you?" Quill looked like a bear in boxer shorts. "For Godsakes, kill the lights." He walked to the vehicle on the driver's side.

Stroup climbed out, nodding to Gunther. "Vic, brought this fella up from the lodge. Says he had to talk to you tonight. Says you two used to work together."

Quill poked his head through the window.

"Hello, Quill," Gunther said. "It's been a long time." He didn't offer his hand.

"Alec Gunther!" Quill said in blank surprise. "Well, I'll be goddamned." He said it as if it were true.

"I have to talk to you tonight." Gunther made no gesture to get out of the Land Rover. "It's company business."

From the tent another head popped through the flap, sleepily inquiring about Stroup and the headlights. Quill sent him back to bed and, after a short discussion, Stroup decided to sleep in Quill's bunk, as long as Quill was going to be up anyway. Five minutes later Quill was dressed. He and Gunther walked to the rise where the lift station overlooked a downslope clearing. Gunther sat against the little cabin on the side protected from the chilly breeze. Quill climbed into the wooden lift chair and swung the metal safety bar down across his lap.

"All right, Alec," he said in a deep, tired voice. "What have you come all this way to wake me out of a sound sleep to talk about?"

If anyone approaching six feet was tall in Gunther's eyes, then Victor Quill was a giant. He might have been a wrestler or a lumberjack. His flannel plaid shirt sleeves were rolled up to below the elbow, exposing thickly haired forearms. His denim jeans were tucked neatly into the tops of his black leather boots, paratrooper fashion. He wore no rings and no watch and kept his hands in front of him, resting on his thighs, elbows slightly out, his weight distributed evenly, ready to spring forward at an instant's notice. He sat keenly erect, though he appeared relaxed and attuned to his environment, and Gunther supposed that little escaped his senses. He seemed, in spite of himself, a gentle and agile man. It was as if time had had no hold on him; he hadn't changed since the months of training in the mountain tropics of Central America. If anything, Quill seemed larger. His brown hair was longer—a concession to the style of the times—and matted in light curls along his straight forehead. The mountain breeze caught several loose strands at the back of his head and caused them to ripple slightly, like the fringe of a waving ensign. Gunther wondered if he was bothered by wood ticks.

"I'm afraid you're in danger," Gunther said. When he said it, he wished he'd put it a different way. "Someone is looking for you." That wasn't any better.

"Besides you?"

"A man named Ollie Vargas. Do you remember him."

Quill said nothing.

"It was the Cuban operation," Gunther said. He buttoned the top button of his jacket and turned up the collar against the mountain chill. He ought to have brought something warmer. The smell of pine and fir was heavy in the air. There was a quarter moon and many stars and only a few cirrus clouds. To the southwest was Mount Torrye's snow-capped peak. It seemed odd to bring up the subject of a dirty, unsuccessful amphibious assault on a derelict island, in scenery such as this. "Operation Jupiter, officially. Vargas commanded Red Beach."

"Vargas is looking for me?" Quill repeated slowly to himself. It seemed to amuse him. "The big black one. The one they called The Horse? The only one in the brigade who could stay with me on our little outings?"

"Yes, that's him. Ollie Vargas."

"What's he looking for me for?" Quill said without moving.

"Revenge, apparently." Gunther stood up and stuffed his hands into his pockets. "He's killed eight agents in the last two months or so. All of them had something to do with the invasion. He seems to hold us responsible." Gunther looked down the ski run. He could see the lights of the lodge faintly in the distance. Turning back to Quill, he said, "It's my job to find him and stop him. You're next on his list."

"Am I?"

"I believe so. It isn't very long anymore, the list, I mean. Of forty-six agents directly involved, twenty-two are dead, one way or another." Gunther remembered Miles standing at the wall in Berlin, saw him cut down by a volley of small arms. "The point is, we think you will be his next target."

"We?"

"I'm working for Mackensen. A special assignment."

In the darkness, Gunther could see the big man smile. "So, Vargas is looking for me, is he, because of Cuba?" Gunther nodded his head. "And you're going to protect *me*?" Quill ran one hand through his hair and placed it back on his knee as if not to would put him off balance. "Aren't you a little old for this kind of thing?"

"Probably," Gunther replied.

"Was that you they ran all the stink about a while back? East Germany? I remember the workname. Shelley or something."

"Sheldon."

"That's it," Quill said with a nod, his eyes on Gunther. "Same workname you used on the Jupiter operation."

Gunther nodded.

"I wonder if you remember mine."

"Not offhand," Gunther said. "It was a long time ago."

"Velquez," Quill said. "Real nice spic name, eh? You were Alec Sheldon, the coordinator, and I was Victor Velquez, the Mountain Man."

Gunther remembered the name now. It sounded familiar.

Quill shook his head. He watched Gunther very closely. "So, you're still active."

"Recently revived, as they say." Gunther glanced up to see a cloud float across the black sky, seeming to touch the moon. Somewhere an owl cried out. It was getting colder. "Specially for Vargas," he continued. "Tactically, Cuba was mine. It seems Mackensen is putting me back in to tie all the loose ends." He glanced up at Quill. "And Vargas is a very loose end at the moment."

"Mackensen is running this?" Quill rubbed his hands together. It was the first indication he'd made that there was a chill about. "A Special Ops job, is it?"

"Yes."

Quill sighed, his breath visible in the night air as he exhaled. "I've done a job or two for Mackensen." He nodded his head approvingly. "He's thorough . . . professional." Quill looked away again, searching the darkness as if he expected to see someone else. "I got out in seventy-one . . . getting tired of the routine. That's why I live here. Away from people. That sound strange to you?"

"No."

"You city boys won't last long up there in those big crowded places." Quill was grinning in the darkness. "Too much pollution. Too many cars, people, airplanes. . . . I hear they mug you in the daylight these days."

"Yeah, well, we do our best."

Quill didn't seem to be particularly bothered that a man was searching to kill him, and that bothered Gunther. Perhaps, he thought, it was because Vargas was black. To a man like Quill it simply wouldn't do to show concern; after all, Vargas was only a nigger. Gunther took a deep breath of the cold mountain air and burned his nostrils.

"You're married, aren't you? I recollect you had quite a beauty waiting in Panama while we were training. Judy, was it?"

"Judith." Gunther looked down the slope toward the lodge. "Divorced now. She's taken up real estate."

"Any kids?"

Gunther shook his head. "I don't know," he said, then realized he was talking about himself. "Oh. No," he said. "We never had much time." He meant *he* hadn't. He remembered Mackensen had asked him the same question and wondered why everyone was so interested.

They were silent for a time. Gunther paced back and forth beside the cabin and Quill spread his arms out across the back of the chair lift and rocked gently in the breeze. Gunther supposed the man was embarrassed about asking so many questions. Gunther was just cold.

"When do you expect this Vargas will show up?" Quill finally asked. He hadn't turned to look at Gunther; his eyes were fixed on something farther up the mountain.

"I don't expect him to show at all. He knows we're looking for him now. He'll probably try something at a distance. With a rifle." Quill turned his head to look at Gunther. "I'm guessing," Gunther said. "But those are tactics we taught him. He's been very good so far."

Quill was quiet for a moment. Finally he said, "How long have you been on this? Searching for Vargas, I mean?"

"Does it make a difference?"

Quill smiled. "Well, if he's already made several hits and you're supposedly some kind of guardian . . . to me, it would make a difference." He stared at Gunther. "Especially if I'm next."

"Mackensen brought me into it after number seven went down. They want Vargas very badly."

"That makes you zero for one, then. I hope your statistics improve." Quill extracted a pack of brown cigarettes from his shirt pocket and lit one. "Maybe you'd better tell me about it. You said eight so far, didn't you?

"Kenneth Tripp was the last. Monday. He was on leave in L.A."

"How?"

"Shot," Gunther said. "Nine millimeter automatic. Close range."

"It's reliable at close range." Quill smiled at a private joke. "I've used it myself."

"The others were made to look like accidents. Harry, Harry Phillips—went off a cliff in his car in Arizona."

Quill nodded as if he agreed it would have been a fatal accident.

"Mat Levin, James Barkham, Jack O'Brien, Dave Cronin—Cronin fell off a mountain near Boulder. It doesn't always pay to be outdoorsy."

"This Vargas moves around, doesn't he?"

"Yes," Gunther said sadly. "José Franzone and Albert Peloquin. That makes eight."

"And I'm number nine?"

"Not unless you want to be. I'm here to stop him."

Quill swung the safety bar up out of his lap and stepped down from the lift chair. "Like chasing a ghost, I imagine." He walked to the edge of the lift runway and squashed the cigarette in the dirt under his boot. "Are you carrying?"

Gunther nodded. "I'd be a little ridiculous not to under the circumstances." He gestured under his arm. "Colt .38 Cobra."

"You carry it well. I hadn't noticed."

"It won't do much good unless Vargas comes after us with a shovel. Do you have a rifle up here?"

Quill nodded his head toward the Land Rover. "John carries a 30-30 Marline lever-action carbine behind the seat. Shells too."

"Lever-action?"

Quill shrugged. "John fancies himself as some kind of cowboy."

"Tube magazine?"

"Right. Six shot."

It was Gunther's turn to shrug. "Isn't much, is it?"

"That depends on the game, Alec," the big man said. "Isn't much on ghosts, but it'll blow the guts out of a man, sure enough."

"Sure enough." Gunther was staring down at the lights of the lodge. It looked to be a long way away.

14

A guerrilla must be audacious and optimistic, even amidst unfavorable conditions and circumstances. He must be adaptable, imaginative and inventive.

Gunther sat in the Land Rover most of the morning while Quill and the others went about their work. He was parked in the shade of a large pine about ten feet inside the tree line further up the slope. From there he could see all the men and had a clear view of most of the rest of the ski run where anyone with a rifle might take a shot. It wasn't an ideal setup, but it was the best he could do, since Quill absolutely refused to leave. He sat with the loaded carbine across his lap and he had shells in both pockets of his jacket.

They all went together for lunch at the lodge. Gunther called Mackensen for an update on Vargas, which was pointless since no one had any idea where he was. Two blacks had arrived earlier in the morning at Silver Bow County Airport, but they were found to be laborers who worked at the Anaconda mine. When Gunther returned to the dining room, he was frustrated and tired.

"You gonna eat the pie?" Quill asked. They were at a table near a large window with a view of the ski runs. Quill had devoured everything in front of him and now he was greedily eyeing the food that Gunther had only played with.

"Be my guest."

Quill pulled the little plate toward him and shoved a heaping forkful into his mouth. "What's a matter, Alec?" he said between bites. "Bad news from the old man?"

"No news at all," Gunther said, staring out at the sunlit slopes.

"Don't be so glum. No news is good news." Quill grinned. "A couple of the guys on the crew have been making funny remarks about you sitting up in the Land Rover all morning. I didn't tell them what you were doing."

"It would make things a lot more comfortable if you and I just left," Gunther said unpleasantly. It had been very warm in the cab and not all the wood ticks were in the woods.

"I told you I wasn't running off, Alec." Quill finished the pie and wiped his mouth delicately with a napkin. "Besides, where would we go? If you intend to catch Vargas, this is the ideal setting. I know these mountains. There's nowhere he could go that I haven't been. He has to take the road up to the lodge unless he's a billy goat, and the assistant manager has been tipped to watch for any blacks that wander in. I'm safer—we're safer here than anywhere else."

"Vargas is an unusual man," Gunther said, recalling what Pelado had said. "I don't trust him to do the simple, logical thing." His eyes scanned the mountains.

"Then trust me. When he shows up—if he shows up—we'll know."

"Maybe," Gunther offered without conviction. He got to his feet. "In the meantime, let's you and me move away from this window. It makes me nervous." He nodded toward the slope. "With a scope, a man could see this table from the top of that ridge."

Quill shook his head. "Boy, you really take this seriously."

"It's kept me alive for thirty years."

"No one could hit me from that far away." Quill was looking up the mountain.

"Exactly," Gunther said. "He might hit me."

He sat in the Land Rover the rest of the afternoon, swatting flies, picking ticks out of his clothes and watching. Surveillance was the most boring job in the world and Gunther recalled some of the jobs he'd had in his checkered career. Whether it was legwork or manning a telephone tap or sweating through earphones on a housebug, it was always the same drudging routine. Waiting was the name of the game and it never failed to give him a headache and put him in a sour temper.

It wasn't until after dark that they stopped work. Gunther drove the truck down to the camp. They ate supper together by an open fire and about nine o'clock Stroup took the Land Rover down to the lodge for the night. The tent was crowded with five men, but as long as Quill wouldn't go back to the lodge to take a room, Gunther stayed at the camp. Quill was being a horse's ass about the whole thing, but Gunther had no authority to force him to do anything. Quill just laughed.

It was the same the next day and that night. The routine was always the same. They went for lunch at the lodge and had supper at the camp.

The following day, when Gunther returned to the dining room after talking to Mackensen, Quill was not in his usual complacent mood. "Alec, I'm getting tired of all this," he said wearily. They were at a different table, away from the window. "It's been three days. You're getting on my nerves just sitting up there all day watching me." He brushed a hand through his hair. "I don't think this character is going to show up. You've scared him away."

"I doubt it," Gunther said.

"We've got another two weeks' work up here. Are you going to hang around waiting until then."

"I'll be here until I know he's somewhere else," he said impatiently. "You might as well get used to the idea."

"He's not coming, for Chrissake, Alec!" A waitress across the room looked up in surprise. Quill leaned forward over the table toward Gunther, his long arms reaching almost to the other side. "He's not coming," he said again, almost in a whisper. "You're wasting your time. I don't want protection. I don't need it, anyway."

"No."

"Look, Alec, for the last—"

Gunther slapped the palm of his hand down hard on the tabletop. "Don't 'look Alec' me! Vargas is setting something up. I know it. I can sense it. Goddammit, Quill, I know he's already here." He nodded toward the window. "Out there." He meant the mountains.

"I can watch out for myself," Quill said angrily.

Gunther said nothing. He wouldn't look at the big man.

"I'm a grown-up. I can look after myself."

"The thing is I'm not really concerned about you," Gunther said. "You're only incidental to me. You are here and that means Vargas will be here sooner or later. I don't care what you do, but I'm not letting you out of my sight." Gunther slipped the glasses off his nose and polished them with a handkerchief. "I'm after Ollie Vargas," he said in a fiercely determined voice. "And by God I'm going to have him. *This is my work!*"

"You won't find him, Alec." Quill stared at Gunther angrily. "Vargas isn't coming. Not today and not tomorrow—not ever. This is a waste of time and I'm getting tired of it." He nodded to himself as if it were obvious what he should do. "I'm going to call Mackensen myself. I don't like you around. There's no reason."

"It isn't up to Mackensen. This is my show."

"We'll see about that," Quill stood up from the table. "You're a fool, Gunther. You shouldn't have accepted this one. You're too old and too stupid to see it."

Gunther shrugged pleasantly, but said nothing and watched as Quill walked quickly to the lobby where the telephone booths were located. At least, Gunther thought, Quill had enough sense to use a pay station. He wondered what Mackensen would say.

15

The guerrilla relies on mobility. This permits him to quickly flee the area of action whenever necessary, constantly shifting his front, to evade encirclement and even to counterencircle the enemy.

For any other man the climb would have been an absurd undertaking. He'd flown into Helena dressed as a United States Army Special Forces captain and stayed at a motor hotel near the airport. He went by bus to Garrison in Powell County and checked into a small motel, paying for three days in advance. Carrying pack and hunting gear and dressed in camouflage suit, Vargas looked like any other hunter that roamed these mountain regions. He set out early in the morning, first along the Clark Fork River, south toward Deer Lodge, then he slanted west into the humpbacks of the Continental Divide.

It was an ambitious climb. From the river flats to the back of Deer Lodge Mountain, it was ten miles—double that for a hiker—up steep ridges and across scores of washboard folds and rockslides. He walked southeasterly on 120-degree course by his compass and kept the peak of Jack Mountain ahead of him through the tall evergreens. Vargas took his first break after four hours, his second after three more. When he reached his pivoting point—the place where he would turn directly west and approach the ski-lodge run from the east—he stopped and made a small camp without a fire. He would approach the lodge from the top of the mountain, three miles away.

He opened a can of peaches from his pack and also ate four strips of beef jerky. He changed his socks. After a short nap Vargas prepared his rifle for the task ahead. It was an Austrian Dschullnigg bolt-action known for its accuracy at long range and its durability. In the hike from the river he'd used it as walking stick, crutch and lever to pull him through rock formations. By the time he'd made camp, it was filthy; the front barrel was clogged with dirt and the stock and receiver assembly was grimy and dirty with mud and sweat. The weapon was stripped down completely, each piece oiled and lubricated, the bore and rifling cleaned, then it was reassembled.

Vargas fired half a box of ammunition using .308 Winchester cartridges. He picked his targets carefully—tree limbs and pinecones—at a medium distance of seventy-five to one hundred yards without a scope. He'd chosen the Winchester ammunition particularly for its weight, two hundred grains, which was heavier than the standard NATO military round. It was not a jacketed bullet, but silver-tipped, which aided accuracy; besides, he preferred center-fire cartridges over rimfire. The greater sectional density of the heavier Winchester bullet ensured penetration and resistance to deflection by wind or brush. With a muzzle velocity of more than twenty-four hundred feet per second, he was assured of a flat trajectory and high residual energy—impact power—at long range.

Next he fixed the round ends of the tin peach can to trees at two hundred and three hundred yards from his camp. He unwrapped a Weatherby Imperial 6x telescopic sight from a cloth in his pack and attached it to the weapon. It was a scope Vargas was used to handling, with grub screws for wind, elevation, and minute-of-angle adjustments, and a post and cross-hair reticle.

At the two-hundred-yard target his first three shots were grouped low to the right in an area about the size of a paperback novel. After an adjustment the second group was above, though in line with, the shiny silver target. Vargas made a final adjustment and lay prone behind a fallen evergreen, resting the Dschullnigg on top at its center. He sighted carefully and fired three times, reloading the single-shot weapon each time between shots. The grouping this time was two jagged penetrations in the target and another about two inches away at ten o'clock position. At the three-hundred-yard target, after five shots, the grouping was in area about the size of a man's head. One of the bullets had pierced the edge of the target. Satisfied, Vargas smeared the grub screws with airplane glue he'd brought along for just that purpose, so the scope adjustments could not be moved accidentally, and set it aside to dry.

The day's work had been long and tiring. He figured he'd hiked twenty-five miles through some of the toughest country in the Rocky Mountains, but still he was eager for the work ahead. He stripped down to his shorts to allow his sweat-soaked shirt and pants to dry before dark, when the temperature would drop fifteen to twenty degrees. The sun was visible in the west. There would probably be three more hours of daylight, so he decided to sleep. He would clean the rifle again, before starting out after dark, and eat. If he timed it right, he could be in position above the ski run shortly before dawn and be ready to do what he'd come here to do. Vargas was accustomed to night exercises and they were what he preferred. As the afternoon sun began casting shadows across the small clearing where he lay, the Taskmaster drifted off into a peaceful sleep, unencumbered by dreams or thoughts of the past.

16

The "minuet" is a maneuver used to wear down the larger-sized enemy force. The enemy is surrounded on all four sides. The dance begins as one side fires on the enemy, who naturally move toward that side and are thus drawn out. Then another guerrilla side begins firing. Thus, as the partners on all sides participate in the dance, the enemy is rendered immobile, expends vast quantities of ammunition, and loses morale, while the guerrilla band remains unharmed.

Gunther was not so fortunate. His cot was uneven and uncomfortable. He was cold and couldn't sleep more than an hour or two at a time. They'd gone to bed early, about nine o'clock, and Gunther lay fully dressed under his blanket, with Stroup's carbine beside him. He couldn't get used to the chilliness of mountain nights at that altitude. He'd sleep for a time, then come awake quickly at the sound of some mountain creature squawking in the night. Twice he'd gotten up and walked to the lift station to smoke a cigarette and piss against the corner of the cabin's log structure. The night was blacker than it had been, clouds had formed late in the afternoon, and by nightfall the stars and moon had been blotted out of the sky. Someone had mentioned snow, but nothing came of it.

The day hadn't gone well at all. One of the workmen had smashed his hand when it was caught in a tree-removing operation involving a wrench. Quill was reticent and edgy in the afternoon after the accident, and when they ate supper he hardly said a word. Evidently his talk with Mackensen hadn't been successful.

Gunther's last trip to the lift station was shortly before 2:00 A.M. When he returned he was determined to sleep no matter how cold or how uncomfortable he was or how many owls tried to keep him awake. He would not get up again, he told himself; besides, he didn't think he had any piss left. At 5:30 when the others roused themselves out of bed, Gunther was groggy and tired. He decided not to shave or eat breakfast, though he did drink coffee. He was not looking forward to this day.

The climb hadn't been difficult. Vargas took his time, walking through the tall pines casually, enjoying the sounds and smells of the evergreens as if he were on a picnic. The rifle was slung over his shoulder, butt down, trigger housing to the front. His night vision was extremely keen and he glided through the trees and brush like a wily panther stalking an unwary prey. He rested only once, and then only to verify his bearings. He moved steadily upward at a constant pace, neither fast nor slow, but at a rate that enabled the night's numbing, energy-sapping cold to balance his physical exertion. Vargas found the chill refreshing and it helped him not to tire or perspire.

It was sometime after three that Vargas made the crest of the mountain. In the last hour a slight breeze had gathered and the night was stirred by the hauntingly serene rhythm of the mountain's rustling pines. It was a music that transcended time and distance as if the mountains were alive and speaking through the gentle thrash of needle leaves in the wind, and Vargas was aware of his own vibrant mood beckoning him onward. He could see the white-capped outline of a hundred lofty peaks against the dark horizon and hear their lonely, whistling sounds. If it was cold, he didn't notice it when he finally stopped. He was at home here.

The Taskmaster welcomed the coming of dawn by searching for a strategic location through the telescopic sight. He was lying in a bed of pine needles at the fringe of the uppermost part of the western ski run. He would have to find a spot that afforded a view of the lodge and the area where Quill and the clearing crews would be working. It would need to be near enough to the target area to assure a reasonable shot—since he would have only one—yet far enough away to make undetected escape successful. It was a sniper's game; all the advantages would be on his side. He had also to consider that Gunther was here somewhere, waiting. That was the challenge.

He found several places along both sides of the run, but chose one on the south side of the slope, below a slight rise of firs. It was an ideal location, about 230 yards from the campsite of the work crew. He'd be shooting across the run's clearing. As he fired into the clearing from that position, with the rise behind him acting like a sounding board, the report of the rifle shot would echo across the mountain like a sonic boom. No one would know where it had come from.

Vargas took his time circling around the slope to get to the place he'd chosen. He had only to wait for Quill to show himself and to pick the moment of execution.

"What the hell do you mean I can't use it?" Gunther said angrily. He was standing with Quill near the front of the tent. Stroup was beside Quill, absently watching the men working on the tree stump that yesterday had stubbornly refused to be pried from the ground.

"Just that," said Quill. "He doesn't want you to use the Land Rover after today. We're going to be hauling—"

"Oh, Christ!"

"I didn't know you were going to show up, you know, Alec. Maybe if I'd known, I could have got you a nice green jeep all your own." Quill nodded toward the slope. "And you could run up and down this goddamn mountain looking for ghosts until the tourists run you out next winter. It's a favor to me that John lets you use it at all."

"Thanks." Gunther sneered.

"It's his fucking truck!" Quill pointed to the vehicle. "And his fucking rifle! The only thing you've contributed to this effort is to piss me off. I don't like it. I'm fed up with this whole game of yours and Mackensen's. I don't need a babysitter. Can't you leave me alone?"

Gunther shook his head. "I don't think it'll be much longer. And I need wheels, I need mobility. If Vargas gets past the lodge without being noticed, how am I going to find him?"

"*I* can find him," Quill said. "*If* he shows up."

"Count on it."

"All right," he said quietly. "Do what you want." Gunther recognized a subtle menace in Quill's voice. "I don't care what you do anymore, but starting in the morning you're on foot unless you want to bring that rented Ford up here. I'm finished talking to you, Alec. Just stay out of my way."

"I'll do my goddamn best, Quill," Gunther said. He stomped to the truck and drove it recklessly to the parking place under the pine tree where he'd spent so many hours killing wood ticks. He didn't notice anything unusual about the tree line to the south as he passed within fifteen yards of Vargas's sniper position.

Vargas, however, did notice Gunther. The way he was driving, speeding and bouncing all over the slope, Vargas thought for an instant that Gunther had spotted him. He lay motionless on the ground with the Dschullnigg trained on the driver of the truck until it had passed.

For an hour he watched Gunther. The Land Rover was parked about two hundred yards further up the slope, placing Vargas almost in the middle of a line separating him from his target and his pursuer. But Gunther hadn't given any indication that he'd seen him, so Vargas felt safe for the moment. He'd always known he'd have to contend with Gunther during the hunt. The added risk of his being this close only made Vargas more determined.

Gunther could just sit there and watch.

It was half a mile from the lodge to where Gunther chose to park the Land Rover. He could see all the approaches to the first lift station and most of the grounds surrounding the lodge. Strategically, it was a good choice to watch the activity of anyone who might try to get to the work crew's camp from the direction of the lodge. He could even see the last three hundred yards of the only road into Deer Lodge Ski Resort. The ski lodge was flanked by rocky, mountainous outcroppings that were also visible from his high ground. Anyone foolish enough to come from either direction could be spotted easily, even from the lodge. Gunther never expected Vargas to come from the east, over the top of the mountain. No one could be that determined.

The men were working with a T wrench and lever. A chain was

attached to the top of the tree stump, and as Quill dug below it with a long four-by-four timber to raise it, the wrench locked each link of the chain so that the stump could not slip back down. Gunther was fascinated by Quill's strength. The man worked the timber lever single-handedly while the others manned the wrenching rig. Quill was just ready to begin another series of downward thrusts on the timber when the whole mountain rang with the explosion of the rifle, which was like a rumbling crack of thunder.

The force of the impact threw Quill backward, arms raised, into the beam, like a man falling from an airplane. The bullet struck him below the collarbone on the left side and didn't stop. His hand went to his throat in a horrifying slow-motion gesture like that of Kennedy after the first wound in Dallas. Quill fell against the beam like a drunken bear. His shirtfront was covered with blood.

Almost instantly, Gunther had the truck rolling, speeding crazily down the mountain. He didn't know exactly where the shot had come from, but it had to be somewhere from the southern side of the clearing. The carbine was in his left hand, banging against the open window of the driver's door. He'd driven fifty yards when he saw Quill again. He couldn't believe it. Quill was on his feet, staggering forward, one hand to his throat, screaming, pointing with his other arm. He's seen Vargas, Gunther thought. He's pointing at him!

The second shot struck Quill in the middle of the chest. He came off his feet and landed on his back, arms and feet splayed out. He didn't get up. That second bullet, Gunther knew, was a mistake. He saw where it came from and aimed the truck directly for the spot; his foot pressed the accelerator to the floor. The truck bucked and crashed over holes and limbs so fast at the speed Gunther was forcing it that he couldn't aim the carbine. He held it out the window, braced against the side-mirror strut. He was less than 120 yards away when he saw Vargas. He was against a tree, rifle sling around his arm in the correct standing position, with the weapon pointed directly at Gunther. Gunther fired the carbine, saw the dirt fly up yards away from Vargas. He cocked the lever-action rifle with his left hand and fired again. Missed again. He knew he was traveling more than fifty miles an hour with less than 70 yards to go. Still Vargas didn't fire. Gunther was close enough to see the black eye of the large scope trained on him. Go ahead you bastard! he thought. Go on and shoot!

Gunther got one more shot before Vargas fired the rifle. He knew he was looking directly into the muzzle. He saw the flash, but he knew he wasn't hit. Suddenly, the Land Rover collapsed to the left and he lost control. He felt the carbine being ripped out of his hand as the truck slid slowly over on its side and crashed into a group of saplings on the fringe of the tree line. Gunther was thrown forward first, colliding with the windshield, then backward, as the vehicle slid sideways into the brush.

Finally, he was stopped. His head reeling with pain, he felt his face and chest. No gushing wounds. He'd held on to the steering wheel and was now lying on his left shoulder; his head touched the shattered side-view mirror that had been bent completely back along the side of the truck and out through the driver's window. Somewhere, he heard voices, yelling and running footsteps. The windshield was shattered in three places, but he could still see. Before he passed out, he saw the chess piece. Ten feet away, near the spot Vargas had lain in ambush, was a short stump of a tree, flat across the top where it had been cut with a saw by workmen some summer before. Centered on the stump was a single black knight. As he drifted warmly into unconsciousness, Gunther wondered if it was plastic or the more expensive wooden kind.

17

The guerrilla, at times, must be a consummate liar.

Gunther woke slowly. He could see before he could hear, and several seconds passed before he could smell an odor of lilacs mixed with tobacco. He was in a room at the lodge. The curtains were drawn and a lamp in the corner was lit. When he turned his head, a wave of intense pain passed through his brain.

Someone must have been watching him because, when he groaned, he heard a door open and close softly. In a few minutes someone entered the room. Then John Stroup was standing in front of him, at the foot of his bed. He was wearing work clothes, and his face was not friendly.

"How do you feel?" Stroup asked.

"Bloody awful," Gunther said.

"Do you feel like throwing up?" By his expression, Gunther didn't think Stroup was at all concerned. It was just a question to be asked. Then there was something to test motor functions: "How many fingers do you see?" Gunther had been asked the questions before.

"No, I don't feel like throwing up."

"The doctor said to ask if you were nauseated. You'll be all right."

Stroup glanced around the room as if he were missing something, then settled his gaze on Gunther again. "Slight concussion. Mild," he said. "You might feel like throwing up." He stood there stolidly, watching Gunther like he half expected it.

"I won't," Gunther promised. His head throbbed. Maybe he would.

"You're scratched up some," Stroup went on. "Cuts and bruises. Nothing serious. You're going to be all right." He seemed to be convinced of that and, Gunther noticed, it bothered him. "Your glasses got broken in the wreck, too."

"I have another pair."

Stroup grasped the footboard of the bed in both hands and leaned forward. "Vic is dead," he said grimly, as if Gunther didn't know. His face was suddenly ashen. The knuckles of his fingers were white where they gripped the bed. "Goddammit, mister, he's dead!"

"I know," Gunther said softly.

"Goddammit, goddammit!" Stroup pounded the bed with his hand. He trembled with rage and despair. "Who killed him? You knew what was going on. Who killed Vic?"

"A man," Gunther said helplessly. Stroup's screams were hurting his ears. "Someone who—" He had no way to explain it.

"You knew he was coming, didn't you? You knew and you just sat on your goddamn fucking ass and watched. Who the hell are you?"

Gunther said nothing. His eyes were burning and he felt a growing queasiness in his stomach. The image of Stroup was blurring in the mad throbbing of his head.

"You'd better talk to me, mister," he said angrily.

"I work for a group of people who would rather not have it known that I work for them," Gunther managed to say.

"The Marines?"

"No. You wouldn't know them if I told you." Gunther was very thirsty. "Quill used to work for them too. Nothing illegal, but we did work in other countries."

"What kind of work?"

"We didn't make a lot of friends at it."

Stroup eyed Gunther suspiciously. "You mean Vic was killed because of what he used to do?"

"That's it. I can't say any more except that the man who shot him also killed several others who worked with us." Gunther's head cleared when he closed his eyes, but he still sweated. "I'm trying to stop him."

"What is he?" Stroup demanded. "Mafia?"

Gunther shook his head. It didn't hurt as much as he thought it would. "No."

"He's gone. Whoever he is, he's gone. I found two empty Winchester cartridges." Stroup lumbered slowly to a chair and dropped himself into it like an exhausted athlete. Gunther remembered the chess piece, but decided not to ask about it. Stroup wouldn't understand. "Why did he kill him like that?" Stroup said. He looked drained, his anger expended for the moment. "I've never seen a man look like that. The middle of Vic's back was—" He looked to Gunther for an answer.

"I know," Gunther said. Stroup had moved beyond Gunther's clear vision. He wished he had his glasses.

"You knew this joker was coming? The guy who killed Vic. You knew, didn't you?"

Gunther nodded again. "We both expected him," he said. He was tired of having everything his fault. "Vic knew about him, too."

"But it was your job?" Stroup made an angry face. Gunther couldn't see him clearly, but there was no mistaking the man's expression, even without glasses. "You said you were supposed to stop him, didn't you? Protect Vic. Isn't that right? You really fucked it, Gunther. I thought people like you were supposed to be efficient." He shook his head.

Gunther said nothing. He felt like death, but he had to try to move, to get up. He must call Mackensen. With great effort Gunther sat up slowly. The throbbing in his head returned, but not the dizziness.

"What do you think you're doing?" Stroup said.

"Glasses," Gunther said, pointing to the small airline bag on the bureau. "I need my glasses."

Stroup retrieved the bag, dropping it on the bed beside Gunther.

"I hope you don't think you're going anywhere," Stroup said.

The man's features came clear as Gunther fitted the spectacles on his face. In the hairline of his right sideburn Stroup had a small wart that Gunther hadn't noticed before. "I have to make a phone call," he said.

"To who?"

Gunther eased himself down from the bed. He had a nasty bruise on his left hip, from the feel of it, and his knees were sore, but he could walk.

"I asked you who you were calling," Stroup said. He was standing off to Gunther's right, at more than an arm's distance.

"I didn't say."

"You're not going to tell me, then," Stroup challenged.

"No," he said, and added, "It's none of your business."

"I think it is, mister." Stroup reached for his wallet. If he'd reached for anything else, Gunther would have hit him. Fastened to an inside pocket of the wallet was a miniature sheriff's deputy's badge. In one of the cracked cellophane frames for snapshots was a card identifying Stroup as an auxiliary deputy for Silver Bow County. "Sheriff Wagner gave me this four, five years ago. I kind of keep the peace. Comes in handy sometimes when we get rowdy workers."

Gunther nodded.

"I talked to the sheriff right after we brought you and Vic's body down here to the lodge. He'll be here soon." He studied Gunther with a resentful stare. "Technically, you're in protective custody until he gets here. You clear any calls through me."

"Protective custody," Gunther repeated. "Protection from what, may I ask?"

Stroup shrugged. "Whatever." He made a hand gesture toward the window. "Him." He meant Vargas. "When we pulled you out of the Land Rover, I found you were carrying a concealed weapon. A .38. Do you have a license?"

"Why, do you want to see one?"

"I want to see a Montana license," Stroup said. "Do you have one?"

"No."

"I didn't think so. That's only one violation; I can think of several more. If you want any cooperation from me, Gunther, you'd better start giving me some information."

"For instance," Gunther said.

"For instance, who is the guy that killed Vic?"

"He's not from Montana either."

"His name," Stroup demanded.

"I don't know his name." Gunther walked to the edge of the bed and sat. "When can I use the phone?"

"How did you know he was coming here?" Stroup said, ignoring the question. "How did you know he was after Vic?"

"He left me a message in Sacramento."

Stroup stared at Gunther for a moment. "Left you a message? What do you mean, he left you a message?"

"He told someone he was coming here and that person told me," he said. "Usual kind of message. Look, Stroup, you're not going to accomplish anything by getting in my way. I really do need to make a phone call."

"Vic Quill was a good friend of mine," Stroup said in a low voice. He was staring at Gunther defiantly. His eyes gleamed black in the room's light. "I want to find the man who killed him."

"You won't find him in Montana." Gunther remembered Rockwell and the map with the little pins in it. Vargas would be moving east. He had to talk to Mackensen. "I doubt if anyone could find him now. He's somewhere out in those mountains. He won't stay in this state, anyway. He's moving fast now. He knows he's being searched for."

"I could find him," Stroup said. "I know a dozen men who live in these mountains who could help—"

"No. It's too late for that."

"Goddammit! Don't tell me what I can do!"

Gunther sighed heavily. "Sorry."

"What's he look like?"

"I wish I knew. I haven't seen him in fifteen years. But he's tall and strong, very bright, and he's black."

Stroup's eyes flickered with interest. "Black!" It seemed to enrage him. "You mean Vic was murdered by a goddamn nigger?"

Gunther paused a moment before responding. "No," he said slowly, "He's black. A Negro."

"A nigger's a nigger," Stroup shot back. "Good for nothing cocksuckers."

"This one is very good at something," Gunther said. He was familiar with racial prejudice, mostly against Jews, which he had learned to cope with, but it was always a subject he found boring and stupid. "He's not your run-of-the-mill shoe shuffler, if there is one. I would think that was quite clear."

"There aren't many niggers around these parts," Stroup said, thinking. "We can alert airports, buses, motels. You didn't say he was a nigger. We can find him."

Gunther nodded again. "Good. You won't find him, but it would be a good training exercise."

"Don't give me that. You think he's some kind of superman, but he's only a nigger." Stroup shook his head in disgust. "But you let him get away." He started for the door. "You ain't too good, eh, Gunther. I'm calling the highway patrol. Let them know what we're looking for."

"May I use the telephone now?"

"Call anybody you damn please," Stroup said. "Just don't try leaving."

"Wouldn't think of it," Gunther said. The call was received by Rockwell. There wasn't much to say. Afterwards, he left the lodge via his window. He'd locked the door and turned the shower on full blast. There wasn't any problem in pushing his rented car to the inclined road that led up to the lodge. He drove to Butte in an hour and was on a plane to Cheyenne by ten o'clock.

18

Like a snail, the guerrilla fighter carries his home on his back and therefore his pack must contain the smallest quantity of items of the greatest possible utility.

He made the connecting flight out of Cheyenne to Denver early the next morning. By early afternoon Gunther was in the Marriott Hotel in Park Ridge, near Chicago's O'Hare International Airport. He had dinner in his room and slept until shortly before midnight. He was to call Mackensen at 1:00 A.M. EST.

"Taskmaster calling for Mackensen." Gunther was sitting at the small desk in his room. He'd just taken a shower and was dressed in clean underwear purchased from an airport shop. There was a roll left from the dinner on the tray, and Gunther nibbled at it while the secretary switched him to Mackensen's line.

"Hello," Mackensen said. It was a very good connection. "Alec, where are you?"

"Chicago."

"Where exactly?" Mackensen sounded tired, as if he'd been up all night.

"Marriott," Gunther said. "Room 311."

"What the hell have you done in Montana?" Gunther heard a sneeze. "Damn." Another sneeze. "It's that damn New Jersey house," Mackensen said finally. "Caught cold. What's happened, Alec? Montana is searching for you."

"Vargas got to Quill. I told Rockwell that before I left."

"Yes, yes, I know about that. What have you done to get the highway patrol after you? They've got out a fugitive warrant. Your name and description went out to the National Crime Information Center, then to the FBI, who contacted us."

John Stroup and the Silver Bow County Sheriff's Office, Gunther thought. So he really was a deputy. "Questions," Gunther said. "They want to talk to me about Quill's death. I didn't have time to wait around for the authorities. Vargas is moving east now. Besides, you said no police involvement."

"Christ, Alec—" Mackensen sneezed violently into the telephone. "Did you have to cause such a goddamn stir? The bureau's in on it now. I got a message this afternoon from them requesting information on you. Interstate flight. Alec Gunther, your own name for Godsakes."

"You're the one who told me not to use cover," Gunther said angrily. "You can get me out of it. I can't go back to Montana with Vargas running around loose."

"I don't know," Mackensen said, straining against another sneeze.

"You'd better. Look, there's no way to know where Vargas is going to show up next. The nine names left on the list all live in the East—from Massachusetts to Maryland. I want each one of them given a babysitter. Round-the-clock babysitters."

"I'm not worried about them right now."

"You'd better be. I have to have some time. This isn't any game anymore with him. Vargas is determined to kill every man on that list."

"I'm not so sure he's so interested in them anymore," Mackensen said. "I'm getting pressure here, Alec. Did you talk to Quill after he was hit?"

"No. What difference would it make? Vargas did what he said he would do."

"How?" Mackensen asked. "How did Vargas get through?"

Gunther paused a moment before responding. "Quill wouldn't cooperate for one thing"—he stared dumbly at the tray of dirty dishes—"and I made a stupid mistake in underrating Vargas's ingenuity. But now it's his turn to make a mistake. I've made all I'm going to make.''

"That's reassuring, Alec. Very reassuring.''

"If you don't like it, then take me off,'' Gunther said hotly. "Put your expert on Vargas. See how long Rockwell lasts against him. I'd like to watch that.''

"I'm not taking you off, but I am changing the emphasis of this assignment, for the moment, at least. Peter has found something of value.''

"Has he?'' Gunther doubted it. "What do you mean by changing the emphasis? Am I after Vargas or not?''

"Yes, of course, but we've got something new. Simon Pelado's story. We've been digging into it. The Istanbul incident. Pelado said he saw Vargas there. We've come up with something on that. There was a man who fits Vargas's description that did have something to do with Turkey's black market. It wasn't poppy fields, as Pelado said, but running Israeli agents in Syria.''

"Israelis?''

"Queer, isn't it?'' Mackensen sounded not at all surprised. "He wasn't using the name Vargas, of course. But we've come up with an associate, a woman contact. Several tracks lead to her. I want you to check her out.''

"Where?''

"Buenos Aires.''

"B.A.? Christ, Vargas is up here!''

"You just let me worry about that, Alec,'' Mackensen said testily. "Besides, you did *almost* get him in Montana. He's going to have to think carefully about his next move. He'll go to ground. We won't find him by waiting around with our thumbs up our rumps. This woman—this lead might just flush him out.''

Gunther wasn't convinced. "I don't like the idea of Vargas running loose.''

"Nobody asked you to like it,'' Mackensen said quickly. "My intuition tells me he won't be active, at least not for some time. And I trust my intuition.''

Gunther sighed heavily into the phone. "You're calling the shots.''

Mackensen said nothing.

"Who is the chief of station in Argentina?" Gunther said.

"Pruett."

"Ed Pruett? From Barcelona?"

"Used to be Barcelona," Mackensen said. "After the cock-up in Berlin"—he paused—"we had to do some reshuffling. Now he's in Buenos Aires."

Gunther did not need to be reminded about the cock-up in Berlin again. "I guess I should be leaving soon," he said.

"Exactly what I was thinking. Peter left here about eight o'clock this evening. He has your passport and details about this woman—not really details, but some information to go on."

"Rockwell is coming here?"

"I thought you should leave for South America as soon as possible. You will need the passport. It's your own name."

"What about Rockwell?" Gunther asked impatiently. "He's not coming along for some sort of on-the-job training?"

Gunther heard Mackensen's short laugh dissolve into a sneeze. "No, Alec. Unless you want him along."

"I don't."

"Fine, Alec. Fine." Gunther could imagine Mackensen nodding his head.

"Don't forget the babysitters. Get them out today. And good people—make sure they know what they're doing. Will you see to that personally?"

Mackensen said he would.

"And get the FBI off my back. Tell them anything you like, but keep them away from me."

"I'll do what I can," Mackensen said. "Peter will be staying at O'Hare Inn. He may be there now. I suggest you leave for Argentina as quickly as you can."

"I will."

"And Alec—"

"Yes."

"Don't stay down there too long," Mackensen said firmly. "Remember, Vargas is up here somewhere. You're after *him*."

Gunther nodded to himself. "I wasn't going to forget," he said.

* * *

It was ten after six in the morning when Gunther rang Rockwell's room. He wasn't sure when Rockwell had checked in and he didn't care: nephews of important United States senators could sleep on their own time.

Rockwell answered on the fourth ring. "Hello?" It was not an alert voice. Gunther had wakened him. He liked that.

"This is Gunther," he said loudly. "Wake up, get dressed. I'll be there in twenty minutes."

"Gunther," the voice said. "Where are you?"

"I'm checking out now," Gunther said. "I'll meet you in the restaurant there. Twenty minutes." He waited a moment, then said, "Rockwell! Wake up, dammit. Did you hear me?"

"Yeah . . . yes, Gunther." A pause. "Christ, you don't have to scream." Now he was awake.

"Twenty minutes," he repeated. "Be there."

"I'll be there," Rockwell answered angrily.

"Good boy," Gunther said, smiling. He enjoyed this. "Wear something red—so I'll know it's you."

Gunther was late, as he'd expected to be, and he found Rockwell at a corner table at the end of the dining room. He was dressed in coat and tie, conservatively, in the Princeton manner, and sat impatiently erect like an unhappy scarecrow, drumming his fingers on the linen tablecloth. When he saw Gunther approach, he did not rise to greet him.

"Morning," Gunther said pleasantly as he sat down.

"You said twenty minutes, Gunther." He was still drumming his fingers.

Gunther shrugged. "Cab got hung up in traffic. Have you eaten?"

"Yes, half an hour ago."

"Sorry."

Gunther ordered breakfast: toast and orange juice and coffee. He spread marmalade on the toast cheerfully, and when the waitress had left he said, "Do you have the passport?"

"Yes." Rockwell passed it across the table. "There's a smallpox certificate card inside also. I don't know if you've had a vaccination in the last three years as you're supposed to, but the card says you had one in February." He'd stopped tapping his fingers. Now he rested his elbows on the table, fingers laced. "Have you?" His expression said he hoped not.

"I don't know," Gunther said. "I suppose." He finished the toast and juice. The coffee was hot, but tasted like instant. "Mackensen says you may have a lead. Tell me about her."

Rockwell leaned forward, touching his chin to the knuckles of his fingers. "You know, I think someone else should go. Someone else should talk to this woman—if she can be found. You should stay here—hunt for Vargas."

"You, perhaps?"

"Why not?"

Gunther nodded and sipped his coffee. "Do you speak Spanish?"

"Of course I speak Spanish," Rockwell shot back. "Four years."

"Four years," Gunther repeated. He nodded appreciatively. "College Spanish. How about Latin Spanish—Cuban, Nicaraguan, Argentinian?"

"I can manage," Rockwell said sullenly.

Gunther nodded again. "*Todos ustedes,*" he said quickly. "*¡Al paredon!*"

Rockwell's eyes flickered, momentarily confused. "What?"

Gunther repeated, but in a slightly different rhythm, altering inflection, slurring word forms. "Back . . . something . . . wall," Rockwell said. "You'll have to speak plainer than that, Gunther, and slower."

"How do you think they talk? Distinctly? Slowly? In verbs that agree and sentences that are parallel? Do you know Latin idioms?" Gunther shook his head. "You'd stick out like a tourist. No, Peter, I'll go. Now tell me about the woman."

"Christ! You really enjoy putting me down, don't you?"

He shook his head, his face suddenly serious. "This business we're in, it wasn't meant to be run by the likes of you. Do you know what it's like to hold a man's life on a piece of paper in your wallet? Do you feel any responsibility when you pull a name from a file and assign it to a case? You'll never understand the grit and grime, Peter, because you're a puppeteer, because you stay very clean and safe up there in the central office. It's all a game of blocks to you. The white American blocks and the red Russian blocks and the yellow Chinese blocks—'' Gunther paused to place the coffee cup back in its saucer. "I've seen the mountains of junk you people call intelligence,'' he said, staring intensely at Rockwell. "How many thousnds of reports and so-called intelligence data do you suppose are right now sitting in a locked storage vault on the second floor waiting for someone with the time to sort them out? Not read, just sort. You and your fucking generation of specialists can only measure intelligence by weighing it first. The August survey of collected information from Bhutan was twenty-seven pounds and was estimated to take one point five linear drawer feet to store. I actually saw that report. And do you know what the substance of the vital intelligence concerned? Yak butter. The kingdom of Bhutan was building highways to connect with existing roads in India, and they were worried about what the effect would be on the yak-butter industry.''

"You're being ridiculous, Gunther.'' Rockwell almost smiled. "Bhutan is almost inconsequential, but it borders China and that makes it important.''

"I hesitate to guess what the monthly poundage from China might be. Tons, I would think.''

Rockwell smiled and Gunther felt a sudden urge to slap him in the face. "Do you know your trouble, Gunther,'' Rockwell said in his debate-team voice. "You grew up in the cloak-and-dagger days and you're too stubborn or too stupid to recognize the fact that those times are over. There has been a technological explosion in intelligence gathering. We aren't agent-oriented anymore. One satellite flyover can do the work of a hundred field agents in twenty seconds' time. Your style of espionage is dying, if not dead. You're an old man, Gunther, and you don't fit here anymore. There will be dreg work like this Vargas assignment—there'll always be that—but any hoodlum can do it.''

Gunther shook his head sadly. "And missiles will replace troops and submarines will replace surface ships and Christmas will come on Mondays—convenience in the name of progress. Very neat.''

"And nothing you can do about it," Rockwell replied. "That really digs the hell out of you, doesn't it, Gunther? No conquests, no challenge . . ."

"No morality."

"That's very funny coming from you." Rockwell snickered.

"Is it?"

"What have you ever done in your life that smacked of virtue—socially redeeming traits?"

"It would be a short list," Gunther said.

"You're a professional liar, thief, cheat, flimflam artist, briber"—Rockwell made a wave with his hand—"and worse."

Gunther nodded his head in agreement. "True," he said. "Just another dreg to you." He lifted his cup and sipped the coffee. "But I'm not a message boy." Gunther glanced pleasantly at Rockwell. "There is still some purpose to my work, which I'd like to get back to. You have some information to deliver?"

"You can't intimidate me, Gunther," Rockwell said angrily.

"Fine. Just tell me about the woman in Argentina; that's all you have to do."

Rockwell produced an envelope from inside his tailored jacket. "Everything is in here. Her name is De Rosas. Camila Marie de Rosas. It isn't much. It wasn't easy to get that, but at least there is an address. Old by a year or more."

"Description?"

Rockwell shrugged. "What little we could get. Most of it was compiled from Pelado's former associates. There isn't any picture. No family names. Mainly, this is information about suspected ties with Vargas—nothing confirmed."

"How did you get the name?"

"I told you—through one of Pelado's old buddies in the smuggling business. It seems that this man who we suspect may have been Vargas had brought her along from Buenos Aires a few years ago. Pelado met her once in Istanbul and said he remembers one of his traffickers mentioned seeing her again in Buenos Aires at a park . . . alone."

"Anything else?"

"Some," Rockwell said. "What there is you'll find in that."

Gunther nodded and put the envelope in his pocket. He counted out two dollars in change and set it on the check. "I'm leaving tonight. Connecting with Miami. Tell Mackensen I'll be in Argentina tomorrow afternoon. He can contact me through Ed Pruett there. I've some shopping to do right now."

"You think you can find her?" Rockwell asked.

"That's the bet, isn't it?" Gunther got to his feet. He liked the idea of looking down at Rockwell. "But just to be sure, why don't you do me a favor?"

"Such as?"

"Have one of your satellites fly over," Gunther said. "I could do with a picture of Camila Marie de Rosas. Nothing fancy. A three-by-five contact print will be fine. Either profile." Gunther smiled. "See you, Peter."

19

The guerrilla has no regrets.

He made reservations with Eastern to Miami, and from there a Braniff flight would fly him to Argentina. It was still early, just after seven, and Gunther took a cab to Grant Park, on the east side of Chicago, because he'd never seen Buckingham Fountain. He walked aimlessly around like a tourist for an hour, freshened by the breeze from a choppy Lake Michigan. Gunther especially enjoyed walking alone in a place without traits to remind him of himself, where he was responsible to no one. It gave him a freedom to think, if he wished, or to blot everything from his mind and relax. It was his escape, to walk in a park. The great cities of Europe have always recognized the value of greenbelts, undeveloped land where a man can go if for no other purpose than to escape the strain of his own accountability for a short while.

A large ship moved slowly toward the dock at Navy Pier, carefully, as if it were a bashful whale maneuvering between walruses. Gunther watched for the ensign to identify it, but the ship was too far away to make it out.

He remembered a small park in Berlin, where he used to go. It was about a mile south of the Wall from Checkpoint Charlie, near Gitschiner Strasse. Bill Nester had taken him there once the week

131

before Nester was reassigned to Kiel. It was the only park Gunther had ever visited that had seemed so isolated in such a large city. He went there usually in late afternoons two or three times a month to air himself out. He would call Judith, tell her he would be late, then drive to the park alone. It seemed to help.

Gunther bought cigarettes from a newsstand. He inhaled deeply as he lit one and studied the tedious city skyline. Rockwell had struck a nerve this morning. There was something to what he'd said and it irritated Gunther to admit it. He *was* getting old. The work *was* changing, but he couldn't bring himself to acknowledge it. There was something the matter with faceless intelligence machinery. It was too much a reflection of big business. Rockwell may have been right about him, but he was dead wrong about the means and purpose of gathering intelligence. Mackensen would know the difference. There were many others who knew the difference, but they, too, were getting old. The Rockwells, like an unchecked blight in a cornfield, were slowly winning, taking over.

Gunther made his way out of the park when the first of the vendors and professional bench sitters began their invasion. He walked east on Roosevelt to a small surplus store near the University of Illinois at Chicago Circle. He bought two gray cotton workshirts for a dollar each from a pile of used clothing and one pair of khaki trousers from another pile. He also purchased a faded blue kerchief, a pair of black lace shoes, a cap, a long-sleeved turtleneck jersey, a windbreaker jacket and a small leather suitcase. Before he left the store, Gunther made sure that each of his purchases had been stripped of labels.

With the makings of his Buenos Aires identity in the suitcase, Gunther walked to the university's walk-in clinic and got a smallpox vaccination. There was no reason not to be careful.

By the time Gunther arrived at O'Hare, there was less than an hour to wait for his flight. The walking he'd done had help loosen the stiffness in his legs and the soreness in his shoulder that he'd felt since the wreck in the Land Rover. There would be much more leg-work in Argentina, and he knew there wasn't a satellite or computer in the world that could make it one step less. He sat in the flight waiting area, smoking a cigarette, studying the other passengers. Gunther knew he would find Camila Marie de Rosas. She was the key with which he could unwrap the enigma that was Ollie Vargas. Finding him now was more than just a challenge—it was a means whereby Gunther could recoup the dignity he'd only recently realized was lost. It was men like Rockwell who had no honor, no morality or purpose, because such terms cannot be qualitatively evaluated on a punch-card balance sheet. Finding Vargas would restore Gunther's faith in himself. Killing him would reunite Gunther and the company as if reconfirming the vows of fidelity. It was a strange dignity he was striving to recover, Gunther thought, but it was a purposeful pursuit, nonetheless. He was not particularly eager to have the confrontation; he was just eager to have it over with. Ironically, a man like Vargas would understand. Rockwell could never see it.

When the Eastern flight number was called, Gunther stubbed out his cigarette and made his way behind a crowd of Miami-bound passengers to the boarding tunnel. Ahead of him were almost fourteen hours of traveling. Standing in the crowd, he wondered where Ollie was and what he was thinking.

20

It is the commander's duty to insulate his plan and his men against the enemy's intelligence apparatus.

The Taskmaster waited patiently at the hotel's front desk until a short pleasant-faced manager with a boutonniere in his lapel greeted him.

"Good evening, sir," said the manager, whose name tag identified him as Mr. James.

"Good evening. I have a reservation. Hughes. J. Allen Hughes." Vargas was dressed in an expensive, but conservatively cut, gray suit. He sported a neatly trimmed mustache and goatee. By his appearance and manner, he was plainly an executive.

Mr. James thumbed through a stack of reservation cards. "Yes, sir, Mr. Hughes. Here it is. Strictland Oil." He pulled the card from the stack and nodded at Vargas. "One night only, Mr. Hughes?"

"Yes."

"Very good, sir. Luggage?"

"Just the one bag."

While Vargas signed the card, Mr. James rang for a bellboy and handed him a key. He smiled as Vargas handed back the pen. "Have a pleasant stay, Mr. Hughes. We have you in Room 533."

"I have several overseas business calls to make," Vargas said,

134

pausing at the counter. "Do you handle it through your switchboard or do I dial directly through the operator?"

"Europe, sir?"

"And one to Japan."

The hotel manager smiled. "That will be no problem, Mr. Hughes. We can handle it for you."

"I expect to be finished before midnight," Vargas said. "Since I will be leaving early in the morning and so there isn't any mistake, please have the calls prepared on my bill."

"Of course, sir. Is this a credit account, Mr. Hughes?"

Vargas shook his head. "No. Cash."

"Very good, sir," Mr. James repeated. "I will see to it myself. Have a pleasant stay."

Vargas had dinner sent to his room. Afterwards, he showered and shaved and made notes on a pad from his suitcase. About 11:00 P.M. he made his first call.

"Overseas operator. What country, please?"

"Israel."

"One moment, please." Vargas was lying in bed, the pillows propped against his back. The picture on the wall opposite him was a landscape with a river and a small dock jutting out from shore. There seemed to be a man or boy sitting at the end, fishing.

There was a light clatter of static when the operator came back on the line. "What city, sir?"

"Haifa."

"Yes, sir?"

"This is a person-to-person to Charles Forbes. F-O-R-B-E-S. The number is 555-3988."

The operator repeated the name and number. "Do you wish to place the call now, sir?"

"Yes."

"Yes, sir. For your information, sir, the time in Haifa right now is six minutes after six in the morning."

"Yes, I know," Vargas said.

"One moment, sir."

Vargas waited a short time until the operator made the connection in Israel and had a voice on the line who said he was Charles Forbes.

"Charles, good morning," Vargas said. "This is Allen. I'm calling from the East Coast." Vargas was looking at the fisherman in the landscape.

"Hello, Allen," the voice said slowly. "Are you well?"

"Yes, quite well, thank you." Vargas decided that the figure in the picture was a boy. "Do you recognize my voice?"

A pause. "The cruelest lies are often told in bed," the voice named Forbes said.

"No, my friend, they are told in silence."

The Forbes voice laughed shortly. "Yes, Allen, it is you. It is you. It is difficult to know on the telephone."

"The time has come," Vargas said. "You may begin."

"I thought it would be soon. I had the feeling."

"You understand what you are to do?" Vargas said.

"Yes."

"You are ready?"

"I am ready."

"Good." Vargas lifted his wrist to see his watch. "Today is Wednesday. You know you have five days, no more. I will be waiting for word of your transaction."

"It will be as we agreed. Within the week you will know."

"Good luck to you, Charles," Vargas said. "I wish you Godspeed."

"And to you, my friend," the voice said solemnly. "Shalom."

"Shalom."

He made six more calls, all similar and all as brief as the call to Haifa. He spoke with Dimitri Struve in Stockholm, Paul Millet in Paris, George Hillard in London, Hidevo Yamamoto in Osaka and Karl Frohm in Amsterdam. His last call was to Arshile Rajab in Cairo.

"It is good to hear from you, Allen," Rajab said.

"The task we discussed," Vargas said carefully. "It is time."

"The same period to accomplish it as we spoke of?"

"Yes. As soon as you are able."

"It will be as you say, Allen."

"You won't hear from me again," Vargas said. "You understand that?"

"Unfortunately, I do." Rajab sighed. "It is necessary, this way, yes?"

"It is, yes."

"One thing, Allen. You may wish to know. There have been several inquiries lately at Istanbul and also Ankara. Inquiries about a black man and a woman who accompanied him two years ago to Istanbul."

Vargas nodded. "How long ago?"

"A few days. It is said the Americans are very interested about this man and this woman."

"Response?"

"It is possible they will learn the woman's identity. I think they will not find the man." Rajab laughed loudly. "No, I think they will not find him."

"Thank you, Rajab," Vargas said. "Your long ears are helpful once again." He paused a moment, then said, "Thank you again, Rajab."

"It is sad to say good-bye this way, Allen. One day we shall meet again."

Vargas nodded again. "Until then, Rajab. Until then."

He was not disturbed by Rajab's information. Gunther was moving fast now. It was bound to happen this way, especially with Mackensen's support, he thought. Besides, Gunther was extremely good at what he did. If Gunther knew about Istanbul, it would be only a short time until he found his way to Camila. Vargas turned out the light on the nightstand and lay in the dark. The hotel's central air conditioning made a low humming in the room. If Gunther moved too fast, it would put the plan slightly off schedule, Vargas thought. There must be something he could do that would interrupt Gunther's attack for a few days. Few, if any, men have no weaknesses and Gunther was no exception. But there are men, like Gunther, who protect or hide their own Achilles' heel so tenaciously that they fool themselves.

Vargas knew what the weakness was. It would work because he knew the mind of a lonely man responsible to irresponsible men.

They enjoyed the same characteristics as soldiers in battle. No matter how mean or tough or callous the man may be, there is always one tender place that he will protect at all costs. It is a foible of gladiators. And Vargas knew how to get past Gunther's guard. Gunther would respond like an enraged bull when he learned of the threat. It was his only weakness and now was the time to use it. Judith.

21

The guerrilla strives to blend with new surroundings.

Gunther was seated behind a group of skiers bound for Santiago. He slept for short periods in naps between boisterous interruptions by the skiers, who were determined to sing despite warnings from the senior stewardess not to disturb the other passengers. He was awake for much the flight that followed the white-and-gray line of the Andes down to Santiago.

When the plane arrived at Ezeiza airport, he was met at the customs line by Ed Pruett, chief of station at Buenos Aires. Pruett was a dark man with bright brooding eyes and short legs. Gunther once had told Pruett he liked him because he was one of few men he knew who was shorter than himself. He was also professional and intelligent, with a retentive mind. He was a man Gunther knew he could trust.

"Alec—so, they've let you out of the box." He shook Gunther's hand vigorously. Pruett was dressed in an American-designed leisure suit; it was dark blue with a white shirt open at the collar, exposing the neck band of his T-shirt. He was the one who had told Gunther it was un-American not to wear a T-shirt. "How was the trip?"

"Hot in Miami, cold in Santiago."

Pruett nodded. "Winter season now. I'm in my second year here now and it's still goddamn hard to adjust to two-blanket nights in July." He raised the black line of his eyebrows resignedly. "There'll be frost on and off till September." He said it with the despair of an Iowan farmer.

They collected Gunther's two bags and walked to Pruett's car, passing a passenger from Gunther's flight who had slept in a seat across from him. The man was awake now; he turned away as they passed, reading with transparent non-interest a brochure on Buenos Aires.

"We get by with what we can manage down here, Alec," he said, indicating his car. "To look at her, you wouldn't know how well she runs. The drivers in this city are crazier than anything you saw in Europe. You hungry? We can stop and get something."

Gunther slammed the door after him and stretched back in the seat, massaging his shoulder. "No, thanks. Couldn't eat that stuff on the plane, either. I'm not much of a traveler." He turned to Pruett. "Why don't we just drive around a bit, show me the city. We'll talk."

"Fine, Alec." He put the car into gear and slid into the flow of traffic. "I don't know how much I'll be able to help you with the woman you're after. Mack said it was a one-man show."

"That's the way Mackensen is," Gunther observed with a laugh. "Trusting."

"You know how it usually goes. We get a message to check somebody out and we check them out. Routine. Sometimes we know why; sometimes we don't care. But Mack wasn't giving any details on this one. Wait for you is the word." Pruett glanced at Gunther and flashed his deprecating smile. "What's up?"

An airport limousine that had been tailgating found an opening in the traffic and accelerated noisily past Pruett's Fiat. It passed several cars and nearly collided with the rear of a microbus as it changed lanes again. Gunther recognized some of the limousine's passengers as being from the flight from Miami. One of them was the sleeping man, who looked away again, but not as quickly as before. If their stunned reactions were any indication, Gunther guessed this was their first trip to Buenos Aires and their first ride with an Argentinean driver.

"I told you they were crazy," Pruett said. He sounded the Fiat's horn and shrugged in Gunther's direction. "That's about all you can do. The bigger the car they drive, the more reckless they are. You should see them try to park."

Gunther nodded. "Someone's trying to kill off our people back home. Someone who knows what he's doing. That's what this is about."

"Company people?" Pruett frowned and his eyes seemed to disappear in the dark recess below his eyebrows.

"At last count, he's eliminated nine."

"He?"

"One man. His name is Vargas. Black. Cuban." Gunther turned down the sun visor to shade his eyes. "I knew him during the Jupiter operation."

"You mean he's just wacking off agents? By himself?" Pruett let out a low whistle. "No wonder Mack didn't say anything."

"You still don't know about it."

Pruett nodded. "He isn't headed down here, is he? My staff is small enough as it is. I don't need any outside help cutting it shorter."

"No. Vargas is after people who worked the invasion. He's working from a list of names and the list is getting shorter."

"You're on it?"

"Jupiter was my responsibility."

"You're on it." Pruett sighed. "Let's hope you're near the bottom."

"Vargas disappeared when Castro released the prisoners. Actually, he was presumed dead. Now we know he's alive. I have to find him."

"Lucky you," Pruett said. "So what's in Buenos Aires?"

"The only lead I have on him. We don't know where he's been or what he's been up to since the Bay of Pigs, except for this information about a woman, Camila Marie de Rosas. Maybe. It might be a dead end."

"I've checked the name," Pruett said. "We don't have anything on her. I suppose you expected that?"

"They only give me the easy ones." Gunther watched as they passed through a large greenbelt area of meadow and long stretches of trees. The park was landscaped for rose gardens and picnickers. To the right was a bridle path that led to a large, well-kept polo field. To the left was a kidney-shaped lagoon and a walking bridge to an island with grassy plots and shade trees. There were only a few people; all wore jackets or light coats. The only rider he saw was a mounted federal policeman.

"You're the one who likes parks," Pruett said, as if he'd remembered something important. "Jimmy West used to call you The Thinker—Walking." He shook his head slowly, with a remember-when look. "Jimmy was something, all right. Couldn't drive worth a shit. Always hitting something"—he nodded toward the traffic—"like these jokers. But a hell of a control."

"I remember him," Gunther said. West was control for Spain when Mackensen was chief of Western Hemisphere Operations before he took over Special Ops. West was Gunther's first teacher and he did a good job. But that was years ago, when Gunther and Pruett had first joined the Spanish network in Madrid. West retired in the late sixties during a shuffle within the agency. Gunther had heard he had committed suicide.

"You know, Alec, it isn't any of my business, but—" Pruett glanced at him, like a man does when he asks a cab driver where he can find some action, carefully, but with interest. "Well, what happened in Berlin?"

"I was caught," Gunther said, a note of surprise in his voice. "Signals got switched and nobody bothered to tell us."

"What was Miles doing with a gun? That wasn't smart. Not on the East side."

"It wasn't Miles," Gunther said irritably. He'd explained this before. "Roberts had the gun. When he killed the guard, he took the gun. Miles was shot at the wall. Ten more seconds and Miles would have made it." He shook his head. "No, it wasn't Miles who had the gun. The Vopos said it was Miles, but it wasn't."

"They were both shot dead—Miles and Roberts?" Pruett asked. "I mean, there at the wall." He shrugged, embarrassed. "That's what I heard."

"They looked dead to me," Gunther said. "I really didn't see them close up."

"And you weren't hit?"

Gunther remembered his nightmare, how it should have been. "No," he said as if he regretted it. "Not by a bullet." Always, the same question. Everyone was interested in why the Vopos did not shoot him, too. He didn't know why. He'd told them maybe it was because of the rain and they couldn't see him as well or because he was farthest away from the wall. He just didn't know. He suspected that some of them thought he'd been turned. He didn't care anymore what they thought.

"Did they treat you badly, Alec?"

"Gunther was caught in mid-thought. "Who?"

"The East Germans."

"The Germans are a precise and philosophizing people," he said. "It helps them to be superb interrogators. They have ways of asking questions without leaving marks."

Pruett breathed in deeply and let it out slowly. "I'm sorry, Alec. I know it's a helpless thing to say, but I'm sorry it happened to you."

Gunther said nothing. He was not good at consoling or being consoled. He might have said he was sorry, too, but it was better to let it pass. He wondered whom it should have happened to.

They were coming into the federal district now. Ahead was the skyline of the city. Traffic was heavy and Gunther was aware of the distinctive if subtle difference in the air: carbon monoxide and industrial fumes. Buenos Aires was not so unlike Chicago, after all.

"What can I help you with first?" Pruett said finally. "I don't work the field, so my Spanish isn't street talk, mostly straight. You should feel at home because almost the entire population is European. Predominantly Spanish and Italian, but a lot of German and French. Have you ever been here before?"

"Once, briefly. A few days."

"Then you know the Spanish spoken here is a hodgepodge of pronunciation and grammatical changes. Waterfront districts have an Italianized dialect I've never been able to penetrate. It isn't all that great a handicap, since the people who live here don't know what some of their neighbors are saying."

"Everything helps."

"Will you be needing a car, Alec?"

"No," he said. "I'm going to use cover and a car wouldn't fit."

Pruett turned right at an intersection with a wide boulevard that was dotted with trees and grassy areas. He hadn't remembered the city having so much greenery.

"You shouldn't have much trouble getting around here," Pruett said. "The subway and microbuses are cheap. The city itself is laid out fairly logically in blocks. The *centro,* expecially the downtown capital area, is easy to get around in. It gets more complicated the further away from the core you go. Avenida 9 de Julio and Avenido de Mayo divide it into quadrants, roughly."

Gunther nodded. "I may need a legman. Someone with a forgettable face who knows the city well. Someone local."

"Arturo Madanes is your man," Pruett said quickly. "A gaucho. He's reliable and he's helped me before. Arturo might help you with your cover, unless you're already decided on it."

"Fine. I'd like to see him tonight. I need to get started."

"I'll arrange it."

Gunther closed his eyes and laid his head on the rest. "God, I'm tired. Didn't get much sleep on the plane. Where am I staying?"

"There's a small hotel in the San Telmo barrio," Pruett said. "It's very old and very Spanish . . . a good place to start. If I were you I'd find another place tomorrow, after you see Arturo, to make your cover secure. You can contact me anytime, but I don't expect you will—if you still work the same—until you have what you're after."

"There are a couple of things. First, the information I have on this De Rosas woman is very sketchy, but one name that comes up is Hector Comi. I'd like you to run down what you can on him for me. I suspect it has to do with smuggling. Also, there is a mention of Cecilio Arbano. Evidently, he is local. All I have is the name."

Pruett nodded. "I'll have something tonight. Arbano rings a bell." He gestured with his thumb to the rear seat of the Fiat. "In the meantime, I brought some material I give to all my people when they check in here for the first time. Something to familiarize you with the city and people—from our slant. You might take a look at it."

"I will," Gunther promised.

"This building with the green dome"—Pruett nodded to his left—"is the National Congress building. This park is the Congressional Plaza. They're all over the place, these little parks. And big ones, too." He smiled at Gunther. "You'd love it here. Prepare yourself, Alec. You're about to get the grand Pruett nickel tour of the capital zone. I don't have much chance to get out like this and seldom do I have the chance to dazzle anyone with my limited knowledge of these government buildings. We'll begin with the Plaza de Mayo and work our way down past the Mint to the Secretarial Office of Agriculture and into San Telmo." He squinted at Gunther. "Are you ready?"

Gunther sighed then smiled. "Why not," he said. "Tour away, Ed. Dazzle me."

22

It is important that guerrilla fighters trust their comrades.

They came about nine oclock.

Gunther's room was small and crowded with its few pieces of furniture. There was one window that looked down into an empty courtyard, and the yellowing wallpaper had begun to peel in several places near the ceiling. A crucifix on the wall beside the door was the room's only ornament. It might have been the room of a Jesuit monk.

"This is my friend, the one from the United States," Pruett was saying when they were inside the room. The man with him was dressed similarly to Gunther, in work clothes, and he smelled slightly of cattle. Madanes did not take off his cap. His arms hung straight down from his shoulders, along the seam of his trousers, and his hands were heavily calloused. He was neither a large nor a small man, but his eyes were alert, and Gunther sensed he was physically quick. He looked like an Argentine cowboy.

"I am happy to make your acquaintance, señor," he said with a short nod. "I am Arturo Madanes."

"Señor Pruett said you were a good man to know," Gunther replied.

The Argentine nodded again. "We have mutual friendships." Gunther had difficulty deciding if Madanes was at all interested in

146

working with a stranger. He was not a smiler. Then Gunther noticed the man was sizing him up, analyzing Gunther's appearance and manner, glancing at Gunther's hands and face, just as Gunther was sizing him up. He liked that.

"Let me tell you about Arturo's working agreement with me," Pruett said, pulling off his jacket. "He does not want to know your real name and I prefer it that way. He knows what I do and he trusts me. He knows only that you and I work for the same outfit and he believes that our work is necessary. Beyond that, Arturo does not ask any questions except what is pertinent to the assignment."

"A sensible arrangement," Gunther said. "Who am I?"

"A German," Pruett said. "That should fit you nicely . . . help you with the language a bit here. Peter Beckmann. You've been here two months. That's what the papers say. The rest you can fill in for yourself, to fit your cover." He turned to Madanes. "What do you think, Arturo?"

Again, he nodded. "It is good, señor." He was speaking directly to Gunther. "You look German." Madanes pulled the cap from his head, sliding it back down his neck. "I think, señores, it would better to speak Spanish. My English . . . it is not so better."

Pruett smiled. "Sí." They talked for nearly an hour. Madanes sat in the straight-backed chair at the desk, Pruett was perched on the edge of the bed, and Gunther was in the armchair. The name Camila Marie de Rosas was mentioned only one time. Pruett had brought plenty of information about Hector Comi, an Italian immigrant who'd come to Argentina two weeks before the Russians took Berlin. Comi was known to have had Nazi connections during the war, but it wasn't until Adolf Eichmann was captured in 1960 that he was exposed as the leader of a vanguard of Nazi sympathizers who'd come to South America to set up a haven for escaping Nazi officials. There were rumors that Comi had successfully hidden Martin Bormann, but nothing was ever proved.

Cecilio Arbano was definitely a smuggler, Pruett said, and operated an import-export warehouse in the Puerto Madero barrio near the south canal. Comi had never left the country, but Arbano, in the past four years, had made seventeen trips to Europe. He'd visited Istanbul nine times in that period.

"I don't know the connection between Comi and Arbano,"

Pruett said finally, wetting his lips as if he were ready for a drink. "Comi lives in a villa north of the city in San Isidro and he doesn't go out. Arbano has an apartment in Palermo inside the federal district of Buenos Aires. Very expensive. Comi is the old Nazi, Arbano is just a crook. I don't know what they have to do with the woman."

"The direct approach is always the best, I've found," Gunther said. "Why don't I just go ask them?"

Madanes's passive expression broke into a smile. His first. "I know of this Arbano, señor. He is a very hard man." He made a fist and held it for them to see. "It is not easy to see this Arbano because he has many enemies."

"Former customers, probably," Pruett said.

Gunther nodded. "What about Comi? Could I see him?"

"I suppose." Pruett shrugged. "My people tell me he doesn't have many guests. He especially doesn't like anyone from the press. But you can give it a try. I can't think of any reason why he would help you." He glanced at Gunther, raising an eyebrow. "Maybe you could make one up."

"Maybe I could."

"Using your cover?"

"Depends on how deep he probes. I'm safe as long as we stick to the topic of Germany." Gunther spoke quickly, forgetting Pruett didn't command the language as well, and he had to repeat himself. Gunther's Spanish was coming back to him now and he felt relaxed using it.

"Good." Pruett got up from the edge of the bed. He brushed at the creases in his trousers. "In the meantime, I'll see what else we can dig up for you. You will check with me?"

"From time to time," Gunther said. "Right now I need to work on this cover." He looked at Madanes. "What would be best for me, Arturo?"

The Argentine cocked his head slightly to one side as if he could see Gunther better when he didn't look at him straight on. "Gaucho, I think, señor." Madanes nodded like he'd made up his mind. "Like me."

Pruett laughed. "Gaucho! That means you'll be out in Mataderos barrio."

"Is that bad?"

"Have you ever been near a stockyard?"

Gunther shook his head. "Does New York count?"

Gunther met Madanes the next morning at a cafe near Avellaneda Park in Mataderos barrio. They ate a breakfast of beefsteak, bread and wine. The scent of the stockyard hung in the air like a fog.

"This is your work permit, señor Beckmann," Madanes said. He passed the gray card across the table to Gunther. "It is more valuable than gold with so many men looking for work. It is helpful also for identification."

Gunther slid the card into his shirt pocket. "Thanks." He didn't ask where it came from.

"We are on the morning shift. Today is a lucky day for us, señor Beckmann. We will unload trucks from a small ranch in the pampas. Have you ever been around beef cattle before?"

"No."

Madanes nodded. "Do not worry, señor. I have for you a job of counter. It is easy work. We will be finished by noon. Afterwards I can take you to the villa of señor Comi."

"I'm not going to have time for this every day, Arturo," Gunther said. "I have to find the señora de Rosas."

"*Sí*, this is understood by me." The Argentine shuffled his chair closer to the table and leaned toward Gunther. The wooden table creaked with the weight of Madanes's elbows. "Only today must you work in the stockyard. The gauchos are paid by the week and their names go to the office of finance. It is important that you establish this Beckmann identity, *sí*?"

Gunther nodded.

"My cousin Juan, he is *superintendente*. He has added your name to the list of gauchos who work here, but you must sign the paymaster's ledger in the presence of the *pagador*. This is so a cheque will be posted to the Beckmann name in the future."

"But I'm not coming back, right?"

"*Sí*. After today you will not return to the stockyards, but you will have an occupation if anyone is interested to check."

Gunther cleaned his spectacles on his shirttail. "And the Beckmann name will be paid even though nobody shows up to work?"

"That is correct, señor."

"For how long?"

"Several weeks," Madanes said. He offered something of a smile. "You see, señor, my cousin, he is feeding a large family and a *superintendente* does not make very much. He will be able to collect your checque for you." He shrugged with an upturned-palm-gesture of his hands. "Such things are done."

The stockyard area was enormous. Thousands of head of cattle were unloaded from trucks and railroad cars into pens at the perimeter of the yard. Activity was loud and furious. The cattle moved in bunches—three and four together—through the narrow corrals to the large pens beyond. They clawed up the dust in clouds, crashing together, bumping pen posts; their brown eyes rolled back, exposing white, and all the while they filled the air with their choking smell and gutteral cries of protest, as if they knew where they were headed.

Gunther had never seen anything like it. He sat straddling the top rail at the head of a pen with two other gauchos, counting, recording groups of twenty animals with knots on a hemp rope. For almost four hours he counted cattle in lots by ranch name. The dust and the smell never let up and Gunther wore his kerchief around his face, but it didn't help much. Everything stank of cattle dung. He thought about Madanes's cousin, Juan, the *superintendente* who would be collecting Peter Beckmann's check, but mostly he counted cows.

San Isidro is a city within the greater metropolitan area of Buenos Aires about ten miles north of downtown. It is an elite suburban district where the city's wealthier citizens migrated in the sixties when the slums of the *barrio pobre,* with their tiny shacks of tin with cardboard roofs and wood-crate walls, began to encroach upon the view of the city. Madanes told Gunther one of the chief complaints was about the nightly cries of starving babies.

They took a cab, and for the twenty-minute drive the driver demanded that they keep all the windows rolled down. Gunther was getting used to the smell of cattle.

"How do you intend to see the señor Comi?" Madanes asked. "It is not so easy, I think, even for *los ricos.* And you—a gaucho."

Gunther held up a finger as if he were making a point. "Yes," he said with a smile, "but a German gaucho."

"It makes a difference?"

"This one will." Gunther glanced out the window. He was surprised to see so many nightclubs. "I hope."

The cab pulled off the road about a hundred meters short of the sprawling Comi villa. Gunther instructed Madanes to wait at his hotel room and sleep if he could. They were going to be working late tonight, Gunther said.

He watched until the cab was out of sight, then walked to the villa. Gunther was surprised when the door opened and a short Argentine houseboy, elderly and dressed in white, answered. He expected someone bigger. German.

"Ist Herr Comi da?" Gunther hoped to God Pruett knew what he was talking about.

"Ja." The little man stood his ground. *"Haben Sie eine Verabredung mit Herrn Comi?* He spoke German perfectly. It was something strange to see—a Latin speaking a north German dialect. So Pruett was right. German was the required language on the premises.

Gunther explained that he had no appointment, but that he was sent by a man named Muller. Curt Muller. The little man nodded politely and closed the door. In a short while he returned. *"Hereinkommen, bitte,"* he said with a pleasant smile, gesturing with a wide sweeping motion of his hand for Gunther to enter.

Gunther had seen lavishly decorated interiors in his life, but he was not prepared to find such extravagance in a suburb of Buenos Aires—even in a rich suburb. He was escorted down a mirrored hall facing columned French windows with a view of a large courtyard. The hall lead to a large high-ceilinged room that was straight out of an English manor house in the Tudor tradition. The floor was textured slate and the walls were recessed in carved oak panels. A dark hand-sculptured frieze seemed to prevent the ceiling, with its three chandeliers, from caving in. The dominent feature of the room was an immense fireplace flanked by what appeared to be genuine suits of armor standing on pedestals and facing the opposite wall, which was distinctive in itself with cathedral-like stained-glass bay windows. High on the walls were paintings of different sizes in elaborate frames. Gunther counted seventeen.

"Herr Comi will be with you shortly," the Argentine said in crisp German. He nodded then and with a short bow left the room.

Gunther walked to the bay windows and stood beside a short oak table with spirally turned legs. It looked very old. Outside, the grounds were green and well-kept behind the high brick wall that apparently surrounded the villa. It was an impressive place.

"Herr Beckmann."

Gunther turned to see Comi enter from a door near the fireplace. He was somewhat taller than Gunther and moved with the briskness of a man in advanced years who was beginning to lose weight. He was dressed casually in trousers and a print shirt, and strands of his flaxen hair, the color of a nicotine stain, protruded from beneath a faded yellow cap. Gunther knew he was in his seventies, but he looked fifteen years younger.

"*Guten Tag,* Herr Comi," Gunther said. "Your villa is most beautiful."

Comi smiled with a modest nod. "I have been fortunate." He motioned with his hand, indicating the room. "This is my English room. Some pieces here date back to before Charles II. The paintings are more contemporary." He turned and moved to a Queen Anne secretary. "May I offer you a sherry, Herr Beckmann?"

"Thank you," Gunther said.

"I have developed a taste for sherry. I think every man should develop a taste for one particular drink. Many years ago I visited a small town in the southwest of Spain . . . Jerez de la Frontera." Comi raised his glass and bowed his head slightly toward Gunther. "This is from that same vineyard. Not richly sweet or very dry, but mellow with a distinctive tang."

Gunther sipped from his glass. He didn't like sherry, but he smiled anyway.

"You approve, Herr Beckman?"

"Excellent."

"It is seldom that I entertain," Comi said. He sighed and walked to the fireplace. "It is good to know that I am still a hospitable host." Comi set the sherry glass on the mantel near one of the suits of armor and studied Gunther a moment. "Pancho tells me you are sent by Curt Muller." A smile. A slightly raised eyebrow, a questioning look.

"Muller is dead," Gunther said. He held his glass in both hands, rolling it slowly between his fingers. "Has been for ten years."

"Nine years," Comi replied. "A small matter. But you have resurrected him. Why?"

"It is important that I speak with you, Herr Comi. I understand that it is difficult to do." Gunther sipped the sherry, keeping his eyes on Comi. "I thought you would be curious enough to admit a man who said he was from a former partner of yours."

Comi nodded and smiled. "Business associate. Curt and I had certain mutual business arrangements. Yes, I was curious. Did you know him?"

"Not personally. I dealt mainly with Brauer and Eicke—Alfred Brauer and Hans Eicke. You remember them?"

"I am an old man, Herr Beckmann, not a silly schoolboy. To presume I knew Brauer and Eicke would be to presume I knew their occupation, which I believe was smuggling. Presuming that, one might suspect I had had dealings with them. The Argentine authorities are quite particular who I see on a business relationship. I am subject to deportation. But, of course, you must know that. I must be careful of what I say and who I say it to. You understand."

"Yes."

"How did you know Brauer and Eicke?"

"We—they made some purchases for me and helped me in other ways."

"Illegal?"

"Very."

It was true as far as it went. One of Gunther's agents in Bonn had penetrated Brauer's smuggling ring in the late sixties, five years after Muller died. Muller had been running it since the war, but was never exposed. Brauer and his new partner Eicke were greedier and not as careful. Eicke was found floating in the Seine River near Notre Dame Cathedral in 1973. Brauer disappeared. There was never physical proof, but according to the CIA file, both Brauer and Eicke were victims of a special branch of the Mossad that eliminated them because of their dealings with Palestinian guerrillas. Gunther figured Comi was aware that they had died. He was careful, Gunther thought, because he knew how they died.

"So, you have worked with these two men on transactions that were not legal?"

"That's right. Some were operated out of Argentina."

"And you tell me this freely?" Comi collected his glass from the mantel, but did not drink. "You know that I can give this information to the police?"

Gunther said nothing.

"These two men—Brauer and Eicke—I never met them. I don't know, but it is a possibility that Brauer had Muller killed so that he might take over his . . . business. Curt Muller was a close friend, Herr Beckmann. I don't think I want to help you."

"I'm looking for Brauer," Gunther lied. "He is alive."

"Alfred Brauer?" Comi squinted angrily. The wrinkles in his face deepened until he looked his age. "He is alive?"

"I believe he is. He is somewhere in the eastern Mediterranean." Gunther shrugged. "Perhaps in a Black Sea resort . . . perhaps Istanbul. He was last seen in Istanbul. I am to find him." Gunther was making everything up now and he concentrated to keep his story straight.

Comi stared past Gunther. "Brauer. I thought the Jews killed him." He sipped his sherry. "You are sure?"

"I am sure."

"What is your interest, Herr Beckmann? Why do you seek him?"

"Several reasons," Gunther said. "He stole from me and caused me much trouble in Hamburg with the *polizei*. He ruined my business."

"Yes, yes. I remember Curt telling me of his trouble with—" Comi cut himself short. "And when you find him? What then?"

"I am not a Jew, Herr Comi," Gunther said. "But I think the Jews would appreciate my intentions regarding this man."

"You would kill him?" Comi's eyes sparkled beneath raised eyebrows. It seemed to interest him.

"Yes, Gunther said tersely. "There would be no mistake with me."

Comi smiled warmly. "I see. Tell me, Herr Beckmann, if I were to help you, how would I be of service?"

"Information. I need information that concerns Istanbul." Gunther sipped again at his drink. "I know that he was there recently. And I have good reason to believe that someone who lives in Buenos Aires also knows him. This person was seen with him several months ago."

"Does this person have a name?"

"Yes," Gunther said. "Her name is Camila Marie de Rosas."

23

Do not ever assume the enemy's weakness; carry the fight to his doorstep.

Gunther returned to his room shortly before dark. The place was in shadows and Madanes was nowhere around. He walked to the window and saw a boy and a girl together on a bench in the courtyard below. His bed had been slept in and there was a note on the pillow:

Señor Beckmann,

Our friend called. I am to pick up some information from him that may help the search.

Arturo

He crumpled the paper and ripped it into pieces. Gunther didn't like people leaving him notes. He flushed the pieces down the toilet, then undressed and showered. He could still smell the cattle until he doused himself with cologne. Now he smelled like a German. The cologne was French.

Gunther was tying a shoe, with his foot on the bed, when the door exploded open, ripping the metal latch plate from the doorjamb and sending it careening across the floor. There were two of them. The

156

one that put his shoulder to the door was large, about 250 pounds, and wore a stevedore cap and dirty pullover sweater with wide horizontal stripes that made his chest look three feet wide. The other one was smaller, but he had the gun.

"Señor Beckmann, do not move, please." The little one was the talker. The big one just stood there grinning as if he was very pleased with himself and rubbing his shoulder. They must have been waiting in the hall for quite a while. Gunther hadn't heard a sound.

"You might have knocked," Gunther said. "It wasn't even locked."

"Your hands, señor, up please."

Gunther obeyed. The little man was holding the gun much too tightly, his knuckles were white around the butt and his index finger was wrapped around the trigger at the second joint. Whoever he was, he wasn't a gunman and that made Gunther uneasy and terribly agreeable. Amateurs with guns were the most dangerous lot of all. The big man patted him down, then stepped backwards beside his partner.

"No pistola."

"Of course not," Gunther objected. "What's this about?" If this was going to be a hit, it would be over by now, Gunther thought. He brought his hands down slowly.

"No questions, señor," the little man said nervously. "You are to come with us." He pointed with the gun, swinging it to indicate the big man with the striped sweater, then bringing it back toward Gunther. He definitely was not a professional. "Please, do not try to get away from us, señor Beckmann. Guido can snap a man's arm at the elbow. I have seen it. It looked very painful." Gunther glanced at the big man, who smiled.

"Where are we going?"

"Do not ask questions. I am in charge here."

The little man was not a killer and Gunther decided to stall, carefully. Guido looked like a man who enjoyed snapping elbows.

"I don't know what the hell you think you're doing, but I'll be goddamned if I'll go anywhere with you to get a slug in my back,"

Gunther said. He took a slow step back when the big man clamped his huge hands together. The nearest throwable object was a lamp on the desk, but it wasn't near enough.

"I am instructed not to kill you, señor Beckmann." The little man tried on a smile. "I am—Guido and I are instructed to persuade you to come with us. Someone wishes to speak with you."

"You should have said that," Gunther replied. "Who?"

"No questions!" He was having to say that a lot, as if someone were prompting him.

"All right, all right, no questions." Gunther nodded toward his jacket on the arm of the easy chair. "Can I take that?"

The little man stepped away from the door and motioned with the gun for him to leave. "Guido will bring it. Go now."

Gunther started out past the splintered doorjamb. The force of Guido's blow to the door had stripped a length of door trim back away from the opening. As he walked by, Gunther grabbed it, turned, dropped to one knee and struck at the gun as hard as he could. The gun exploded almost against his ear before the little man dropped it. Gunther scurried across the floor for it and had it in both hands, pointing it up at Guido as he lay on his back. The big man was standing less than two feet away, stupidly holding Gunther's jacket in one hand.

"Now just back off slowly, you goddamn gorilla," Gunther snapped. "Nobody told me I couldn't use this!" The little man was at the door, moaning and holding his wrist.

"My hand! It is broken!"

Gunther's head was ringing with the explosion of the gun. There was a hole in the door about six inches from the knob. It might just as easily have been in his head. If either one of them had acted like a pro, he wouldn't have dreamed of pulling such a stunt.

"Anybody tell you what assholes you are?" He got up from the floor, keeping the gun trained on Guido.

"Señor, my hand—"

"Shut up!"

"Señor—"

"Goddammit. I told you to shut up." Gunther looked at Guido. "Do you have a car downstairs?"

The big man nodded.

"Throw the keys on the bed. Gently."

Guido did as he was told.

"Now gentlemen, tell me who we're about to meet. I don't much like surprises."

Guido glanced at the little man, then looked back at Gunther and the gun. "Señor Arbano. He wishes to speak with you."

"Guido!"

"The señor has the gun now, Raul," the big man said hotly. He looked at Gunther. "We were not to harm you, señor Beckmann. It is the truth."

Gunther shook his head. "He has a poor way of extending invitations."

"He thought you might resist."

"Really?" Gunther took the keys from the bed. "Well, I'm ready now. Let's all go. You two first."

Raul backed out the door, holding his hand. He was more nervous than when he had had the gun. "But, señor, what will you do with us?"

"Ah, ah," Gunther said, shaking his head solemnly. "No questions."

Guido parked the little English Ford near the channel in front of a row of several large warehouses. They had driven in silence. Gunther sat in the back seat with the muzzle of the gun pressed against the neck of Raul, who sat in the front passenger seat. The little man was keenly interested in Guido's driving, pleading with the big man to avoid every bump.

Guido leading, they walked briskly to one of the warehouses, then up an exposed stairway on the side of the building to the third level. The evening was getting cooler, and Gunther glimpsed the lights of a barge trailing behind a tugboat in the channel as they stepped into a long hallway.

"Which door is Arbano's office?" Gunther whispered in Raul's ear.

The little man pointed to the third door on the right. Gunther nodded for Guido to approach it, touching a finger to his lips and indicating he use his shoulder to open it. When Guido frowned, Gunther pointed the gun in his face. There was a click as Gunther removed the safety with his thumb. A moment before Guido crashed through the door, the tugboat could be heard chugging along outside in the dark channel.

Gunther shoved the little man through the opening. Raul fell sprawling over Guido, who was off balance after breaking the door, and both crashed to the floor. The room was well lit by three rows of fluorescent lights in the ceiling. A balding man sat at a large desk near a wide window and another, younger, man sat with his feet propped up in a chair. When the door burst open, the younger one reacted a second too slowly. Gunther was in the room, on one knee, ready to shoot.

"*¡No se muevan!*" Gunther shouted.

The man's reaction time increased noticeably. He quickly held his hands out away from his sides, palms out, indicating to Gunther he had no intention of protecting himself or anyone else.

Gunther glanced at the balding man behind the desk. "Señor Arbano, I presume?"

He looked at Gunther, then at the two on the floor. "And you are—"

"Señor Beckmann," Gunther said. "We have something of an appointment."

Arbano stared a moment, then smiled. It was a nervous smile, exposing large white teeth, but it was infectious. The young man smiled. Guido smiled. After a moment, even Raul smiled.

"*Sí*, we have, señor."

"I don't like being rousted," Gunther said. "Your two messengers weren't very polite. I don't like that." Gunther got to his feet carefully. He spoke to Arbano, but kept his eyes on the man with his hands out. There was a distinctive bulge under the man's coat, below the shoulder, and it wasn't cigarettes.

"Please, excuse them, señor Beckmann. Sometimes they are not very smart."

"Tell your friend to remove the *pistola*," Gunther said. "Instruct him to use the fingertips of his left hand." He aimed the gun at the man's head. "I'm very good with one of these."

Arbano nodded. "Carlos, do as you are told."

Carlos's smile waned slightly. Gunther wasn't sure whether it was because the man was being separated from his weapon or because he was unhappy at the prospect of being shot in the head. The gun was a Swiss custom-grade automatic with ornate scroll engravings on the external surfaces. With his index finger and thumb, Carlos extracted it slowly by the lanyard swivel in the butt as if it were a dead mouse he held by the tail. He set it on the corner of the desk, then put his hands out as before, smiling again like he and Gunther were the best of friends.

"There," Arbano said. "Now can we be friends, señor?"

"Maybe. You don't happen to have any surprises in your desk?"

"A *pistola*, señor? Me?" Arbano looked almost hurt.

Gunther said nothing. He reached for the automatic and slid the magazine out of the butt. It was full.

"Señor Beckmann, if I carried a *pistola*, I would not need Carlos."

"Just the same, keep your hands on top of the desk. Carlos, you and these two"—he nodded to Guido and Raul, still sitting on the floor—"go sit down over there on that sofa in the corner." When all three were seated, Gunther moved the chair Carlos had used to a spot where he could see everyone clearly and sat down. "Now, Arbano, about you wanting to see me." Gunther placed the gun on the arm of the chair. Across the room someone sighed. It was Raul.

"I was curious about you, señor," Arbano said. "For a German, you speak very good Spanish."

"Yes, I know," Gunther said. "Why were you curious?"

Arbano reached for a handkerchief in the outside pocket of his suit coat, stopped to ask Gunther's permission with his eyes. Gunther nodded. Arbano wiped his face and the top of his bald head. "Señor Beckmann, I am not in the habit of discussing business in the presence of —" He jerked his head toward the trio on the sofa.

"This is my party now. We'll do what I say we'll do. I say you'll answer the questions I put to you."

Arbano's smile turned sour. The corners of his mouth twitched. He was a man accustomed to giving orders and this turning of tables was uncomfortable for him. Gunther had seen it before in other men. He rather liked seeing them uncomfortable.

"How did you happen to know about me in the first place?" Gunther prodded.

"I received a call from a friend today." Arbano touched the handkerchief to his forehead. "Someone you spoke with earlier today."

"Hector Comi," Gunther said.

The bald man closed his eyes as if in pain. It was clear he didn't want the name spoken. After a moment Arbano nodded his head.

"And what did Hector want?"

"He told me about your visit. He said perhaps I could be of some help."

"Can you?"

"Perhaps. You are looking for someone." He dabbed the kerchief at his upper lip.

Gunther said nothing. He heard the sound of another tugboat and glanced at the window. There was nothing to see but the reflection of the room. Carlos, Guido and Raul sat together like three children in a crowded church pew, bored but attentive.

"You are seeking information about a man who might be living in Turkey. This is so?" Arbano smiled again.

"Hector talks a lot, doesn't he?"

"The señor called me because I may have some knowledge of this man. He has taken an interest in your search for personal reasons." Arbano arched his eyebrows as if he knew what the reasons were.

"I'm only interested in finding the woman at this point," Gunther said. "Did he tell you about her?"

He gave a casual shrug. "Possibly, señor."

Gunther took the gun from the arm of the chair and, with one eye closed, sighted down the short barrel at a point above Arbano's head. "You want to try that again?"

"Señor Beckmann, this woman is not so important, but the—"

The gun was a small caliber and the noise of its firing was like a small firecracker. The bullet crashed into the plaster wall about two feet above the bald man's head, sending flakes of white chalky substance down upon a file cabinet. Everyone in the room jumped, except Gunther.

"She's important to me," Gunther said. He cocked the hammer back. Everyone watched as the cylinder turned, aligning a new bullet with the chamber. Raul trembled with his mouth open.

"Señor Beckmann! Please!" Arbano dabbed at his forehead more vigorously than before.

"Her name is Camila Marie de Rosas." Gunther opened his eye and set the gun back on the arm of the chair. "Do you know the lady?"

"Please, señor, no more shooting."

"I want you to know how anxious I am to find her. She's important to me."

The bald man nodded rapidly. "Yes, yes, I know of her. Please, señor—"

"What do you know about her?" Gunther sat forward in his chair, and as he did, Raul flinched, shielding his face with his hands.

"I know that De Rosas is not her real name."

"What else?"

Arbano wiped his face with the kerchief. He licked his lips in a way that reminded Gunther of Pelado—nervously, as if his mouth were coated with chalk dust. "I do not know much about her." Gunther made a move toward the gun. "Truth! It is the truth, señor! She is said to live here . . . in Buenos Aires. But I have never seen her. I have seen her two times—perhaps three times—in Istanbul when I was there."

"With who?"

"With no one, señor." He wiped his fingers across his mouth. "I have done some business—my business takes me to many countries. I have dealt with her as a buyer."

"Buyer of what?"

"Different things." Arbano watched Gunther's hand. When it moved, he said, "Weapons. Very small weapons. *Pistolas,* carbines, some ammunition."

"Nothing else?"

"No, señor. They were very small consignments. No more than a few each time."

"How was the contact made in Istanbul?"

Arbano shrugged. "In Istanbul it is not difficult to find dealers of small arms."

"I said, how?"

"Referrals from other dealers." He mopped the top of his head with the kerchief. "It was always the same, her order. She only purchased NATO arms and ammunition—seven-point-six-two millimeter rimless. Once I offered Russian rimmed and she got very angry and cancelled an order for six American M fourteens."

"Why would she come to you?"

"I offer only the very best," Arbano said pridefully. "It is my reputation. There are many dealers, especially in Istanbul, but it is known that I deliver exactly what I promise."

"Who was she buying for?"

Arbano held his hands up as if he expected to be shoved. "Please, señor. A dealer does not ask such questions of a buyer. In the case of the señora, the transaction was a simple cash delivery."

Gunther thought for a moment, handling the gun and stroking it along the line of his jaw. Everyone waited patiently for him to speak. From somewhere far away came the whistle of a tug, answered lazily by the throaty blast of a distant foghorn. Only Gunther seemed to notice it.

"And you don't know who she is?" Gunther finally said.

"I did not say that, señor."

"Either you do or you don't."

"When I learned that the señora was from here—Buenos Aires—I became curious as to why she never contacted me here. Always, our transactions were in Istanbul."

"So?"

"I made some discreet inquiries," Arbano said. "Just a few questions to appease my curiosity. You understand, it is not good for business to ask too many questions about a buyer."

"Yes, I understand," Gunther replied.

"A man who asks too many questions is likely to lose his regular—"

"Yes, yes," Gunther said impatiently. "Get on with it."

"Puentes. Her name is Puentes. That is what I learned. I thought one day I might call on her." He nodded his head knowingly. "She is an attractive woman, señora Puentes."

"Call on her where?"

"In the barrio Flores. The older district, I am told. There are some villas there, but it is too crowded for my taste."

Gunther nodded to himself and rose from the chair. "Your information had better be good or I'll be back."

"You can locate this man through the woman, señor Beckmann? This one who hides in the eastern Mediterranean? The one responsible for señor Comi's friend's death?"

"We'll see," Gunther said. "Call Hector and thank him for me tomorrow. I'm obliged for his efforts. You've been helpful."

"If I may be of any further service to you—" Arbano smiled his business smile. "We seem to be in a similar line of work."

Now Gunther smiled and everyone sitting on the sofa smiled back. "That may be possible," he said. "Yes, I think I have some associates who may very well look you up."

"It would be my pleasure, señor."

"The pleasure will be all mine," Gunther replied.

A tugboat whistle sounded from somewhere near and the same foghorn answered. It was a game sailors played.

24

To attain the stature of a true crusader, the guerrilla must display impeccable moral conduct and strict self-control.

"I'm sorry about it, Alec. I'm just goddamn sorry as hell."

Pruett was pacing Gunther's room when Gunther arrived and he continued to pace, swearing oaths against Arbano, Peronism and gangsters while he stared at the floor as if it were his fault that Gunther had been visited by two of Arbano's hoodlums. Gunther listened patiently, leaning in the doorway to the bathroom, and Madanes was in his usual place, in the straight-backed chair near the desk.

"Don't you worry, Alec. I'll do something about our friend Arbano. We'll do something about his little arms deals. I'll—"

"All right!" Gunther said. "Do whatever you like—draw and quarter the bastard—but at least he came up with a solid lead on the woman I'm after."

"The little bald-headed gangster, I'll—"

"Jesus Christ, Ed, will you get off it!"

Pruett stopped pacing long enough to light a cigarette. He walked to the window and opened it a few inches as if the cool night air would calm him down. It didn't. "I'm sorry, Alec. It's just the idea—"

"Stop apologizing."

"Okay, okay."

"This Arbano isn't so all-fired tough as you're led to believe. Lots of bark, but not much guts. That's the way most of these people are." Gunther shook his head; he meant would-be South American dictators of second-rate empires. "And while I'm thinking about it, I don't like people leaving me little notes on my pillow." Gunther was watching Arturo. The gaucho solemnly agreed with a nod of his head. "What was so damned important anyway?"

"Got a message from Mackensen." Pruett sat on the ledge of the windowsill and flicked an ash out the opening. "The rest of the Taskmaster's list have babysitters. That was the message. He also advised me that you may be staying an extra day or two." He shrugged. "I didn't even know how long you were staying in the first place."

"Mackensen thinks that just because those people are being watched, they're safe." Gunther looked at Pruett. "Well, he's wrong. I've got to find that woman and get back before someone else gets shot up."

"You don't mean to take her with you?"

"Can I?"

Pruett shook his head. "No. Maybe if she was American or anything but Argentine. You can't just run off with a foreign national, Alec."

"Either way, I have to find her first." He turned to Madanes. "That's your job tonight. If she's in Flores, find out where, by morning."

"So late, señor?" Madanes stirred in his chair. "I have friends, señor Beckmann, but they also work. I will have to wake them."

"Then do it. I can't afford to keep bankers' hours."

Madanes was on his feet. "*Sí.*" He smiled as he pulled his cap down over his head. "I enjoy this. If the señora Puentes can be found in Flores, I will find her."

"And don't scare anyone away. I just want to know where she is. I'll see her myself. *¿Comprende?*"

Madanes nodded. "*Comprendo.* You will be here, señor?"

"Right here."

Gunther had to force the door closed after Madanes left. Pieces of wood hung broken and splintered around the frame, fragmented mementos of the visit from Raul and Guido. He wondered if Argentine hotels were insured against vandalism.

"You said you took a gun away from them," Pruett said.

"Yes. The littler of the two." The bottom edge of the door wouldn't fit into the jamb due to a bent hinge and Gunther had to kick it shut.

"You're getting bold in your old age."

"Instinct," Gunther replied. "Stupid instinct, but instinct all the same. If I'd thought about it first, I probably wouldn't have tried it."

"Whatever works."

Gunther nodded. Pruett had raised the window a few inches and the room was rapidly getting chilly. Pruett didn't seem to notice the cold, just as Quill hadn't noticed it. Gunther sat in the armchair, away from the draft.

"Our señora Puentes was buying small consginments of arms." Gunther folded his arms across his chest. "That's what she was doing in Istanbul. She bought from Arbano, but she probably bought from others, too. Arbano seems to think he's got the market cornered on NATO small arms and ammunition."

"Buying for Vargas?"

"That's my guess. Why, I don't know."

"Maybe he is a supplier," Pruett said. He flicked his cigarette out the window and lit another.

"Not a supplier. We know the suppliers. Besides the orders were too small and weren't regular, at least as far as Arbano is concerned." He pulled off his glasses, held them to the light, then polished them with a handkerchief. "Whatever it is sounds very small time."

"Why buy in Istanbul?"

Gunther shrugged. "That's where the crowd is. Lots of dealers. And with a buyer who wanted only a few weapons at a time, it's easy to get lost in the shuffle for bigger buyers. The little fish are easily forgotten." He placed the glasses back on his face and looked at Pruett. "Whatever Vargas was up to, buying in small lots with the girl as a front would doubly protect his anonymity."

"Cagey fellow."

"He's learned some new tricks since Cuba. I wonder where he's been learning and at whose knee."

They were silent for a long while. Pruett smoked his cigarette almost down to the filter before he flicked it outside. Gunther watched the smoke swirl, mixing with the cold air from the window and disappearing against the white ceiling.

"There's something from your old stomping grounds, Alec," Pruett said, as if he had found something amusing while reading a paper. "It came in today. It will interest you."

Gunther nodded for him to go on.

"Remember Jodl?"

"Erik Jodl?" Gunther said. "*Abteilung?*"

"Right. Deputy Head of Counterespionage, GDR. Your opposite number in Berlin." He smiled. "Well, Erik let the pressure get to him, I guess. He pulled the big number on himself."

"Did what?"

Pruett put his index finger to his temple and pulled the trigger with his thumb. "Bang. No more Erik."

Gunther squeezed up his face. "Jodl? Shot himself?" He shook his head. "Not possible."

"He sure did." Pruett nodded proudly like a schoolboy who knew the capital of Tanzania. "His apartment."

It had been Gunther's job, when he was a controller, to know the other side. He'd studied files and photographs and dossiers of all the department heads and their immediate subordinates when he took over the Berlin network, and he'd found Jodl to be the most aggressive, ambitious and savage of them all. He had a quick mind and used it vindictively against his enemies, and some of them were in the *Abteilung*. He was feared, disliked and mistrusted within his own department for his cruelty and ambition, but he was not a man who pointed a gun to his own head. Not Erik Jodl, unless the world really was going mad.

"I don't believe it," Gunther said. "Jodl would never have committed suicide."

"He's dead, Alec. You can't argue with the facts."

Gunther shook his head gently. "If he's dead, he had some help, whether he asked for it or not.'' He rubbed the coldness out of his shoulder. "You know, if I didn't know better, I'd say Vargas moved to Berlin. He's very good at arranging this kind of thing."

"Too bad he didn't." Pruett smiled. "That would solve your problems."

Gunther didn't reply. He knew it wouldn't solve anything. Mackensen would just send him back to Germany. With the right incentive, Mackensen could be a vengeful character. He wouldn't forget that Vargas had caused the death of nine of his agents. Just as Vargas had not forgotten Cuba. It was a game men played to prove themselves that the test of honor had no limits.

"If you don't mind terribly, Alec, I'd like to hang around awhile."

Gunther nodded indifferently. "You're chief of station, I guess you can do what you like. Just do me one favor."

"Yes?"

"Shut that goddamn window before I freeze to death!"

Pruett laughed. He pulled the middle sash until the window was closed. "It's not that I miss fieldwork," he said, staring into the darkness outside. "But every once in a while I get fed up with this overseer work. I'm continually filing this or checking that . . . pins and paper clips. You know what I mean?"

Gunther said he did.

"It can be an unwholesome bore at times." He glanced away from the window to look at Gunther. "You came along at the right time. I need this diversion."

"Is that a rusty feeling or just self-pity?"

"Both, I imagine. I feel old. Shit, I'm only forty-seven."

"In this business we are old," Gunther said.

"Dick Patton told me about a dream he used to have," Pruett said, continuing as if he hadn't heard. "He said he was climbing this old tower, a circular stairway on the inside against the walls, and the longer he climbed, the more he wondered what he was chasing and feared the trip back down. It's kind of like this job. Sometimes I wonder where I'm going. It's like standing in the middle of a tightwire. You can see the net below you, but the longer you stand there, the more the crowd roars for you to walk, and you know that if you do and you fall, you'll miss the net."

"Good grief, Ed."

"Don't you ever dream? Have bad ones?" Pruett seemed to be pleading to be understood.

"No," Gunther said, "I don't." For an instant he remembered the rain and the searchlights and Roberts's death smirk as he lay on his side in the mud. "I wouldn't go around repeating that drivel if I were you," he added hotly. "It's the kind of thing people get recalled for."

"You're a friend, Alec. I can talk to you." Pruett was watching Gunther closely. He seemed surprised, as if all these years he'd been visiting the confessional of the wrong church. "I thought I could—"

"You think too much," Gunther said. He shook his head as if it were the only way he knew to apologize. "I'm not a person you can talk to like that, Ed. Maybe I was back in Spain, but I'm not anymore. Spain was a long time ago. We're what we are because we chose to be. This is one goddamn hell of a time to be having second thoughts!"

"It's not that." Pruett shrugged his shoulders in a sad gesture of defeat and returned his glance to the window. "I guess that's why I was never that great in the field. No guts."

"No." Gunther sighed and shook his head again. "No, Ed, you're one of the few enigmas in the service. You're an honest man and you care. That's your problem."

"Oh? And what are you?"

Gunther remembered the young courier who'd brought him the dispatches at the house in New Jersey. "I'm a prototype," he said wearily. "Something to be studied, but not imitated. That's the hypocrisy of doing this kind of work in a democracy. We all began as basically honest men, but fieldwork makes you cynical and mean and turns you into something else. But it takes cynical bastards like me to make the system work. Only I'm so good at it they can't find a niche to put me in." Gunther had been staring at his hands, palms resting flat on his thighs, and now he looked up at Pruett. "That's why Mackensen loves me so. I don't care."

Judging from his expression, Pruett was embarrassed. He'd never heard Gunther talk like that. He turned to the window and after a moment lit another cigarette. It had started to rain and he watched for several minutes as it gently washed the courtyard below and pattered against the window. Finally he said, "I don't believe you, Alec." He didn't look away from the window. "I think you probably care more than any of us."

Gunther didn't respond. It was easier to listen to the rain.

25

Do not underestimate the value of women in a revolutionary process. This must be emphasized, for those of a colonial mentality tend to discriminate against women. They are capable of the most difficult deeds.

Gunther unfastened his seat belt as soon as the car was stopped. He'd changed into his brown suit and wore a long, belted raincoat against the gray misty morning that threatened but didn't rain.

They had left as soon as Madanes returned, about half past seven. Pruett drove and Madanes sat in the back, giving directions. The street was wide, by Buenos Aires standards, in this old section of the barrio Flores, but the houses were crowded against one another as if a giant hand had shoved them together to make room for a tiny park at the end of the block. From a distance these homes looked like one huge, ugly, rambling Spanish villa with two shiny television antennas for every one of its hundred grimy chimneys' blemishes on an already unattractive landscape. Gunther pulled up the collar of his raincoat against a coldness he only sensed. The overcast sky sprayed the buildings with a bland diffusion of light that left them two-tone gray-and-white like a grainy reproduction of a photograph from a Xerox copier.

"You're sure this is the place?" Pruett asked. He tapped a cigarette against the center of the steering wheel as he studied the buildings across the street.

"*Sí*. The señora Puentes, she lives here, with her mother and her sister's family.'' Arturo leaned forward on the front seat between Pruett and Gunther. ''This is the house, señores.''

Pruett turned to look at Gunther. ''Not exactly what I had expected, Alec. With the money she must have been making . . .'' He shrugged. ''You want me to go with you?''

He shook his head. ''No. Wait about ten minutes. If I'm not back by then, you might as well go. I'll probably be here awhile. I can find my way back.''

''Call me at the office?''

''The office?''

''Yeah,'' Pruett said. He lit his cigarette, cupping the light between his hands as if there were a draft in the car. ''Have to stop by anyway. Besides, Jean stopped worrying about me coming home every night years ago. You'll give me a call?''

Gunther nodded and got out of the car.

The house was of wood and dried brick and was painted robin's-egg blue. He walked through a small canopied, tiled patio and collided with a small boy who'd just appeared, running from the front door that had just opened. He caught the boy before he fell and knelt down to see his face.

''*¿Está bien?*'' Gunther asked. He held him by his shoulders as if the boy needed support.

''*Sí*, señor.'' The boy's brown eyes were large with surprise or sudden fear, Gunther couldn't tell which. He'd never felt comfortable with children; he thought his awkward self-consciousness frightened them. The boy appeared to be about five or six, if Gunther was any judge, and he squirmed until Gunther let him go. He always forgot to smile when he was with children.

''*¡Felipe! Qué vergüenza!*''

She was standing in the doorway, her hands on her hips, holding a wooden spoon, frowning at the boy. Tall, slender, she had an oval face with classical lines, high cheekbones and wide, full lips that parted to offer an embarrassed smile. ''*Perdón,* señor.''

Gunther smiled, finally. ''Your son?'' he asked in Spanish.

''My nephew,'' she said. ''Clumsy nephew,'' she added for Felipe's benefit. ''May I help you, señor?'' There was a flickering of concern in her voice, in her eyes, in the way she pulled the boy to her as if she'd met strangers before on this patio and wished she hadn't.

"I am looking for the señora Camila Puentes."

"Señorita," she said, holding the fidgety boy closer. "I am not married, señor."

Gunther was surprised and not sure why. Arbano had said she was attractive. She was that and more. He guessed her age to be about thirty-five, no more than forty. She wore no makeup (or so little it didn't matter) and her face had the smoothness of a young girl's except for the tiny lines at the corners of her eyes. Her skin was slightly dark with the coloration of a true Latin and her long dark hair was tied up with a band. She was a beautiful woman, not stunning or artificial, but, rather, she was naturally attractive with an air of sophistication in the way she held her head.

"Señor, you are staring."

Gunther felt his face flush. "I am sorry, señorita Puentes. I had expected someone different." This was not going right. The boy was restless. Finally he pulled away from the woman, produced a plastic whistle and disappeared down the alley, blaring away. Gunther decided to try again. "My name is Peter Beckmann. I thought perhaps we could talk."

"Talk, señor? About what, please?"

"It is a matter that requires some privacy, señorita."

She frowned and glanced quickly to either side of Gunther as if she expected to see someone else lurking about. When she returned her gaze to Gunther, she held her head a bit higher, looking slightly down at him. "Señor Beckmann, I do not know you. Perhaps where you come from, it is different, but in this country it is a discourtesy for a *caballero* to come calling in this manner without a proper introduction."

She smiled with a reservation Gunther had come to recognize in people who thought they were being polite.

"I am sorry," Gunther said. "We do have a mutual friend."

"Yes?"

"A man from Turkey, señorita. A man from Istanbul."

She wasn't fast enough to cover herself. She had glanced quickly at Gunther before averting her eyes to something else, but Gunther caught it. There was recognition in her eyes, and fear.

"I am sorry, señor, I—"

"You have forgotten him? But he has not forgotten you." Gunther smiled. "Señor Arbano. Cecilio Arbano." He watched her hands; her long delicate fingers played restlessly with the handle of the spoon, which clicked against an inexpensive onyx ring. "When you used the name De Rosas."

Camila glanced up sharply. For an instant Gunther saw an expression of hatred. "You are from the National Ministry?"

He shook his head no.

"Turco?"

"German," Gunther said. "I found you through señor Comi. We have a similar interest."

"Comí?" She did not look surprised to hear the name, but the spoon ceased to move between her fingers. "I know no such—"

"Please, señorita Puentes. I'm only here for information. I mean you no harm. I am not from the police." Gunther offered another smile.

"German, señor Beckmann?"

"Yes."

She was quiet a moment; then her expression changed as if she saw the whole game. Camila returned Gunther's smile.

"You are not German, señor," she said with certainty. "You are not señor Peter Beckmann, a German, I think."

"No?"

"No. You are American," Camila Puentes said in English. "You are Alec Gunther."

26

Women should be entrusted with carrying confidential messages, ammunition, etc. If captured, they will invariably be treated better than men, no matter how brutal the enemy.

Her full name was Camila Delores Magdalena de Rosas Marie Puentes. She had traveled in Europe, Africa and Asia on a forged passport as De Rosas, an old family name from her mother's side. She knew Comi and Arbano and several other smugglers in the munitions business, but resisted any acknowledgment of Vargas. She was totally relaxed now, almost as if she'd expected him, and she conversed with Gunther in flawless English. They were sitting at a table in a small living room with a fireplace and wooden furniture. It was a distinctive room to Gunther because under every lamp or vase and on the arms and backs of chairs were lace doilies. He remembered that when he was a boy his mother's house was full of the things.

"How did you know who I was?" Gunther was saying. He could feel the warmth of the fire at his back.

"You look just like you were described to me," she said. "You have eyes of ice. Blue. Terrifying eyes. Sad eyes. You are not a large man, but you exude a feeling of strength. Physical strength—and tenacity—like a bulldog." She touched a cloth napkin to her lips. "I do not mean to offend. You do not look like a tourist or a businessman or a policeman. You are a thoughtful man—I don't mean that you are polite, though you may be. You are thoughtful in that you judge people, analyze them, as you are judging and analyzing me at this moment."

The Thinker, walking, Gunther thought. "Anything else?"

"Yes, of course," she said. "You are a spy for the United States government." She sipped her coffee, then added, "Excuse me, Central Intelligence. Sometimes I forget the Americans have different spies for different organizations."

"I don't suppose it would matter if I told you that you were mistaken."

"As you are mistaken about me?" She smiled. "No, I think not."

"Do you know why I'm here?"

She leaned forward slightly as if she were suddenly interested. "You would like perhaps to tour the *Banco Central* with me? Sometimes I go there . . . to work."

Gunther shook his head. "Thank you, no. Perhaps another time. I'm in a bit of a hurry."

"Then why are you here?"

"Ollie Vargas," Gunther said. "Oliva Raul Vargas. Cuban. I think you were buying small arms and ammunition for him."

Camila shook her head. Her hair tousled slightly with the movement. She was a beautiful woman, and the light from the fire softened the lines of her face, helping her to look even younger. She didn't look like a gun runner. "The name is not familiar. I've never bought anything for a Cuban. My purchases were for Israel."

"Who told you about me?"

"A man. Perhaps, even, he was an Israeli."

"Even Israelis have names."

She nodded, smiling. "Yes. Allen. Just Allen. Probably not even that was real. Do you suppose, Mr. Beckmann?"

"What did he look like?"

"Tall. Is it so important?"

"To me," Gunther said. "Was he black?"

"Black?" She sighed, looked away. "Even blacks can be Jews, you know."

"Was he?" Gunther insisted.

"Black?" She nodded. "Yes. Jew? I don't know."

"Tell me about him."

She had been looking away from him, studying some object at the end of the room, and now she turned quickly back toward him. "You are a guest in my home, Mr. Gunther. I am willing to talk to you. Allen told me you might come. All I ask in return is that you treat me courteously. I am not an animal to respond to commands." She placed her hands together on the table, long fingers interlaced with long fingers. "Now, what was it?"

Gunther removed his glasses, polished them with a napkin, put them back on. He couldn't remember the last time he'd interrogated a woman—was it Cologne? Madrid, in the old days? The industrial worker who'd come over the wall? He'd never quite felt comfortable with the job, whenever it was. Be patient, that was the rule, that was always the rule. Be more patient with women than with men because they are more liable to fits of hysteria. Gunther blinked at the woman across from him. She was not that kind of woman. He wondered if the same rule applied and decided it did, but not for the same reasons.

"If you don't mind, tell me about him," he said finally. "Please."

"And don't patronize me."

"I promise."

"We were business associates," she said, looking at her hands.

Gunther nodded.

"And lovers," she added.

Gunther nodded again. "You and Vargas?"

"Allen and me. I don't know a Vargas." She looked up at him. "Does it surprise you that I slept with a black? It does not matter, I am just curious."

"Blacks can be lovers, too, you know."

She smiled at that. Gunther was just noticing how white her teeth were, how perfect her smile. Lovely.

"Allen said you had a sense of humor. That's rare, you know, in men like you, I mean. He said you were very good at your job. Do you enjoy what you do?"

"Do you mind if I ask the questions?"

"Sorry," she said. Gunther believed her. "He talked about you quite a lot, you know. Allen did. He was a very unusual man." Camila flexed her fingers, curled them around her coffee cup. "I loved him very much."

"You sound as if it's over."

"It is. Not that I don't still feel the same way, but I won't see him again. He told me that. He's dead, or will be soon. That he didn't tell me, but we both knew." She looked at Gunther again. It was she who had the sad eyes. "He's in the same kind of work as you."

"Yes, I know," Gunther said.

"You're looking for him, aren't you?"

"Yes."

She nodded her head sadly, like a child. "I don't know where he is. You don't have to believe me, but I don't."

"Would you tell me, if you did?"

She said nothing.

"Do you know about him? His background? Where he came from? Anything?

"Will it help you to find him?"

Gunther shrugged slightly. "I don't know."

"Are you his friend?" She wasn't smiling now. Her incisors, white as snow, bit into her lower lip, but did not hold back the tears at the corners of her large brown eyes. She looked less like a child now, more her age. "He talked about you so much, but he never said you were friends."

"We were, once," Gunther said. "I have to find him. He's . . ." Gunther started to tell her, then decided against it. She already knew he was a dead man, just not dead yet. "He's somewhere in the United States."

She didn't make a sound as the wetness around her eyes streaked in tiny droplets down across her high cheekbones, down the beautiful smooth face to the delicate line of her jaw. *"Superintende de tarea,"* she said quietly to herself, then again louder for Gunther. "It is something . . . I don't know. Something to do with you. Something about his life . . . a goal . . ."

"Taskmaster," Gunther repeated in English. "Do you know—"

"I know nothing!" The tears were coming faster now. "He did not discuss it."

"I'm sorry about this," Gunther said, not sure what he meant by it. "But I must know more about Var—Allen. How did you meet?

When? Where? What was he doing? What had he been doing?'' Gunther was dry in the mouth. He looked into his empty cup, decided this was not the time to ask for coffee. He could feel the fire, still warm at his back. That must be why he was so thirsty, he thought. *Why was this woman so goddamn affecting?* She was nothing to him, he told himself. She was an object, a source of information like the thousands he had dealt with before. No, she was different. She *was* different, goddammit! Gunther watched her, saw the glistening eyes that looked past him at nothing, eyes that looked into the past, remembering moments, moments no one could rob her of. With Allen. With Vargas. Are you his friend? Yes, once. No, that was a long time ago. No, Vargas was a killer. No, Gunther thought. No! "Do you feel like talking now?" he heard himself ask.

Camila Puentes nodded slowly, as if answering a voice in the dark. "Yes." Softly.

"Tell me," Gunther said. "Please."

"He was always Allen," she began. "He has always been Allen to me." Long slender fingers reached for the cloth napkin, touched it gently to the streaks on her face. She spoke without looking at Gunther. She spoke to the fire behind him, the light reflecting in her eyes. "There were other names, you know, because of his work, but he was always Allen with me. I met him here . . . in Buenos Aires. It was in June, 1970, at the university here. My father was speaking to a student group—he was a professor at the university in Córdoba until we moved here in the late sixties. He was truly a gentle man, my father, but he was anti-Peron and he was killed for it. It was that night, after the lecture; a car ran him down. It was the same night that the government fell. The military, you know."

Gunther nodded, but she didn't notice.

"Allen was the one who took charge at the place"—she glanced at Gunther briefly—"were my father was lying. He held the people back and forced a man with a car to take Father to the hospital. It was an accident, really, that I met him. He said he admired my father. I remember, at the hospital, when my father was dead, he—Allen—said, 'They've taken over and your father was the first casualty. Enlightened men are always first.' That was our beginning. From death comes life, Mr. Gunther.''

"So he persuaded you to become a revolutionary.''

"Not a revolutionary." Her eyes met Gunther's again and held. She was not crying anymore. "We were not that, ever. It is easy to label a person's belief as revolutionary if he is an activist, political, social, anything . . . It is something the Americans are good at, labels. I think it is something drummed into your culture by television advertising. If it's different, it's revolutionary. Tires are revolutionary. Detergent is revolutionary. Baby food, cigarettes, books, clothes, cars . . . It does sound silly to say in your country, even now. The Land of the Free?"

Gunther shifted in his chair. "When did he start working for the Israelis?"

"When?" She shook her head. "I don't know. Always, I suppose. He liked them. I think it was because they started against such great odds—after the war, I mean. He's always wished he could write. Write books. He thought Exodus was the greatest book ever written because it was about the people who created a nation. People he knew."

"Was he involved in the Six Day War?"

"Against the Egyptians?" She smiled. "Of course. He said it was his duty. He wanted to see the Red Sea open up again. He said it was his greatest disappointment not to have been around when Moses did it to them the first time." She glanced past him again at the fire. "That was before we met. Not that it mattered, but he never told what he was doing. Oh, I was his buyer sometimes, but I never knew details. Allen said it was best I never know. It was for his protection, more than for mine. He told me that, too."

"He never talked about it?"

"It?"

"What he did."

"Names, sometimes," she said. "Sometimes he would wake up sweating, calling names. I never saw him frightened except in his dreams. He would talk then, but only generally. He was in prison a long time. I don't know where. He almost died there. Did you know about that?"

"Very little."

"I don't want to know about it." She sighed and glanced at her hands. "That's when he talked about you, after a bad dream. There were two people he talked about most. You were one." A pause.

"He respected you very much, but he never called you his friend. I don't understand."

Gunther studied her a moment, wondering how it was between them, between Vargas and this woman. "You said there were two. Who was the other?"

"Ramon," she said, letting her eyes drift back to the fire. "It was funny because he always asked me about him. I lived for many years in Córdoba, where he was born, but I never knew him. People always do that, you know."

"Ramon?" Gunther repeated.

She looked at Gunther again as if she'd forgotten where she was. "I'm sorry." She smiled. "Ramon was what they called him. Ernesto Guevara de la Serna. Che Guevara."

"Vargas knew Che?"

"Allen knew him," she said. "Before he was a legend. He spoke of Ramon a great deal. I think he was with him in Bolivia . . . before he was killed. He had much respect for Ramon. He told me he knew Ramon, but he did not know Che. No one knew Che until after he died. This is true of all myths."

"And knowing that, it didn't occur to you that he might be Cuban?"

"No, because I was not interested to know. Besides, Ramon himself was not Cuban. He was Argentine, Alec. Do you mind if I call you Alec?"

"Not at all."

"Allen spoke of the Congo also," she continued. "It is known that Guevara was in the Congo for a short time—Zaire now. I thought perhaps Allen came from there. But Allen would not tell me when I asked. He said blacks have no home, only a final resting place. 'We are like the Jews before Israel,' he told me once, 'except for us there is no Promised Land, no Moses.' "

They were silent again for a long while, then she said, "More coffee, Alec?"

Gunther nodded and watched as she poured. He drank it without milk.

"About this Taskmaster," he said between sips, "did he say anything about it? Anything at all?"

"No."

"Do you know what he meant?"

"No. I told you, he never discussed it."

"But he must have said something. You heard the name. He must have mentioned something about it or you wouldn't have heard the name."

"If I knew, why should I tell you?"

Gunther looked into her eyes. She didn't know the man he was hunting, only Allen, the man who tried to save her father, the man who fought injustices. Gunther answered finally, "Because he knows he will be caught. There's no escaping and he knows that. And I think you do, too." He started to drink again, changed his mind and set the cup down. "I think he wants me to find him—I know he does. He's left clues for me. He knew someone would find him and he wants that someone to be me. Vargas is a romantic. He is his own Quixote and he's picked on the biggest windmill around." Gunther watched her, hoping his words would penetrate. She was looking into the fire again. "He *is* going to die. He has a silly, childish notion of vengeance against my country and he has carried out certain threats. People are dead because of him and my government cannot allow that. He will die; he knows he will and he's planned it in such a way that I was chosen to find him. I think I know why now. It's a stupid, senseless reason. Few of us have friends in this business, it's the nature of the work. Your Allen wants to die with a friend."

Gunther waited a moment, but she said nothing.

"Did you hear?"

"Yes." Softly. Her eyes did not move from the fire. "It is a strange friendship, is it not, Alec?"

"Not really." Gunther shook his head. "Maybe. It is impossible to explain."

"I do not know about this Taskmaster," she said quietly, trying to keep control of her voice. "I do not know. I know only of the *Banco Central,* but you are not interested."

"If you say so."

"I have told you everything you would be interested in." She would not look at him. Her voice was cracking; she was losing control. "I would like to be alone, please."

"Yes," Gunther said. "Is there . . . can I do anything for you?"

"No, just to be alone." The long hands were flat against the table like a medium's. They looked blue and cold. He wondered about the bank, tried to picture her as a teller, but couldn't. She was inflicting her loneliness on him and he wanted to finish and leave. Gunther could see she was fighting not to cry. It was a machismo quality he expected only of the men here.

"Do you have any money? Did he provide for that?"

Her eyes did not flicker; the movement of her head almost imperceptible. "I do not take money," the voice whispered. "I am not a *puta.*" It was all Spanish now.

Gunther got up and retrieved his coat from a chair near the door. When he looked back, she had not moved. He stood at the front door a few moments, listening to the quiet of the empty house and the sounds from the room with the fire. Outside, the sky and the street and the grimy little houses were a cardboard gray, but there was no rain. Then he left. Behind him, Gunther heard her, Camila Delores Magdalena de Rosas Marie Puentes, crying before the fire. He did not look back.

The overcast was heavier than before, low enough to make almost indistinguishable the tops of the buildings along the street; it was as if the mist would rub out their sharp lines. Gunther walked toward the park at the end of the narrow avenue, toward the center of the city. He was thinking of Mackensen and the progress of the hunt and his part in it, when he saw the figure. A man in a battered fedora. Gunther saw him for only an instant before he stepped back into the recess of a doorway some way down and across the street—not far, thirty yards, perhaps a bit more. He wore a short jacket and gloves and appeared to be looking for something, perhaps a taxi, which was an odd thing to do on an empty street. Gunther slowed his walk only slightly, ready to dive into any one of several patio terraces along his path. He could feel the weight of the revolver inside his coat and thought of a dozen defensive tactics he might use, but when he was at a place where he could see the doorway clearly, the man was gone, and Gunther felt foolish.

27

It is pointless to take prisoners in a guerrilla conflict.

"I can leave now."

They were sitting in Pruett's office. The chief of the Buenos Aires station was in his shirt sleeves, unshaven, slightly groggy. Gunther was in a chair to the side of the desk, in a shaft of morning light from the window where he could see the city below. The overcast had broken, allowing sunlight through like flashlight beams in a dusty mine shaft.

"That certainly didn't take you long." Pruett was looking for something. He kept patting his pockets, looking in drawers, patting his pockets again. "I can book you out tonight or in the morning."

"Tonight, I think. I'll need to get with Mackensen right away."

Pruett nodded. "Check. Jean will be sorry she missed you, Alec. I was hoping we'd have time to get together for dinner before you left." He felt inside his coat for the third time. "You don't happen to have a cigarette, do you, Alec?"

Gunther shook his head. "You smoke too much."

"I know, I know," he said, nodding. He pressed the intercom. "Cheryl, bring me some cigarettes." Pruett glanced up at Gunther and added, "and coffee, Cheryl, for two."

"You look awful," Gunther said. "Why don't you go home?"

"I will, and sleep for days." He stretched his back, sitting up in his chair, and yawned until his eyes watered. "I don't remember the last time I was up all night. I mean, *all* night. I don't miss fieldwork as much as I thought." His smile was interrupted by another yawn. "You said she was not much help—the Puentes woman?"

"I said she didn't know much." Gunther fought to keep from yawning. He wished Pruett would stop. "She knew Vargas, that's true, but she didn't know anything about his operation. She didn't even know his real name was Vargas."

"What about buying? She talk about that?"

"Some," Gunther said. "I wasn't much interested. She was a buyer and that was it. Knew nothing about who or what the weapons were going to. Vargas used her very carefully."

"Was it worth the trip down here?"

"Everything considered, I would say so. I know some more pieces about Vargas that I didn't know before." Gunther yawned in spite of himself. "I've also learned I'm a very good counter of cows."

The girl came in with the coffee. She put the tray on the corner of Pruett's desk between Gunther and Pruett and handed him a package of cigarettes. "You smoke too much," she said. By the time she'd poured two cups and was gone from the room, Pruett had lighted one of the cigarettes.

"Everybody's a critic," he said, exhaling a blue cloud of smoke. After a moment he looked at Gunther. "This little errand you're on, Alec. It's something of a problem for me, I mean, as chief of station."

"It is?"

"You know the procedure. All fieldwork coordinated through station—especially interrogations—are required to have follow-ups. Normally, I'd send a team to follow up on your initial contact. Do a complete bio, the whole thing, for our files. She obviously knows dealers. We're very interested in dealers these days. But you're here on a solo from Special Operations. Not only that, but special authorization from Mackensen." Pruett shrugged his shoulders sadly. "So what am I supposed to do? Officially, I'm not supposed to know what you're up to. Just cooperate. Do I send a team to talk to Puentes?"

"I wish you wouldn't."

"I'm sure she could be helpful. We're really very interested in dealers, Alec."

Gunther took a long sip of coffee. It was extremely good. Rich and full-bodied, like they claim on television, but don't deliver. Television. He remembered Camila's comment and wondered if coffee beans could be revolutionary. Gunther tried to make his mind relax, to just let it float awhile, but Pruett was staring.

"I don't know, Ed," he said tiredly. "Do what you think is best."

"Send in some people, then. You think it'd be all right to talk to her? It wouldn't interfere?"

"Goddammit, Ed, you're the chief of station here, not me."

"All right, fine, all right," he said defensively. "I'll do it. I just didn't want to mess up something you're into. I'll send someone around to talk to her."

Gunther took off his glasses to rest his eyes. "Give her a little time," he said. "A few days. Don't jump on her right now. She'll be here next week. She hasn't got anywhere to go." He drank more coffee, thinking about her. "You have women here, don't you? Send a woman. Yes, that would be best. Send a woman to see her, Ed."

"Whatever you say, Alec. There's a flight that leaves this afternoon. Santiago–Miami. Same flight you got here on. Shall I put you on it?"

"Yes. What time?"

"Three or four, I think."

"Yes," Gunther said again. He closed his eyes and leaned back in the chair. "That will be fine."

"I'll have someone stop by your motel and pick up your things. You can stay here until you go to the airport. We have a day room with a bed and a shower, if you like."

Gunther nodded. "I need to call Mackensen," he said mechanically. "Tell him I'm coming home." He was thinking about the flight, hoping all the skiers were still in the mountains.

Then he remembered the man at the airport and the man in the Flores barrio. "Ed, you haven't been watching over me like a mother hen, have you?"

"Mother hen?" Pruett gazed at him almost glassily. There was no mistaking his need for sleep. "How's that again?"

"Someone from station watching out for my welfare."

"A babysitter? For you?" Pruett's smile widened into an uncontrolled yawn. "Whatever for?"

"Then there wasn't any?"

"I haven't the manpower, for one thing," he said. "Besides, there was no request for one. But I'd have told you in any case. It isn't the usual thing . . . trailing one of our own. Especially Special Ops." Pruett shook his head. "There hasn't been anyone, Alec. Why do you ask?"

"Shadows," Gunther said, still slightly annoyed. "I've been seeing too many shadows."

"You think Arbano—"

Gunther got up from his chair. "No, no. It's nothing. Forget it."

"Now, Alec, if you think—"

"Forget it. I'm tired is all."

"Well thank God for that. I'm glad to hear you admit it. I feel like an old man watching you go thirty hours without a break as if there was nothing to it."

"I'll need to talk to Mackensen as soon as you can get a stat call through. Then I'll rest until the flight."

Pruett got up to see him to the door. "Fine. I wish you could stay longer. Jean will be disappointed."

"There'll be another time."

"Right." Gunther could hear him yawning again. "And don't be concerned about shadows. You'll be home soon enough."

But Gunther was concerned. He was remembering the plain-faced men in the airport terminals and the man in the Flores barrio who wore the battered fedora.

Gunther felt suddenly cold with the fluttering in his stomach that accompanied alarm, a sign anticipating fear. Someone *was* watching him. But only watching, as if to do more would spoil the game. The question of *who* did not at this point arouse his interest. *Why* did.

The day room was no more than a converted supply storeroom,

almost a cell. There were no windows and the walls were unpainted where shelves had been ripped away. The rusty shower was a simple tiled affair, curtained and set in the corner. Gunther lay on the bed, tired but not sleepy, staring vacantly at the ceiling. He had a headache.

When the telephone rang, he answered it quickly.

"Yes?"

"Your call is ready, sir," a male voice said.

"Okay."

"Hold a moment, sir." The line went dead a few seconds, then he heard a beep as the scrambler equipment was switched on. "This line is secure," the voice said. "I'm leaving the line now, sir. Just hang up when you're through."

After the agency operator rang off, Gunther said, "Hello."

"Alec?" It was Mackensen.

"Yes, I'm leaving this afternoon. I'm finished here."

"Good. How long will it take?"

"I'll be in Miami by three in the morning. Don't you want to know about Vargas?"

"Did the woman tell you where he was?"

"No."

"Where to look?"

"No."

"I want you here by nine, Alec. Take the first available flight from Miami. I will meet you at Dulles. I have disturbing news, Alec. Very disturbing."

Gunther wondered when he'd ever heard Mackensen give him glad news. "I thought you were interested in Vargas."

"Erik Jodl is dead," Mackensen said abruptly.

"I know," Gunther said. "Pruett told me. So what?"

"Ibn Saud Naguib was run over by a train in Cairo. Counterintelligence. Brian Whittish crashed his private plane near Gatwick. Counterintelligence."

Gunther nodded to himself. "Both dead, I presume?"

"Of course they're both dead. They're all three dead. Suicide and two accidental deaths of major intelligence operatives in four days. Germany, Britain and Egypt. I don't like the implications here, Alec."

"You think Vargas is responsible?" Gunther asked. His head pounded worse now.

"Who else? These aren't coincidences, Alec. You can bet your ass they're not coincidences."

"But they had nothing to do with Cuba. Those—"

"Christ, I know that! Just get back here."

"You must have something more solid that intuition to think Vargas is responsible."

"A challenge," Mackensen said. He paused a moment, then said, "An ad was placed in the London *Times* the morning after each of the deaths. The office there picked up on it. It's Vargas, all right."

"What was the ad?"

"I have it here. It says, 'Tell Alec, silent knight moves as secret troopers each removed.' It's an acronym, Alec. T-A-S—"

"Taskmaster," Gunther said without surprise.

"Exactly. It's Vargas, there's no question. It's his perverted way . . . addressing it to you."

It figures, Gunther thought. "Look, I think I've been followed . . . since I left California. Do you know about that?"

Mackensen sighed heavily. "We'll discuss it after you arrive."

"Christ, Mackensen, if you've—"

"I want you back as soon as you can get here," Mackensen shot back. "I know where Vargas is."

Gunther noted something akin to sadness, at least resignation, in his voice. Mackensen was never sad about anything in his life.

"Where?"

"Here . . . the states. New England."

"You *know* where he is?"

A pause. "Yes."

"Don't we have people up there?"

"Yes."

Mackensen was less sad now, more businesslike. His old self.

"But I want you to finish this assignment. You personally. The way it was planned. Do you understand?"

Gunther said he did, but he was only beginning to.

28

The true guerrilla warrior is tireless in the pursuit of his objective.

The flight was uneventful. They always say that, Gunther thought. Unless the plane runs into a goddamn mountain, it is an uneventful flight.

He waited only an hour before boarding an Eastern flight from Miami to Washington. He tried to sleep, couldn't, and read all three magazines in the seat pouch before the plane finally touched down at Dulles.

They were waiting for him when he got off. Mackensen and Rockwell, the team of Mutt and Jeff, standing outside the passenger debarkation area. Mackensen greeted him solemnly with a nod, while Rockwell stood to the side, arms across his chest, like an impatient second ready to take someone's hat.

"Good to see you, Alec," Mackensen said without a smile. "Long trip?"

"Let's go somewhere," Gunther said. "Now."

"You look tired."

"I want to talk. Let's go."

Mackensen nodded and started off toward the nearest exit. "Luggage?"

Gunther indicated the small bag in his hand. "No." They were side by side as if on a stroll. Rockwell walked behind them.

At the taxi stand outside, Mackensen pointed to an empty cab. "We'll take this one. Peter will drive."

"Yours?"

"One of my rogues," Mackensen said, holding the door. "Very handy at airports." In a few moments Rockwell had the car in traffic. "All right, Alec. Talk to me."

"I quit." Gunther had been savoring this for hours. He was going to tell Mackensen exactly where he could stick this job. He was tired and frustrated, but mostly he was angry.

"Do you?" The hint of a smile.

From the front seat Rockwell said, "You can't quit, Gunther. People don't quit."

"Just drive, Peter," Mackensen said before Gunther could respond. "This is something between Alec and myself. Isn't it, Alec?"

"I don't like being followed by my own," Gunther said hotly. "I'm taking myself out. Get someone else to finish it. I don't like being someone else's training exercise and I especially don't like running interference on an operation that I'm only half-informed about. And unofficial at that."

"They weren't mine, Alec. The people you saw, they weren't company."

"Bullshit!" Gunther started to add something and changed his mind. It was useless talking anyway. He looked away from Mackensen and out the window. It would be full daylight soon. It looked like it would be a hot day. The sky was cloudless; traffic was light. He wished he could roll down a window, but the knobs were missing.

Mackensen paused a moment to glance out the window. "Think for a moment, Alec. Why should I have you followed?"

"I don't know—another one of your goddamn tests! Look, you send me after Vargas, then on a whim to South America where I learn he is not, though I already suspected he would not be, and I find you've not only located him here, but have, in the short period of my absence, attributed deaths in England, Germany and Egypt to Vargas. That's a goddamn neat trick for a man with no record of passport. Why shouldn't I wonder?"

Mackensen shook his head. He didn't bother to smile. "You had an assignment in Argentina."

"The assignment was to find Vargas; it was not to be the quarry for your army of solos."

"They weren't my people, Alec. They were his—Taskmasters, they're called."

"His!"

"Vargas's." Mackensen nodded confidently, smiling wryly like a sagacious psychic, as if he had some great secret to reveal. "I think now is the time to fill in the blank spots of this assignment."

"The right time for that was in New Jersey."

"I've been after Vargas for a long time now," Mackensen said, looking nowhere. Gunther thought he saw in his eyes an odd relenting—odd for Mackensen—as if Mackensen was near the end of a long and tiring journey. He looked back at Gunther. "Your friend runs an organization that is trying to destroy us . . . Central Intelligence. The organization is known simply as Taskmaster." Mackensen shook his head. "That's not precisely correct. His organization is not known except to a very limited few. I know. Peter knows. Now you know." He made a weak sweeping gesture with his hand. "Some others, Jodl, Naguib and Whittish, knew."

"What do you mean he's trying to destroy Central Intelligence?"

"You must trust me, Alec. Vargas and this organization are bent on wrecking the company. It's a game of sabotaging our prestige, our manpower. In a way he's a guerrilla terrorist in our community. He knows us very well. He's even adopted the name we gave him in Cuba."

"Why doesn't anyone else know?" Gunther said. "Why doesn't the company—"

"Because there are too many ears and mouths in the company today, Alec. You haven't been in the mainstream of things lately. There are people who have no business knowing our covert operations. I will not have our people looking over their shoulders for Vargas when they have more important duties. If this were made official, it would get out. I'm not going to let it out."

Gunther's eyes locked briefly with Mackensen's, but only briefly.

The explanation wasn't complete. "Why the killings all of a sudden? And why those retired agents in particular?"

"I will explain it to you when the assignment is done, Alec. Right now there just isn't time."

"Make time."

Mackensen glanced at his watch. "There isn't any." He looked at Gunther. "What's bothering you?"

It was the question that Gunther himself could not answer. Something was missing inside him. Desire, perhaps. The work did not have the appeal it once did. He thought about the woman in Buenos Aires and about Pruett's confessions. Maybe a man could be so blindly intent that he would pass himself into a twilight domain of metaphored contradictions where west *does* meet east and he exchanges identities, where the cautious man acts impetuously, the vigilant man sleeps, the indurate man cares. Perhaps.

"Alec?" Mackensen was staring at him.

"Look, maybe . . . maybe I *am* getting too old for this. Odd things bother me now that never bothered me before. Vargas *did* slip by me in Montana. Maybe it's a sign that I shouldn't—"

"Rubbish," Mackensen said. "These things happen."

"But never to me. I've never been this sloppy before."

"You've been on ice for more than a year, that's all it is. You were not quite up to form after so long sorting checks in that dreary little office on Fifth Avenue. But that's over. You're as good as you ever were, Alec." Mackensen was smiling, at least making the effort, as if he weren't really sure himself.

"Always the optimist, aren't you?"

"I pride myself in knowing which man to choose for each assignment. Vargas is yours . . . always has been. From the very beginning, Alec, I knew you were the one to ferret him out. That's why I sent you to B.A. It brought him out in the sunlight. Now you can finish it. I couldn't very well include anyone else from the company, since no one else knows. It's yours, Alec."

"And I should kill him," Gunther said.

"You told me you didn't object. We went over this quite carefully."

"Yes, yes. I know." Gunther nodded slowly, looked at his hands.

Mackensen sat quietly with his arms folded across his chest, a finger across his lip, watching Gunther. "What do you say, Alec?"

"I should run Vargas down. Put a bullet in his brain. Even up the score." Gunther looked at Mackensen.

Mackensen shrugged, said nothing.

"All right," Gunther finally said. "Forget what I said."

"You'll finish the assignment?"

"Yes, I'll finish it! I'll find him . . . and the rest of it."

"Good boy." Mackensen patted him on the knee and hunched forward toward Rockwell. "All right, Peter, you can turn around now." He smiled at Gunther when he was settled back in the seat. "We're going back to Dulles. You're leaving for Montpelier"—he glanced at his watch—"in about forty minutes."

"Vargas is there?" Gunther seemed almost not to care.

"In Vermont, yes," Mackensen said with a genuine smile. "We just have time to discuss it. He sent you a wire—a telegram. I have it with me."

Gunther stared at the little man beside him. "A telegram?"

Mackensen reached inside his pocket. "Vargas still plays games, but he's there, Alec, in Vermont, waiting for you."

29

Guerrilla tactics dictate that there be no clear lines of battle. The guerrilla is an elusive shadow that the enemy will strike at in desperation. We draw strength in the enemy's confusion.

He had not yet met a stewardess who could fix a decent drink.

Gunther sat patiently in his seat by the window, glancing out at the huge pods on the wings so he wouldn't have to watch the girl with the cart of bottles and ice and plastic glasses.

"Here you are, sir," she said, and handed him the drink.

Too much water. Too much ice. The usual thing.

Gunther nodded his thanks and, when she had gone, pulled the telegram from his coat. Mackensen said it had been delivered yesterday. He unfolded the yellow copy and read it once again:

GREETINGS/WAS TRIP SOUTH PRODUCTIVE/HOPE TO CATCH YOU SOON/WILL WAIT TAVERN MOTOR INN HERE/BEST/OLLIE/ NNNN

He was a cheeky bastard, Vargas was, Gunther thought. A telegram! Gunther stared at the clouds beyond the wing tip and sipped his drink. One way or another it was going to be finished in Vermont. Vargas was not after agents any longer, that was plain. He was after Gunther. Well, by damn, we'll play out this end game, he thought. *We'll finish it. The great Alec Gunther will perform. The enemy, Vargas, has offered a challenge and we accept.*

Gunther sipped at his drink and stared beyond the clouds. He *was* getting old. He knew that. He was making mistakes, very bad mistakes. Quill was a mistake. No matter that the son of a bitch wouldn't cooperate, he'd made a fatal error in protecting the man's life. That trick with Raul and Guido wasn't simply a mistake, it was stupid. Nobody wanted to kill him, but he almost forced them into it—slapping the gun away like that. He might easily have caught a slug in the head for his troubles. Stupid and lucky. Gunther remembered the Vopo captain in Berlin. "You are a lucky swine, Mr. Alec Gunther." He was right. It could have been him with his face in the mud instead of Roberts. He was lucky to get out of the Bay of Pigs without being caught. He was lucky he hadn't been dead after a hundred incidents he could think of if he wanted to count them. But now he was Mackensen's lucky piece, his good-luck charm, in this last assignment. Last? Why not? Mackensen had promised a job in the think tank, hadn't he? Why not? Why the hell not! It was time to get out of this fieldwork. This was the time. After Vargas. Finish Vargas and get out. What's wrong with pins and paper clips? He deserved it after all, didn't he? Twenty-one years in the field was enough for any man.

Gunther finished his drink and set it aside. Maybe he *was* lucky. Gunther smiled to himself. He was Alec Gunther, after all. Nobody beats Alec Gunther. Just ask the new fresh faces at the Farm who studied him. They knew. They knew all about him.

He settled back in his seat and closed his eyes. Vargas must—*would*—be stopped. He was the obstacle now. Destroy the obstacle and the road is clear to an unfettered and uncomplicated position with Mackensen and the other thinkers. An office and a secretary and a push-button phone. Pins and paper clips. Security, that was the thing. In a few minutes Gunther was asleep. He hadn't slept as soundly in more than a year.

The Taskmaster had been too busy to sleep much these last few days. As he came out of the Western Union office, Vargas walked briskly to the car and slid into the passenger side beside a woman in sunglasses and a large wide-brimmed hat.

"Did you send the telegram?" she said as she moved the car out of the parking lot.

Vargas nodded. "It will be waiting for him when he checks into the motel. He'll probably rent a car and be here by morning."

"It's started then . . ."

"Yes."

"So long since the beginning," she said. "It's hard to believe we're almost finished." She glanced quickly at Vargas, her eyes hidden behind the dark sunglasses. "The beginning, really. Will he do it?"

"There is no choice now," Vargas said. "Alec has no choice."

Judith nodded her head. She gripped the steering wheel firmly in her gloved hands. "I suppose not. Alec has finally run out of options. Now he's ours."

III. DESTROY

In the underdeveloped countries of the Americas, the rural areas are the best battlefields for revolution. Conventional defenses will not deter the guerrilla warrior. The enemy can be destroyed in its own environment.

Fundamental Three, Che Guevara

30

The guerrilla's numerical inferiority makes it necessary always to attack by surprise.

The telegram was waiting at the Tavern Inn when Gunther arrived: NEW LEXINGTON. POST OFFICE. NOW.

The reservation clerk had never heard of New Lexington, but Gunther found it on a road map in the Avis office when he rented the car. It was only twenty-three miles, but he missed the turn at Waterbury and the detour took him almost an hour.

New Lexington was a small community of farms. The blacktop road led into the hamlet from the south. Gunther could see the steeple of a white frame church through maple and beechwood trees as he approached the city limits sign. Beyond the town the Green Mountains sloped gently upward, culminating in the peak of Mount Mansfield.

Gunther pulled up beside a state police car parked to the side of a large banner stretched across the road that welcomed visitors to "The New Lexington 63rd Annual Cracker Barrel Bazaar." He got out of the car and walked to where the trooper was sitting in a folding chair, propped against the bumper. He was eating a pie. The sounds of marching music echoed from the town.

"Afternoon," the trooper said, smiling. "Come up for the festival?"

204 • *Harold King*

Gunther nodded. "First time for me." He looked around as if he were searching for something. "Supposed to meet some friends at the post office."

The trooper took a last bite of the pie, leaning forward so as not to drip on his uniform, then slid the paper plate under his chair. "Don't have one regular—post office. You'd want Condon's Store. He services the mail hereabouts." He pointed toward the town. "Second building past the church, across the street."

Gunther started back to his car, stopped and turned around. "Lots of people here for the"—he glanced at the banner—"bazaar?"

"More than last year, I'll tell you. Most of the tents are in the church lot. You'll have to park down the street. It's all marked plain enough. Just follow the signs." He settled back into his chair, balancing on the rear legs. "Better get to the fruit-pie tables soon, if you've a mind to. They'll go quick. Always do, you know."

Gunther had no trouble finding his way to the grassy parking area. If anything, there were too many signs and arrows pointing out the way. The only small sign in the town was the one beside the gate of the parking lot that informed drivers of the fifty-cent parking fee.

Condon's Store offered hardware, groceries and lumber goods in long rows of tables and shelves and was crowded almost beyond capacity for this year's annual event. From inside the store marching music bellowed from strategically placed speakers. Gunther was surprised that such a small town could attract so many people and he wondered if Ollie was somewhere near, watching him.

"Say, is this the post office?"

The woman didn't hear him. He was standing before a large bin of nails at the end of the store and a Sousa march was blaring from a wall speaker above him.

"Excuse me, is this—"

"Can't hear," she said. The woman bent forward, cupping a hand to her ear. "What, now?"

"Is this the post office?"

She made a face because of the music. "Don't have a post office. Just general delivery here."

"Here?" Gunther pointed at the bin of nails.

"No pickup till morning," she said. "You got a letter?"

Gunther shook his head. "Looking for someone."

She shook her head, too, and grimaced to the sound of a piercing trumpet-cymbal-piccolo obbligato. "No stamps. Closed today."

The music was too loud. Gunther waited a moment for the noise to stop, but the next recording, "Stars and Stripes Forever," began immediately. The store was like an incredibly small box and the sounds of crashing cymbals and pounding drums and a hundred brass horns were fighting to get out. Gunther searched the crowd for a familiar face. The blaring speaker was too much. He started for the exit, pushing against people to get out away from the noise, when he saw her. She was wearing a large, wide-brimmed hat and she seemed to have been watching him all along. Judith was one of those rare women who could talk with her eyes. And her eyes told Gunther he must come quickly.

She turned and made her way through the crowd to the rear of the store and stopped before a door marked "Office." In seconds Gunther was beside her, his heart beat pounding in his ears. He could smell her now. Touch her.

"Inside, Alec. Hurry."

There was an instant of quiet, then "Semper Fidelis" began. Gunther stood there immobile. *Judith was here!*

"Judith . . . you're . . ." A burst of Sousa drowned him out in his own ears.

"There isn't time, Alec. You must come *now.*" She opened the door and glanced back into the crowd quickly. Gunther followed her inside and watched her as she bolted the door and began quickly to undress. "Take your pants off, Alec. And your jacket." She pointed to a bundle of clothes on a metal desk. "Put those on."

The music from the other side of the door was still intense and she had to raise her voice slightly to be heard. The large hat was on the floor. She was out of the dress and half out of the frilly slip. "Alec, please, will you hurry."

"What the hell are you doing?"

She kicked off her high heels, gathered up the discarded clothes and stuffed them into a plastic wastebasket bag. Judith looked up angrily in her bra and panties. "This isn't a quickie, Alec. Do as I say. You're being followed."

"By who?"

"There isn't time to explain." She pointed at the bundle again. *"Change!"*

Gunther pulled off his sport coat and tie and began shedding his pants. Judith stepped into a faded green jumpsuit and zipped herself in. She nodded at the gun in the holster under Gunther's shoulder. "You'll need that."

"I know I will," Gunther said hotly. In another moment he was in a jumpsuit that matched hers.

"Stuff your clothes in here." She handed him the plastic bag and a jacket. "Wear the jacket. It gets cold here nights."

Gunther zipped the jacket closed after he'd slipped the gun harness over his head, while Judith hid the bag behind a file cabinet.

"We're ready," she said. "Can you drive a motorcycle? A dirt bike?"

"If I have to."

"You do."

"Look, Judith—"

She waved him off. "Must go. They're wondering what happened to us by now." She moved quickly to a place between the desk and the window and pushed a rug away from a trapdoor. "You'll have to open this, Alec. It's too heavy for me."

For Chrissakes, Judith!"

"Please, Alec. We're both in great danger right now. You have to trust me. This will all be explained. Open this trapdoor. I'll follow. This place used to be a mill. Below, you'll find a dirt bike and helmets. Once we are in the open you'll have to drive as fast as you can toward the tree line. West. Straight west into the trees. I'll give directions from there. This was the best we could do under the circumstances."

"We?"

"Hurry, please."

Gunther went down the ladder and saw the cycle leaning on its kickstand. There were two helmets. Light from outside filtered through long splintered cracks in the barn-type doors of the old ground-floor mill. He straddled the bike, moving it off its kickstand as Judith came down the ladder, slamming the trapdoor behind her and locking it with a short length of chain.

"Start it! Start it! They're right behind me."

Gunther heard the music get louder above him as the office door upstairs burst open. Then pounding feet.

Judith ran, stumbling, to the cross latch on the double doors. "Start it, Alec!"

He kicked the starter twice. Suddenly, the trap door above him seemed to explode into splinters of wood. Short bursts of gunfire ripped a hinge from the heavy trapdoor and hurled it noisily into the sawdust floor. Gunther kicked again and this time the engine caught. He pulled the helmet roughly down over his head as Judith waved him to the door.

"Hurry!"

The cycle moved too quickly. Gunther hadn't handled one in years and when he revved the engine, then twisted the gas handgrip down, the single-cycle engine coughed and died.

"Alec! Hurry!" Judith was beside him, shouting, frantically looking from Gunther to the trapdoor to the open mill doors and back to him. "They're shooting!"

Gunther kicked the starter again. And again. From above the remainder of the trapdoor fell away from the floor and careened down the wooden ladder. He could hear voices now. Shouting, cursing above the din of drums and piccolos. The cycle started again on the next kick. He could feel the surge of power through the handlebars as he kept the engine revved high. He yelled for Judith to climb on, but she wasn't looking at him. She was staring up at the hole in the floor above them. A man was stepping down through the hole. It was an awkward position, but he held a small automatic carbine in one hand, trying desperately to get the thing pointed down at them.

Gunther immediately felt stupid. He was going to die sitting on this goddamn motorcycle. With his left hand on the clutch, he released the gas grip with his right and reached inside the jacket for his gun. His face in a snarl, the man on the ladder was yelling, screaming angrily at Gunther or at someone upstairs, but no one could hear with all the noise. It didn't matter. Gunther fired once and missed. The second bullet crashed into the rifle stock with enough impact to knock the man off the ladder, backward into a bin of lumber. He watched the man lying there for one long terrible moment. It was Michael, Simon Pelado's babysitter in New Jersey.

Then Judith was on the cycle behind him and they were bouncing crazily across a long meadow toward the safety of the tree line as fast as the bike would travel. Gunther didn't look back and he didn't try to take any evasive action; he just went straight for the trees. His face was sweating inside the helmet and he could feel the wind in his eyes and Judith's arms around his waist. He drove into the trees and beyond. Branches slapped at him from both sides as he pushed the bike on faster until they began moving up the incline of the mountain. Gunther twisted for more gas and more speed, but the bike would not respond and finally stalled.

He struck a small broken log and lost control, throwing them both off the machine, gasping for air. Then his senses returned and he heard Judith crying beside him.

"Alec. You're going too fast . . . too fast, Alec . . . Alec . . ."

Gunther pulled off the helmet and lay back against a tree. "Judith . . . what is this?"

She was crying and gasping all at once.

"Judith! Answer me!"

"We must go on . . . not out of danger yet. Must go on . . ."

He grasped her by the front of her jacket and pulled her to him. "Goddammit! Tell me." He slapped her once very hard across the face. "Tell me!"

"It's Ollie," she said wild-eyed and panting. "He's waiting for you. It's all right, Alec. We're on your side."

Gunther pushed her away. He tried to stand and only got to his knees. "Vargas! You and Vargas?"

"You have to understand what's going on, Alec. You have to understand. Those men—that man who—"

"I know," Gunther snapped. "I knew him. *I knew him, for Chrissakes!*" Gunther took a deep breath and tried to swallow. "He was Special Ops."

"Yes," Judith said.

"But, so am I, goddammit!" He looked wildly back down the slope, toward the village of New Lexington. In the distance he could still hear the music. "What the hell are they doing? We're the same people!"

Judith shook her head. She took several breaths to normalize her breathing. "You're not the same, Alec. That's exactly why you're here. You've been lied to and tricked all because of an elaborate and nasty little scheme that you were never to know anything about." She got to her feet and went to the cycle, surveying it for damage. "I hope it still runs, Alec. We have a long way to go."

"What scheme?"

"Not now. Ollie will explain it."

"Vargas," Gunther said contemptuously. "He's behind this. He's right in the middle of this whole goddamn thing . . . But you, Judith, what are you doing here?"

Judith turned to face him. "There was a time, Alec, when you knew everything and I knew nothing." She made a face, indicating despair, shrugged as if she were talking to a child who insisted on being stubbornly obtuse. "It's different now. There are people involved in this who are not what they seem. And there are more sides than you realize, but it will be explained. You, most of all, have to understand. It's all a cockeyed fishbowl. Everybody is watching, analyzing, scheming, studying, predicting what the specimen will do and think."

"Am I supposed to know what you're talking about?"

She righted the cycle, dusted the seat. "Of course not," she said. "You're the specimen."

31

The guerrilla revolutionary army must have a well-structured, over-all leadership. In the final analysis, rank itself is of little importance.

With Judith giving directions, Gunther drove the cycle up several mountain paths until finally the incline was too steep for the machine. They'd passed hikers and picnickers and, at the base of a small rocky bluff, a troop of Boy Scouts. They had not seen anyone else on a motorcycle, which would make matters much easier for the men searching for him, Gunther realized. He wondered if Vargas also knew that they could not hope to escape a thorough manhunt for more than several hours. And Gunther wasn't convinced he didn't want to be found quickly. Judith was not anyone's captive. She was somehow involved with Vargas, but she would not explain. "Ollie will explain." Not Vargas. Not even Allen. Ollie. Gunther would find out about that too.

Gunther hid the bike as best he could in a small ravine. The climbing was more difficult now, and from the west he could see dark clouds forming. Sunset would be sooner than usual. There might be rain. He hoped Judith knew where she was going. The light jackets they were wearing might be sufficient against a summer night's chill in these mountains, but they weren't waterproof.

When Judith stopped to rest again, Gunther guessed they had come four or five miles since they'd left the bike. Two hours. Three hours since he'd shot the Special Ops man. He had thought about that a lot in the last hour or so.

"It isn't much farther," Judith said. She was leaning against a birch, taking long, deep breaths. Her long hair that had been done up in a bun some hours before was now hanging in strands from the clip at the back and had small leaves and pieces of twigs clinging in it. Her jumpsuit was wet with perspiration around the neckband, under the arms and down the back and Gunther thought it odd because he'd never seen her sweaty before. He face glistened with moisture in the slowly failing sunlight. Even now, she was the most beautiful woman he'd ever known.

"It's about half a mile from here," she said. "Just a few more minutes."

"You've done this before? This mountain-goating?"

She nodded her head. It was easier than talking.

"This place we're going to—where Vargas is—is anyone else there?"

"No."

"Just the three of us, then?"

She nodded again without looking at him.

Gunther glanced back down the slope reflexively. He wasn't used to being chased. If he were somewhere else, in a subway or on the street, he'd be looking over his shoulder.

"Why are you involved in this, Judith? What are you doing here?"

"I'm taking you to the man," she said. "The real one. It's an enormous charade, Alec. But you are going to find out. Ollie—"

"—will explain," Gunther interrupted. "Yes, I know. I'm looking forward to it."

Judith glanced to the west, then back at Gunther. "Do you think it will rain?"

"Probably. I left the windows down in my car."

She smiled briefly and shook her head. "We'd better go. It will be dark soon."

She was right. They had walked less than fifteen minutes more when the mountain incline became less steep and in a narrow clearing Gunther saw a small frame house. Its location was strategic in that from three sides the house overlooked open terrain, for the most part, and the fourth side practically butted against an almost vertical outcrop. In these last few minutes the sun had all but disappeared, leaving a faint pinkish glow in the underside of the heavy clouds. The wind had also picked up and Gunther was uncomfortable in the feeling that this night promised to be cold and wet. He didn't like nights like that.

They entered through the kitchen. The living room was small and there was a fire in the large fireplace, which was the focal point of the room. All the windows were protected by heavy drapes as much to keep light from escaping, Gunther imagined, as the cold from getting in. This was, after all, a hiding place.

"Where is he?" Gunther searched the room quickly at a glance. "I don't like surprises, Judith."

She walked to the fire. "It's cold. I'm glad Ollie started the fire."

"Where is Vargas?"

"What do you intend to do, Alec?"

Gunther unzipped his jacket. He could reach the Colt easily now if he had to. "I'll listen for a while."

"Then?" Judith shivered slightly, her shadow covered half the room and shivered with her.

"Then we'll see. I have a lot of questions."

"And I have a lot of answers." It was a deep voice, from behind, and familiar.

Gunther swung around in a crouch, dropping to one knee. His Colt was in his hand, pointing at the middle of the huge figure standing in the doorway of the kitchen. Vargas was smiling pleasantly.

His hands were empty, palms out at waist level. Plainly visible.

"Don't shoot me yet, Alec. There's still plenty of time for that."

"Vargas!" Gunther drew the hammer back with his thumb, carefully, letting the quiet room fill with the sound of the click.

"It used to be Ollie," Vargas said.

He was a very cool character, Gunther thought, considering he had a .38 pointed at his belly. Gunther stood erect slowly. Vargas didn't move. He just stood there smiling as if this were a cozy little party where he was waiting for someone to ask him to sit and have some tea.

"I'm not armed, Alec. If you'll let me talk, I'll try to be brief. When I'm finished you're welcome to use that."

"You're finished *now.*"

Vargas nodded. "Yes, I quite agree."

"Turn around slowly until you're facing me again. Very slowly."

Vargas obeyed. He was wearing light cotton pants and a short-sleeved tennis shirt. The light colors contrasted with the dark skin made even darker in this light of the fire. Vargas's arms and neck were as muscular as they had been the last time Gunther had seen him. He had a prizefighter's waist and a linebacker's shoulders and he kept his feet spread comfortably apart, balanced, which indicated to Gunther that he was still quick. Vargas was not carrying a weapon.

"You see, Alec, no funny business," he said when he was facing Gunther again. "No tricks. All I want to do is talk."

"Yes, I've been hearing about that," Gunther said. He glanced quickly at Judith. She had not moved from the fireplace.

"You won't need the gun for a while. There's no one here but the three of us. I'm not going to try and run off, Alec."

"You know this place will be crawling with agents by morning. Good ones. People who know what they're doing in this kind of country." Gunther knew he was not one of them. He'd already proved that in Montana.

"I expect them," Vargas said. "I said I wasn't going to leave. But it gives us enough time to talk. Me, anyway." He nodded toward the sofa and chairs by the fire. "Can we sit down? There are some things you should see. Papers, files, a lot of things. It's all on the table by Judith."

"This is what you brought me here for? This whole goddamn chase? To look at files?"

Vargas's smile disappeared. "Mackensen wants the information here very much, Alec. He has gone to great lengths, schemed an elaborate setup, to get his hands on these files. You can listen."

Judith moved a few steps from the fireplace. "Please, Alec. Listen to him. Is it so much to ask?"

He was silent a moment. "All right, Vargas. Slowly now. I'm terribly anxious to hear your little tale." He watched as Vargas moved to the sofa and sat down; then he went to a chair across from the small coffee table. A place where he could watch them both. "Okay, I'm all ears." Gunther heard the first light peltings on the roof and against a window somewhere in the kitchen. The rain was beginning, and he thought of his car in New Lexington and wondered if anyone had turned off the music in Condon's Store. Sousa would be getting tired.

32

Guerrilla tactics demand extraordinary strategies through the use of imagination and surprise. It would be foolish to discount the possibility of similar counter-tactics by the enemy.

Vargas leaned forward slowly and picked a cigar from the humidor on the table. He lit it casually, careful to hold the flame below the tip as he turned it between his fingers. He seemed totally unafraid, Gunther thought, even relaxed, as if the weapon Gunther held were not a threat.

"Let me begin by saying I greatly admire you, Alec. I'm not trying to be patronizing. You have an incredible facility for organization. You have a rare ability to think in terms of strategic priorities—analysis of the opposition's strong and weak points and how they fit against your own side's abilities. I've seen your case file—please don't be surprised—and I know that you are a terribly efficient man at what you do."

"If I ever need a reference, I'll be sure to use your name," Gunther said without smiling.

The black man nodded and even smiled. Outside, the rain was coming faster, prelude to a storm. Gunther moved the gun to his other hand.

"You can be a valuable asset to the Clandestine Service. These days, men of your caliber are needed at the higher echelons in Central Intelligence. Even Mackensen recognizes your potential."

"You're boring me, Vargas. You know why I'm here."

"Sorry." Vargas stared across the room for a moment and Gunther felt he'd been here before. Camila had paused the same way. He wondered if they'd spent their entire relationship sitting in front of a fireplace. "Do you know what the Clandestine Service is all about, Alec?" Vargas finally said. "Now, I mean, not back in the early days."

"You're the one who wants to talk."

"Economics," Vargas said. "American economics. American multinational corporations have created colossal interests all over the world and wherever you find U.S. business interests, on that scale, you find the American intelligence apparatus. Do you know why?"

"Tell me," Gunther said. "I'm fascinated."

"Domestic prosperity depends on the foreign operations of American business. Twenty years ago it wasn't true, but now it is true. Supply and demand, Alec. The American way of life, like none other in the world, is sophisticated beyond its own capabilities to supply, and the demand is to cater to that sophistication. That means foreign interests. And the multinational corporations expect a peaceful status quo in countries where they have investments so that they have undisturbed access to cheap raw materials, cheap labor and stable markets. The status quo is vital to maintain if their investments are to remain secure. It also suits the ruling groups . . . supported by Central Intelligence abroad. American business runs the CIA these days, Alec. They have a distinct vested interest in the Cold War. There cannot be revolutions in countries where business has huge investments, but revolution is encouraged where it suits business.

"You really are intent on boring me to sleep, aren't you?"

"Not really, no."

Gunther sighed. "The big, bad Wall Street imperialists. Maybe you thought I never heard that song before. This may came as a shock to you, but I don't make policy. And I really don't care that ITT or Campbell's Soup exploits foreign markets. Around here it's all right. We call it capitalism. But I didn't come here to be schooled in that old Marx-line drivel."

"Anything goes, right, Alec?" Vargas said angrily.

Gunther brought the .38 up steadily. "Careful there, Deadeye. I've agreed to humor you with my presence. Just talk; I'll listen."

"Does nothing bother you, Alec?"

"You bother me. Since I got this assignment, you've bothered me. You have something to tell me. Let's get to it."

"What would you say if I told you that Special Ops had backed an African revolution—tried to, I mean?"

"Why? Am I supposed to be surprised?"

Vargas nodded solemnly. "Yes, if it was Communist guerrillas they were supporting."

"I'd say you'd been eating too many bad bananas."

"And if I can prove it?"

The rain was steady and heavy now. In the distance Gunther heard a rumbling clap of thunder. He rested his hand with the gun on the arm of the chair, laying the revolver flat on its side but still pointed toward Vargas. "There's a maxim in fundamental logic," Gunther said, "that states one cannot prove a theorem if the theorem does not exist."

"This one exists." Vargas dropped his cigar into an ashtray. "Do you remember where you were in the spring of 1965?"

Gunther said nothing.

"You were in Berlin. If you'll recall, you were very agitated over the apparent disappearance of a section officer in the East German Ministry for State Security. One of Jodl's men. He just disappeared. Remember?"

"Lots of East Germans disappear. I try not to get upset over it."

"Heydrich was different," Vargas said excitedly. He sat up on the edge of his seat and Gunther followed the movement with the muzzle of the .38. Martin Heydrich. Remember him? Tall, balding man. Spoke Hyde Park English. It bothered you because you were watching over Jodl's section at the time. Counterintelligence. Something funny was going on, but you never found out what it was. And Heydrich never surfaced again."

"You must do a lot of reading."

"He was in Africa—the Congo. I know because I saw him there."

"Bully for you." Gunther nodded toward the east. "That must have been during your visit to Africa with Guevara. He let you out of Castro's hell hole and you joined his eager little band of revolutionaries. Set the black man free. The Congo and the others must have been ripe for revolution, to his thinking. That about the way it was?"

"Close enough. I'd done some other traveling as well, but that's close enough. Ripe for revolution is exactly what he was thinking. But there were others who had the same idea. The Chinese, Russians, African Communist splinter groups—and others. Heydrich was sent secretly to Lake Victoria on the Uganda side. I was there with Guevara. We met with Russians and an element of the Kinshasa rebels. Someone else was there also. He did a lot of the planning—we were working on specific strategies against the loyalist forces of Tshombe who were being aided with arms and advisors by the CIA. Vargas watched Gunther's eyes. "John Miles."

"Miles! That's insane!"

"After a time he left. His strategies were very successful, but then they should have been, since he was CIA in the first place. His sources of information were always accurate as to when and where government forces would be on a given day. Of course, some of the mercenaries killed by the rebels were also CIA agents." Vargas looked at Gunther for a long time. "It's not surprising the agency never loses a battle when you stop to consider they have generals on both sides."

"It isn't true," Gunther said angrily. "Miles wouldn't—"

"It is true, Alec. But I'm not finished. As I said, Miles left. Quit would be more the word. He didn't realize what he was doing until he inspected an ambush site. We were counting bodies, burying them. Miles saw one, someone he obviously recognized, with the government forces. I'm sure it took him some time to figure what was happening, but, anyway, he wasn't with us long after that. But he was there long enough to bring someone else from his sponsor down to our H.Q. We were north of Stanleyville then, south of the Lindi."

"How did you know he was CIA?" Gunther snapped.

"Oh, I didn't at the time, of course. No one did. It was some years later I found out who he was. You see, Alec, Ramon—Che— was running the guerrilla tactical operation by then, with the Kinshasa rebels. The Russians, Chinese, East Germans, they were represented by small groups of advisors offering support, weapons, munitions, material. The thinking was that if Guevara could pull it off—a revolution in the Congo—then one of the groups could move in politically. If the Congo fell, then there would be a political base in Southern Africa. All of southern Africa was the ultimate target and the Republic of South Africa was the plum."

"You can't tell me Miles was involved this way."

"I'm coming to the best part."

"*If* Miles was there, who was he supposedly representing?"

"Jodl," Vargas said. "Eric Jodl and the *Abteilung.*"

"That's crazy."

"No, it was outrageously clever. You see, the first group of East Germans were picked up before they got to Uganda. Miles and two other agents took their places and sent reports back to Berlin. But what no one in the CIA operation expected was for Jodl to send a *second* group. That was Heydrich. As you can guess, Miles was surprised to see him, but by that time he was already putting the operation together."

"If it's true, why didn't Miles get burned right there?"

"Who would believe Heydrich? He wasn't expected. He needed time to get a message back to Jodl. He never did, of course. The next evening headquarters was hit by a surprise ambush. We thought it was government troops who just stumbled upon us, hit and run. But the odd thing was there were only three deaths."

"Jodl's second group."

"Exactly."

Gunther shifted in his chair. He glanced at Judith, who had not moved from her corner of the sofa and had not offered any comment. She just sat there staring at him as if he should believe all this on faith. He noticed her jumpsuit was dry.

"What's the point of all this, Vargas? Even if I thought there was the smallest shred of truth to it, which I don't, where does it get you? It didn't happen. It couldn't have. We don't work that way. The service does unpleasant things, but it's an unpleasant business.

We do not send elements of our own organizations against one another in paramilitary operations. Christ, it's tough enough recruiting agents to fill in attrition.''

"This is background, Alec. Very important background that will bring you up to date on what has come to be a nasty little game . . . the roots of it are in Africa in 1965."

"You're in here too . . . somewhere?"

"Yes," Vargas said. "In the mid-sixties, before the Clandestine Services reorganized its area subdividions, Europe and Africa were run from the same desk."

Gunther acknowledged with a shrug.

"And Mackensen had that account. He ran that division."

"Yes, yes," Gunther said impatiently.

"Do you also know he organized and deployed secret projects unknown to the agency?"

"That's absurd."

"Is it?"

"Can't be done," Gunther said.

"It *was* done . . . by Mackensen . . . in Africa."

"You're accusing the chief of Western Hemisphere Division of outfitting a guerrilla operation in the Congo *against* paramilitary agents working *for* the Congolese?"

"I am."

"And Miles directed the group without knowing what he was doing?" Gunther shook his head. "You really are crazy, Vargas."

"Is it so surprising? You know how Mackensen thinks."

"He's unorthodox," Gunther retorted irritably, "but not . . . " There was a moment's silence.

"Do you know what Heydrich looked like?" Vargas's voice was oddly conciliatory. "Would you recognize his photograph?"

"Of course I would."

He nodded toward the file folders on the table. "I have some photographs here, Alec. I'd like you to see them. There is also a roll of negatives. These pictures are numbered according to the exposures on the negative roll."

"You've gone to a lot of trouble."

"I just want you to see that these photos are from the same roll of film."

Vargas handed him one of the prints. Along the margin someone had written "Kodak Tri X Pan/Jun 9, 1965/exp. #6A." There was a single figure in the picture, sitting on a rock near a stream. The photograph was slightly overexposed, but Martin Heydrich was clearly identifiable. He was facing slightly away from the camera, apparently unaware his picture was being recorded.

"This was taken the morning Heydrich arrived," Vargas said. "Do you recognize him?"

"It's Heydrich."

"Now this one." Vargas handed him another. Four men. Part of a tent or lean-to was visible at the left edge. Che Guevara was standing with one of the others, holding an open newspaper in front of him. "Heydrich had brought a newspaper with him. Che couldn't read German, but for the camera he looked at the pictures. He liked to have pictures made of him and his men."

Gunther studied it a long moment. "This is Guevara, there's no mistaking that. But what proves it was taken in the Congo? This might be Bolivia for all I know."

"Look at the headline, Alec: CHOU EN-LAI ASKS FOR SUMMIT. He was in Tanzania June fourth through the eighth. The date is not easy to see there in that photograph, but I do have a copy of that same edition in one of these files. It was a June seventh edition of *Neues Deutschland*. The same day Heydrich disappeared so mysteriously from Berlin."

Gunther nodded his head impatiently. "All right. It looks as though Heydrich was with Guevara in early June in 1965."

"In the Congo," Vargas said.

"Apparently," Gunther said. "If these aren't doctored."

"They aren't." Vargas picked up the next print. "This is one of Che with some Chinese. That's me on the right." He handed him another. These are Russians. You can see Heydrich in the background there."

"Wonderful."

"This photo is the following morning," Vargas said. "I told you we were hit that night." The photo was of a body laid out beside a shallow grave. It was Heydrich.

Gunther studied it a moment, but said nothing.

"I have one more for you, Alec."

"More bodies?"

"No," Vargas said, "much more important than that." He handed the print over. "As you can see, this one is number fourteen from the roll of film. It's the same roll of film as these others. It's important that you understand it was taken from this same roll. Heydrich's body is number seventeen. I told you Miles left us, but not before someone else came down for a day or two. Look at this picture carefully, Alec."

He did. What he saw stunned him. There were five people in the photograph. They looked to be just standing around the remnants of a smoldering tent. One was Vargas. One was a Chinese. One was a Russian Gunther recognized. One was John Miles. But it was the last person that Gunther stared at with incredulity. He was younger then, with a matted crew cut. Mackensen.

"Tell me, Alec," Vargas said in a low voice. "What is the chief of Western Hemisphere Division for the Central Intelligence Agency doing in the camp of a Communist guerrilla stronghold somewhere in the wilds of the Congo?" He sat back into the cushion of the sofa patiently. "I'd really be interested in an explanation."

33

Victory is the climax of guerrilla life.

"Where did you get these photographs?" Gunther did not raise his voice, but his words contained a sudden urgency now as from a man who had been too long deceived.

"I've had them a very long time, Alec."

Gunther stared at the man in the picture several seconds more, then dropped the stack on the table. He shook his head unbelievingly. "It's impossible."

Now Vargas was silent.

"It's a trick," Gunther said. "It just doesn't add up."

"It's no trick, Alec. Mackensen was there. There is other proof. Che kept a diary. He encouraged all his men to keep diaries. I have portions of some of the entries, including my own, that refer to the night of the ambush and the people in camp at the time. Mackensen was using the name Baade. A very pale man, short. There are several references to him. It can all be easily verified."

"Just like that, I'm supposed to believe this?"

Vargas indicated the file folders on the table. "The proof is here, Alec. It will take you time to read it all, absorb it, but it is all here. I have left nothing out."

"Why didn't you bring this in to someone years ago? Why me? Why now?"

Vargas glanced at Judith briefly, then looked at Gunther. "This brings us to the next phase of your debriefing—the Taskmaster Group."

"Your vendetta against the agency."

He shook his head sadly. "No, Alec. There is a group known as Taskmaster, but it had nothing to do with the deaths of those CIA agents." Vargas paused, then added, "Except one."

"You expect me to believe that?" Gunther stared at Vargas for several seconds, unmoved. "You *do* expect me to believe it! Jesus. I saw you waste Quill."

"That's the one."

"And you almost wasted me!"

"Do you really think I am that poor a marksman, Alec? Quill was several hundred meters away. You were much closer in your truck. Regrettably, it took two shots to finish Quill, but you were a much better target. Did you not wonder why I didn't kill you there?"

Gunther remembered driving at the figure in the trees, remembered looking down the muzzle of the rifle.

"I aimed at the left front tire of the truck. I did not miss."

"Very considerate of you," Gunther hissed.

"Mackensen is a masterful planner, Alec," Vargas continued. "The only mistake he's ever made operationally was in Africa. It was a preposterous idea to infiltrate the rebel command and actually participate in the combat strategy that resulted in the deaths of friendly agents and other Americans that he also happened to command. Anywhere else, one might call it calculated murder."

"If it's true, it was murder."

"The operation was a success in one respect: that is, the rebels were crushed. The only moral law in intelligence work is that it is justified by results. Mackensen was charged with putting down the Communist revolution and that's exactly what he did. No one in the agency, however, knows that he accomplished it in just this way." Vargas paused to wet his lips. "Let me give you some more background. Guevara brought about one-hundred Cubans to Africa. Trained guerrillas."

"Including you."

He nodded his head. "Mackensen learned about us. He's very

big, you know, on choosing personnel who can think like the opposition.''

Gunther recalled his meeting with Mackensen in New York before they went to the house in New Jersey. He was feeling him out, judging, analyzing. ''There may be something for you,'' he'd said. Gunther nodded. ''Yes, I know.''

''The men who worked this special operation of Mackensen's were picked with the Cubans in mind. He wanted people who'd recently been involved with them and could comprehend their thinking. It was a logical choice.''

''Operation Jupiter.'' Gunther could see their faces.

''Yes. Shall I give you the list of names . . . agents who worked this secret operation in Africa?''

Gunther shut his eyes. He had a sickening feeling in the pit of his stomach. In his mind the pieces of a terrible puzzle were beginning to fit together. ''Harry Phillips from Arizona,'' he said almost inaudibly. ''James Barkham. Dave Cronin. Kenneth Tripp.''

''And others,'' Vargas said.

''You're saying Mackensen had them all killed?'' Gunther shook his head. It wasn't possible. It wasn't possible, yet . . .

''That's exactly what I'm saying. I can prove it to you, Alec. That's why I've arranged this meeting. You play a pivotal role in Mackensen's scheme to totally wipe away any connection between himself and this one African campaign.''

Gunther was suddenly cold. He laid the .38 on the table in front of him. The rain pounded furiously outside and he listened to it for a long time before replying. ''You'd better explain it,'' he finally said. Gunther was off balance now, vulnerable. He took the last photograph from the stack and studied Mackensen's picture. ''Tell me everything.''

''They were a threat to him,'' Vargas began. ''Mackensen is in a very powerful position of authority and he has come to believe himself infallible. It's a dangerous combination. Your agency has been dragged through a lot of nasty exposures recently. I suppose he sees exposure of himself as an irreparable injury to the organization as a whole. In his own way, Mackensen is quite patriotic.''

''How could those people be a threat? Christ, half of them were retired." Gunther stared pleadingly at Vargas. "He killed them for no reason."

"There is another organization, Alec." Vargas glanced at Judith. "It involves me and Judith and many, many others. We are a unique intelligence group. You might say spies within a network of spies."

"Representing who?"

"No one, everyone . . . ourselves."

"Great response," Gunther said.

"In the beginning we recruited agents from the services in the European Theater . . . British, German, Russian. We've grown. Now we have agents from every intelligence system in the world. Our accomplishments have been substantial, from our point of view, Alec. Each to his own task . . . an orchestra of Taskmasters. The name borrowed from the Cuban invasion plan because it was a just effort, fouled by deceit."

Gunther said nothing.

"There are too many excesses that pass for the official line . . . expedient results that aren't questioned as to the means used."

"No one claimed it was a gentleman's work."

"Is mass murder worth a secret . . . or anything else? Where does it stop, Alec?"

"We haven't gone that far," Gunther retorted angrily.

"Results by any means. That's how Mackensen views his work. We're after the Mackensens . . . all of them."

"Mackensen knows about you and your group," Gunther said. "He knows you're trying to destroy Central Intelligence."

"Maim it," Vargas said. "We aren't trying to kill the beast. We couldn't anyway. Espionage is an ancient craft and it's beneficial. Know what the other people are up to. It began as a passive art. It has evolved to its present deadly state. Governments are overthrown, rulers of state assassinated, operatives taught the vilest tricks in the name of national security . . . There are Mackensens everywhere. We want a return to sanity. It is not the military that will destroy civilization, though the military will be the tool. It will be one too many unchecked adventures of a Mackensen."

Gunther pulled off his glasses and rubbed his face exhaustedly. He looked across at the solemn face of the large black man. "What you're telling me is—'' He shook his head. A boom of thunder rattled a window.

"There was very little time to get to you."

"What am I supposed to do?" Gunther snapped. "Join up? I certainly don't sign anything. What do you do, prick fingers and mix blood? Jesus!"

"Nothing so arcane as that, Alec. Bloodletting is not our purpose."

"And what do you call Quill's sudden demise?"

"An extreme action," Vargas said. "Believe me, it will be paid for. But it was a necessary action . . . justified under the circumstances."

"That's a tidy rationalization."

"Quill was the exception. It's never been done before. Our other accomplishments far outweigh the episode with Victor Quill."

"Do tell."

"You recall the resignation of General Spinola in Portugal? Suzikaya in Japan? Guillaume? We were instrumental in persuading those close to them to force their stepping aside. The trouble in Brandt's cabinet. We helped expose the spy."

"Which forced out a good man."

"The Chancellor?" Vargas shrugged as if he felt little regret. "In every guerrilla operation—and ours is such an operation—there are casualties. But perhaps you didn't notice, West Germany has not collapsed for lack of leadership. We try to help clean house. We're devious, Alec, but then we wouldn't exist otherwise."

"Do you also expose American presidents or is that out of your purview?"

Vargas smiled. "Politically, Americans seem to come around to cleaning their own house eventually. Your press is a vicious and unrelenting watchdog, Alec. But there are areas even they cannot penetrate."

"Back to Mackensen?"

"Yes," Vargas said. "You're quite right, Mackensen knows about our organization. We've been working this up"—he indicated the files on the table—"for some time and we've been letting pieces of it out to people who can do something about it. But Mackensen is a resourceful fellow. He knows we exist and why we exist and he dealt us a severe blow. Berlin was part of it. He hurt us. It's taken time and a lot of planning to drop the other shoe, and he almost succeeded. But not quite." Vargas sat up slightly, arching his back as if he'd been sitting too long in one spot. "Under the directorate of Intelligence is a department called Internal Intelligence."

"Never heard of it," Gunther said.

"You weren't supposed to. It's new. It came out of the shake-up when Central Intelligence was being exposed for all its assassination plots during the House and Senate investigations. It was implemented just after Colby left as director. The people in that department are watchdogs . . . headhunters. Nobody in Congress wants another surprise revelation like those attempts against Lumumba and Castro."

"Something you helped influence?"

"Peripherally. We have sympathetic ears in the legislature. Our Jack Andersons in the Senate. They know nothing of our organization, but are afraid of what the agency may ultimately lead to if it isn't provided some kind of internal watchdog."

"Who are they watching?"

"Mackensen, for one. As a matter of fact, he is their first job. They just haven't got enough evidence to move. They have only suspicions."

Gunther indicated the files on the table with his eyes. "What about all this?" He looked at Vargas angrily. "Surely this is—"

"It has taken time to get everything together, Alec. Too much time, which I take responsibility for. In the interim Mackensen almost pulled off the operation of his career. It was a slick plan and very professionally done because it accomplished two objectives." Vargas counted on his fingers. "First, he had to separate himself from the Congo operation and, second, discredit our organization. Sooner or later he knew we would get to those agents, so he got to them first. Dead men tell no tales. He made it appear that I was striking back at the agency because of the Bay of Pigs and he even worked in Taskmaster. If he could make the headhunters believe that I was behind the plot, then everything shifted away from him. He comes out clean. We'd never be able to recruit another agent.

"But his plan was supposed to end in California. Hix was last on his list. You were never intended to find me. It was enough that he sent someone to stop these killings. The tracks would end in California with enough evidence to convince the headhunters that I was resonsible.''

"Then who did kill them?" Gunther said. "If Hix was last, then . . . ''

"The Mountain Man," Vargas said. "The big man. Mackensen's man. The one who could pass for black . . . for me."

"Oh, Christ!" And then Gunther remembered. Harry Phillips had tried to tell him, but Gunther was too high on rum to see it. Harry had told him! Gunther pictured Harry in his mind, sweating in a bus-terminal pay phone. Scared. Praying Gunther could help. The great Alec Gunther. Goddammit! Harry had described him and Gunther was drunk.

Big guy. Black. Valdez or something. V like victory.

But it wasn't Valdez. It was Velquez. Victor Velquez. Phillips had known him only by his workname. Victor Velquez was Victor Quill. The big man. The man who could pass for black. Gunther had thought he was talking about Vargas.

"Jesus," Gunther said quietly. "It *was* Quill. The airplane . . . the airport near the lodge. That's how he got in and out . . . quick, efficient." He looked toward the fire. "No wonder he wasn't frightened."

"It was Quill behind you in the subway, Alec. Harry's call got them very nervous. But that was before Mackensen decided you might be useful."

"You know about the subway, too?"

"Mackensen never expected I would get into his little game," Vargas said. "That's why I had to lead you to Quill. It forced Mackensen to send you after me in earnest. We changed his game to fit our needs."

"But why me? Why am I involved in this?"

"Like I said, Alec, Mackensen used you because you fit the job perfectly. You had worked with me. You 'knew me.' It wasn't entirely his own doing that he selected you, but once you were pointed out to him for this assignment, there was no better choice. The chess piece was a clever touch. You were well researched."

No one spoke for a few moments as another clap of thunder broke nearly on top of the house. Strangely, it didn't bother him. He remembered Miles climbing the Wall, reaching for the barbed wire and the safety beyond. "Miles was a part of this—this orchestra, wasn't he?"

"Yes. He was a deputy control then. Mackensen learned about Miles and Taskmaster—a misjudgment on my part—he's still a damn good intelligence officer. It was Mackensen who set up that snafu on the East side. He blew Miles's cover and set up a hit. But he didn't expect you to go over. That's really where you fit into all this, Alec. Miles was very high on you. He wasn't sure where you stood. Anyway, Miles was killed."

"So was Roberts," Gunther added cryptically.

"But not you."

"I remember."

"I've made mistakes. Serious mistakes. Miles's death really threw us. He was our only agent in the company. We have very good people, Alec, but control is not a job that many want or are suited to. It takes a certain kind of man." Vargas studied Gunther a moment, then looked away. "I'll be replaced soon."

Gunther nodded as if he understood. "And Judith? How did she get involved with you people?" She looked up sharply at him when he mentioned her name.

"I wanted to, Alec. Ollie came to me after the separation. He explained everything to me—what you did, what he was doing—everything."

"You should not have brought her into this," Gunther said angrily. He was staring at Vargas. "She never knew. She's not like you and me. Judith is—"

"Judith is a big girl," she said. "Ollie explained the risks. I accepted them."

"Miles had intended to approach you," Vargas said. "Feel you out. Then there was the Berlin thing and operations fell into my lap. Even after you were released, you were being watched. We weren't sure what was in your head. Even the agency watched you for a year. I contacted Judith because no one knew you better."

"Mackensen's tactics are rubbing off," Gunther said hotly.

"Judith was never in the field. She's a useful messenger."

"I believe in what Ollie is doing, Alec. I really do. We want you to come in with us." She acted as if it were no more than an invitation to join a book club.

"You're both crazy." He glanced at Vargas. "Christ, Mackensen's practically got you in the bag now. This organization of yours . . . you admit you're in trouble. The whole thing is going to collapse on top of you."

"Perhaps." Vargas nodded. "Perhaps not. I have a strategy of my own in the works. Special delivery, you might say." He smiled. "It is a very simple adventure, but it requires our participation and cooperation. As I said before, I have made mistakes; therefore, the responsibility for protecting the organization rests with me. I am the one in trouble, Alec, not the organization. Only the control—me— and his deputy know the identity of the operatives. The operation demands this. We know each other through a code word that changes monthly. This month it is *jade*."

"Who is your deputy, Vargas?"

He smiled. "Not just yet, Alec."

"You've gone to a lot of trouble to bring me this far. What do you want, a commitment from me? How do you know I wouldn't just expose everything you've told me?"

"And injure who? Me? You already have me. Judith? Do you want her implicated? The most damaging information you have is against Mackensen. All you know is that the organization exists. Even Mackensen knows that. So what have you got, Alec?" Vargas offered a weak smile. "I want you with us. We need you. Mackensen and his breed must be checked."

"There are still too many things unanswered," Gunther said. "Simon Pelado, for one. How did he get into this? The business with the Israelis, buying small consignments of arms. And Jodl. *Someone* had him put away. Mackensen tells me there were others."

"A final gesture as Taskmaster," Vargas replied drily. "Jodl was one of six. As long as Mackensen had arranged this little charade, it gave me an opportunity to unload other burdens in the world. Central Intelligence is not the only apparatus with a Mackensen. We supplied their people with incriminating files such as this one on

Mackensen. Whatever happened to them was a result of decisions from within their own services." Vargas's expression indicated he knew what those decisions would be. "The London *Times* notices were signals to me that the information had been delivered. I imagine Mackensen was very surprised to hear about the advertisements. Probably as surprised as when he learned you were going to Montana to visit his assassin. He must have been unnerved by that development."

"And the guns in Turkey?"

"I did do some work for the Israelis. Of all the secret services, I think the Jews are the most professional and the most vicious. Of course, they were taught by experts and they have the most to lose, the way they see it. I've been concentrating my recruiting efforts there in the last year. You'd be amazed by the results. Our Mideast operatives tend to be younger than the rest. I suppose they are closer to the fire; they can see where we're all headed. Our Russians are getting younger too. Central Intelligence is the most stubborn in that respect. The fewest young ones, I mean. I wonder if there's a moral there somewhere."

"Low tolerance to propaganda," Gunther said irritably. "Not like us old men." He waved off Vargas's reply. "What about Pelado?"

"Simon happened to be at the right place at the right time. He was my introduction into Mackensen's tidy scheme. I did see him in San Juan. Very talkative fellow when he drinks. We'd known about him and the money for some time. It turned out to be a good leverage to force him to go to the agency. Mackensen didn't know what to do about your poor Simon. He had to do something since he had an assassin running around the country and headhunters breathing down his neck. You see, at the time, Mackensen was still a bit undecided whether or not to bring you into it. Pelado was my insurance that he did."

"Also, I have reason to believe, Alec, that Mackensen's plan—revised plan as it were—is that you will take me out. Then, there will be an unfortunate accident in which you are fatally injured. Perhaps not an accident. Our shooting it out might be an alternative. The point being that Mackensen cannot afford to take the chance that we talked. He is a meticulous man. All the loose ends will be neatly snipped. It might even be that he will implicate you as one of us, in case questions are asked, though they are usually not where Special Ops is concerned. Mackensen will be away cleanly."

"And Pelado . . . where is he now?"

"Pelado is dead. Did you expect Mackensen to let him go?"

Gunther was silent.

"You see, Alec, I have nothing to hide from you."

"Except your deputy."

"In time even that will be made known to you . . . and much more."

Gunther looked thoughtfully at Vargas. His eyes were brown and intense and a bit sad. "You're going to tell me?"

"No."

Gunther felt suddenly stupid. If Vargas was really serious about protecting his organization, why was he giving himself up this way? Gunther felt a prickling at his neck. "You said you had some kind of strategy. What is it?"

"I cannot allow Mackensen to win," Vargas said. "The ultimate triumph would be for him to destroy us. I cannot allow that."

"Killing Mackensen won't help you."

"I don't intend that, Alec." Vargas leaned forward slowly. "There is more to gain for us by what I have in mind. We have an opportunity, thanks to Mackensen, to place a man high within Central Intelligence. It is an extraordinary opportunity, but not without its sacrifices. I said before that I was a good tactician, and this strategy, if it works, would be my crowning achievement. It solves everyone's problems—mine, yours, the organization's, even Mackensen's. It needs only one man's cooperation to make it work . . . and his commitment." He was sitting on the edge of the sofa, watching Gunther's face. He seemed to be very close.

"Me," Gunther said. "You're talking about me."

Vargas didn't take his eyes off him. "Yes. I'm talking about you."

"And do what exactly?"

"What you set out to do from the beginning," Vargas replied softly. "Carry it to its logical conclusion." He reached slowly toward the table, toward the Colt. Gunther didn't react. He knew now. "We end the game here. My part ends and yours begins. Mackensen will exert no effective influence toward us after tonight and you will have cleared away any doubts as to your loyalty." He nodded toward the files once again. "With the information here, Mackensen loses. We survive."

"And I'm the hero," Gunther said bitterly. He stared at Vargas a long time, then glanced at Judith. She was looking away. He could see the light reflected from tears in her eyes. "My God, you've counted on this all along!"

"I'm offering you everything, Alec. We don't want you to join us; we want you to lead." He placed the weapon in Gunther's hand. "Now is the time."

Gunther stared at the revolver as if seeing it for the first time. He remembered Camila. She had understood the inevitability of this confrontation, but not its necessity. That was reserved for Gunther.

Gunther watched his eyes—brown, liquid, confident. Vargas stared straight ahead; he made no movement as Gunther stood. The .38 was cold and heavy in his hand. Then suddenly he dropped it into the chair.

"No," he said. "I won't do it." Gunther moved away from them, away from Vargas, away from Judith, toward the fire, as if the distance would protect him. The pawn was disobeying. "There is another way. Christ, there has to be another way!"

"But there isn't, Alec."

"Nothing is worth this sacrifice. Look at yourself. You're glad to do it, eager for the death blow. For what? Christ, for what?" Gunther shook his head in disgust. He turned to face the fire. Pruett was right. Where does a man escape to if he's already free? Who rescues the liberator? The tightrope stretched endlessly in both directions, but there was no net.

"Please, Alec." Judith's voice pleaded warmly, but, oddly, lacked compassion.

"No."

"Please."

He heard the click that precedes the trigger pull and instinctively began to turn, pushing away from the fire, turning on the balls of his feet, but not quickly enough. The explosion of the Colt filled the room as if it were in a tunnel. For barely seconds, Gunther lost his orientation and stared dumbly as Vargas's body slumped from the couch and slid heavily to the floor. Blood was already collecting in a pool near the leg of the coffee table from the wound in the side of his head. Judith stood stiffly behind the chair as if she were frozen there with the Colt between her outstretched hands.

Judith rapidly became paler. She dropped the gun and supported herself against the chair. "I had to."

Gunther didn't move. For an interminably long time he listened to the quiet interrupted by the steady rain, the far-away cadence of thunder, and the hushed, broken sounds of a woman's weeping. Then the army outside began its assault.

34

Death in combat is honorable. No fallen comrade will be forgotten.

When they came, they came shooting from their hiding places in the rain. The two windows in the front of the house began shattering almost at once, sending shards of glass ripping through the drapes. A wooden plaque over the mantel broke in two from the impact of an automatic rifle slug and fell awkwardly down the wall to the floor. Judith stared dumbly at Gunther.

"Alec, wha—"

"Get down!" He knocked her over like a charging halfback, scrambling for the Colt and its remaining five rounds. He could hear glass breaking and wood splintering in the kitchen from the automatic-rifle fire.

"Alec!"

"Stay down!" Gunther pushed her behind the overturned armchair and crawled to the corner of a window. The drapes were already flapping and dripping with the rain that blew through broken panes. From the muzzle flashes, Gunther counted four of them, blurry shapes in the thunderstorm. They were no more than twenty yards out, spaced roughly equally in front of the house in the classic frontal assault advance.

"Who are they?" Judith screamed.

"Who do you think, for Chrissake!" Gunther took as careful aim as he could, crouched beside the window, and fired at the figure on the right flank. The man went down, but so did the others, diving and rolling, and in the next seconds, the volume of the fire was overwhelming. What remained of the window panes exploded into the room in bits of wood and glass; the shredded drapes pulled away from the hanging rods; the wall opposite took on the appearance of a target backstop.

Gunther, huddled below the window, protected his face. The firing stopped momentarily, then continued in short, choppy bursts as the assaulters maneuvered for positions. He knew the routine. Load and fire and advance. Load. Fire. Advance. They would be moving alternately. One covers while the other moves. There wasn't much time and four bullets were precious little insurance against the odds.

"Judith." Gunther crawled back to her. "How do you get out of here?"

"Oh, Alec, what have I done?"

"Where are the doors?"

"Just the front and the one we came in . . . the kitchen."

"Nothing in back?"

"No."

"Terrific."

A short burst from outside ripped through the wooden molding around the mantel.

"Look, you take this"—he handed her the gun—"I'm going to—"

"No." She wiped a tearstain from her cheek. "I'm all right now, Alec. You're not leaving me. Whatever you do, I'm going to be beside you."

"Judith, there's no reason!"

"Yes, there is." She handed back the gun. "Ollie's deputy . . . it . . . it's me. It wasn't a field job, just organizational paperwork. He wouldn't let me do more than that, but I know who the people are. Everyone. He anticipated you coming in, us working together."

"Jesus Christ!"

She took Gunther's hand. "This is the key, Alec, literally, to

Taskmaster.'' She pressed a small key into his palm and closed his fingers over it. "There is a safe-deposit box in the Central Bank of the Argentine Republic. It's a double-security lock. The other key is in Buenos Aires. Everything is in that file: the organization, lists of all our projects, dossiers, dates, names, places, agent identities . . . It's all there. But instructions have been given that, should something happen to Vargas, the contents of the box be destroyed if no one comes to open it at least once each quarter. It was how we were to protect our people. The organization dissolves if someone doesn't open that safe.'' Judith watched Gunther's eyes. "You.''

"When is the next deadline?''

"Soon, Alec.''

The shooting was random now, but Gunther could hear them yelling to each other. They were getting closer.

"If something happens to you, then it's over,'' she said. "I can't do it.''

Gunther nodded toward the door. "We only have one little problem . . .'' He hoped he'd counted enough of them. If there were four, then two would rush the house and two would cover. And if he'd hit that one from the window, there would be only one to cover. It made for lousy odds if he made a break for it, but the chances of survival just waiting for them to come didn't exist.

"All right, Judith, let's go.'' He pushed her ahead of him in a low crawl past Vargas's feet.

"What are you doing?''

"Just move. We're getting out.''

He bullied her into the kitchen. The side door was ajar, but he couldn't see enough of the front to know exactly where the men outside were positioned. It would be a very risky run to the tree line, twenty yards, but the poor visibility and the so-called element of surprise would work for them. He hoped. At least they would be concentrating on the front entrance for the first few seconds. It should be time enough.

"When I say move, Judith, get out this door and run as goddamn fast as you can toward those trees. Don't think about it, don't look around, just run. I'll be right behind you.''

"What about them?''

"They'll be busy playing Marines. Just do what I tell you."

"What." She started to turn back on her hands and knees toward the living room. Gunther grabbed her arm angrily, pushing her back against the wall.

"Dammit, Judith. We're going *this* way!"

"The files, Alec," she said. "We can't leave the files on Mackensen. There's no other proof except those files."

"Forget it."

"Alec, no. You can't leave them."

"Christ Almighty, I'm trying to keep us alive!" But Gunther was already moving. He ran into the room and shoved handfuls of the papers and photographs into the leather pouch. Then he realized that the shooting had stopped. They'd be coming any second now. He stuffed the pouch with what was left and started back when the explosion of automatic weapons began for the last time. He heard running footsteps and he dove toward the kitchen when the first one hit the front door.

"Now, Judith! Now!"

She was already on her way by the time Gunther was out the door. The inside of the house sounded as if it was coming apart. They must be spraying everything with bullets, he thought. He ran low, ignoring the invasion behind, conscious only of the safety of the tree line ahead. Judith was fifteen feet ahead, her hair a rain-blown snarl of tangles, flapping as she ran. Gunther knew there were men still outside in the rain, somewhere in the dark, confused now, but ready to cut them down. Gunther forced his eyes open against the rain. They were close, almost to the trees, when Judith faltered. Gunther caught her before she fell. He pushed her on roughly, turning back quickly to face their pursuers. "Keep going! Keep moving!"

Then from the blur a figure rose up ten paces to the side. Gunther almost didn't see him except for his quick movement and the distinctively abrupt rhythm of an Armalite's charging handle being hastily cocked into the arming position. Suddenly he remembered it all in one ghastly instant. Berlin. The murderous, racking fire from the tower. The pounding rain. Miles at the Wall. Roberts behind him, running furiously toward freedom, just as Judith was running now. It was happening again. Like some hideous nightmare come to life, it was all happening again! The Vopos and their machine guns were now faceless assassins in rain slickers.

Gunther fired. His target was close, not a murky shadow advancing before glaring headlights. This time there was no searchlight to blind him. This time *he* had the gun. He lunged toward the figure and fired as the muzzle of the man's automatic flashed in a short, rapid arc of flame. The assailant had shot wildly, too quickly, as if he'd been surprised, spraying the area around Gunther and missing him. But Gunther had not missed. He'd shot this image a thousand times in a thousand repeating nightmares. Now the Vopo was hit and Gunther kept firing until the enemy lay sprawled on his back, conscious but dying, moving his lips and watching wide-eyed and helpless as his mortality was reaffirmed in the mud. It was Rockwell. His long, thin face was frightened and speckled with the runny mire of Vermont earth. He'd led his last assault. It might have been Roberts lying there, or Miles.

Or Gunther.

Obedient drones.

Gunther had avenged himself, but the triumph was hollow, like a crushing victory over an outclassed foe. He didn't feel like a winner. He didn't even feel lucky.

Gunther finally noticed that the shooting at the house had stopped and he was aware of Judith, calling him through the rain.

"Alec? Are you hurt, Alec?"

He retrieved the Armalite from the mud beside Rockwell. He heard angry voices cursing loudly from the house.

"Alec, you must get away from here. Hurry, please!" Her voice was strained and slightly out of breath.

He walked to her and followed her into the trees. The smell of wet pines reminded him of Pennsylvania when they were there together, in a different life a hundred years ago.

"There is a small . . . a small settlement that way," Judith said, pointing down a slope to the west. She was panting heavily, steadying herself against a tree.

Gunther glanced back quickly over his shoulder. The men in the house were calling for Rockwell.

"About two miles . . . maybe less."

Gunther moved past her to lead the way as if he knew it, holding branches back for her. They walked only a few hundred yards and she stopped to rest, standing against a spruce.

"I'm sorry, Alec." Her hair was matted in long streaks down her face. She fought weakly to keep the rain out of her eyes. "I wanted to take that damned boat ride to Staten Island with you once more."

"Judith?" Gunther saw her winsome smile bend into a grimace of pain. She dropped to her knees and he caught her before she fell to the ground. "Judith!" He felt the wound in her back, sticky in the rain-soaked suit, tasted the blood on her mouth. "Oh God. Oh Jesus, no, Judith!"

"It isn't much farther, Alec . . . remember the pouch."

Gunther pressed his hand over the hole and she moaned heavily. It isn't too bad he told himself. Oh, Christ! "It isn't bad," he told her. Gunther slung the Armalite over his shoulder and raised her in his arms. "It isn't bad!"

"Camila has the other key."

Gunther started down the slope, half walking, half running. Tree branches slapped his face.

"Camila has the other key," she said, "in B.A."

"Don't talk!"

"She has the key . . . the safe-deposit box. She can help you, Alec."

He was stumbling in the slippery mud, going west. "Please, Judith . . . goddammit, don't . . . don't talk!"

"Robert Bickel . . . Alec, Robert Bickel is who you must give the pouch to. Internal Intelligence. In Washington . . ."

"Please, Judith!"

"He can stop Mackensen. Give the pouch to him." Her words were beginning to slur.

"It isn't bad . . . just don't . . ."

She smiled. "Take me to the ferry, Alec."

"I will. I will!"

"Take me to the ferry. Let's do it one more time."

Gunther felt a spasm wrench her body. He stopped suddenly and almost fell.

"Judith!"

There was a bright redness to her lips. "One more time," she said. Then she died, in his arms, between the leather pouch and the Armalite rifle.

He carried her to the settlement. The rain had stopped, and he found a dry place on someone's wooden porch where he could lay her. He wiped the wetness from her face and combed the strands of hair away from her cheeks with his fingers. Then he left her and called a man named Bickel in Washington.

35

Only after the battle is won—when the enemy scurries away in defeat and the revolutionaries remain to collect the spoils—can victory be savored.

The room was sparsely furnished, but the bed was comfortable. Gunther had little recollection of their arrival except of a car ride to a building with no windows and many corridors. He slept until hunger roused him, and he was fed. His knew the time of day only because they brought him lunch instead of breakfast. A man dressed in khakis escorted him from his room to an office in the same building and told him to wait. After a short time a thin-lipped man entered. He went to the desk, paused as if the room was also unfamiliar to him, then sat down.

"My name is Robert Bickel," he began. "We spoke on the phone."

Gunther nodded.

"The information you delivered has been useful. Very useful. Where did you run across it?"

"Someone sent it to me," Gunther said. "I don't know who." The inside of his mouth was gummy and dry. He didn't remember the last time he'd brushed his teeth.

"This man Vargas, you shot him?"

"Yes."

"On orders from Mackensen?"

243

"It was my assignment." Gunther nodded again. "Yes."

"And Peter Morton Rockwell?"

"I didn't know it was Rockwell until after I'd shot him, but it wouldn't have made any difference. They were blitzing us."

"Yes, I know." Bickel opened a folder in front of him and pretended to read. Gunther hated it when people did that. "I'm heading the investigation concerning the former director of Special Operations. The information you provided pretty well closes the book on Mackensen." He looked up at Gunther and paused a moment before he added, "I'm sorry about your wife."

Gunther said nothing. There was no point in correcting him. He wondered where they had Mackensen.

"We'll want you for debriefing, of course. Otherwise, you're free to take some time off. Reassignment will come after the dust settles." Bickel glanced back at the folder, then at Gunther, appearing slightly embarrassed. "I'm recommending you for the Intelligence Medal." He hesitated a moment as if unsure of what came next. "It's the least we can do, I think, after what you've been through."

Gunther nodded deprecatingly, but Bickel paid no notice. "What happens to Special Ops . . . disbandment?"

"No. It's still a useful section."

"Even now?" Gunther said.

"We're cleaning it up," he said. "Mackensen is gone. That's the important thing. You'd approve of his replacement, I think."

"You don't know what I'd approve of."

Bickel shrugged. "Well, you know him . . . the new director of S.O. I would think you'd approve."

"I knew Mackensen," Gunther said. "I wouldn't say that was much recommendation."

"Marty is different . . . much different than Mackensen."

Gunther looked up sharply. "Marty?"

"Yes," Bickel said. "Marty Burdict . . . from Operations Directorate in New York."

There it was. Vargas's end game complete. His final strategy finally deployed.

Marty Burdict.

The man that was to be placed high in the agency. The man whose promotion required Vargas's sacrifice. A Greek among the Trojans. The Taskmaster's spy. Gunther watched as Bickel shuffled papers together. He couldn't see the point anymore.

"We're going to be involved in a wrapping up of all this. Perhaps you'd be interested in—"

"No," Gunther said quickly. "I wouldn't be interested. Wrap up, clean up, sweep up . . . Do whatever you need to do, but don't include me. I don't want any more to do with it. Debrief me and let me go. Reassign me . . . I just want to go."

"Reassignments are not up to me, but I understand how you feel about all this."

He didn't, of course.

"Where is Mackensen now?" Gunther asked.

Bickel nodded toward the door. "Here."

"What will be done with him?"

"I'm not sure exactly. I don't—"

"I want to see him."

"Mackensen! After—" Bickel wet his thin lips. "What on earth for?"

"A last good-bye," Gunther said. "I think I've earned it."

Gunther was allowed only a short time alone with Mackensen. It was a surprisingly large room with no windows and a high ceiling. He sat at a long table, smoking a cigarette. In the light, Mackensen was even smaller and paler than Gunther remembered.

"Come to gloat, have you, Alec?" He wore a white shirt open at the top. It was slightly soiled around the collar, as if he'd been sweating. Mackensen indicated that Gunther take a seat. "You'd think as much money as we pay for these buildings at the Farm they could maintain a decent thermostat control." He folded his arms across his chest as if he were chilly. "Has it started to rain?"

Gunther shook his head. "I haven't seen."

Mackensen sighed. "Well, no matter. Sit down, Alec, sit down. I don't imagine you'll be here long."

"Just a few minutes." he said. Gunther pulled a chair up to the table and sat down opposite Mackensen. "Why? Tell me why you did it and I'll go."

"Why, indeed." He puffed on the cigarette, coughed and smiled a hollow smile. "Survival, Alec. It always comes down to that in the end."

"It was pointless."

"Perhaps to you. Everything is relative, Alec. When you gamble with such high stakes, it is vital that you subordinate the croupier. That has always been my way. Until recently, it's been good enough."

"Good God, man, you can't—"

"Please, Alec, no lectures just now. Anyway, there is no such thing as right. Not here." He extinguished the cigarette in a small plastic tray. "You know how ironically it all turned out. You and me, and, of course, Vargas. He is dead, at least. And you the scapegoat turned vindicator. I am—" He raised his hands, palms out, a gesture of indifference. "I am Solomon Grundy." Mackensen looked past him. "How does it go? Born on Monday, christened Tuesday, ill Thursday, worse Friday, and Saturday . . . dead!" He glanced back at Gunther. "What day *is* this, Alec?"

Gunther said nothing.

"I'm something of a president forced to resign," Mackensen went on. "They can't shoot me or send me to prison or banish me to Elba Island." He nodded at the ceiling. "This is my San Clemente."

"And if they let you out?"

Mackensen leaned forward, resting his chin on interlaced fingers. "This concern isn't like you, Alec. If you have learned anything, it is that one does not compromise himself, no involvement except with the job, the work. That is your strong suit. It's what I've always admired in you."

"Maybe I'm not too old to learn a new trick," Gunther said.

"A new trick?"

"Double-crossing the double-crossers. Vargas told me everything. Even about Miles. Did you know what he was really doing?"

"It wasn't terribly difficult to figure out, you know, Alec. Vargas didn't like the business I was in." Mackensen shrugged. "I didn't particularly like the threat he posed. The man was insane, clearly. He had no hope of changing the worldwide intelligence system the way we know it. Can you imagine it? The Russians, the Chinese, all of them—he challenged them all with his scheme. We'd be back to knights and dragon slayers."

"You say 'them' as if we weren't included."

"It's all the same game."

"I'm not convinced Vargas didn't have the right idea. He did have some good effect, after all." Gunther nodded toward the walls of Mackensen's white-collar cell.

"Then why did you kill him?"

"I didn't." Gunther noted the surprise in Mackensen's eyes. "Oh, he's dead enough. I just didn't put the bullet in his head." For a fleeting moment he remembered Judith. The old Judith. Before Vargas.

"Dead, nonetheless, and his scheme with him. That is the trouble when you run an organization on the strength of one man's abilities. When the brain dies, the function of the appendages ceases to operate. Remember that, Alec."

"I intend to," Gunther said. "It may be that this organization is not finished." He looked at his hands. "Vargas made me an offer. I'm still thinking about it."

The man across the table studied Gunther a long moment. "You!" Mackensen shook his head and even smiled slightly. "He did it. Vargas turned *you*. I'll be goddamned."

"Don't be too sure."

Mackensen waved him off. "You needn't worry about me, Alec." Now he smiled with enthusiasm. If he were capable of it, Gunther thought, Mackensen would have laughed. "Even if I tried to, no one would believe me, not now. I could never convince anyone what Vargas was really up to." He nodded his head exultantly as if it were a joke and he'd thought it up. "It was clever, Alec. Everyone was used . . . was a part of this, even you, and no one knew it except Vargas himself."

"You think it was clever?"

Mackensen smiled bitterly. "You have the last laugh, Alec. You and Vargas."

"Except I turned him down, Mackensen. I wasn't going to go along until Rockwell and your maniacs showed up. Maybe it's true that you have to lose something you value before you can appreciate what you had. That's what convinced me that some way, even against such odds, Vargas had the right idea."

Mackensen was silent for several moments, frowning his Medici frown. "Why are you telling me this?"

Gunther got up from his chair, walked to the door and turned back. "I wanted you to know how close I came to stepping off the tightrope," he said in a low voice, almost to himself. "The trouble with clever plans, Mackensen, is that they can be too ingenious. That was your mistake. Vargas went to a lot of trouble to make me see it. That may have been his."

36

There is no such thing as the perfect guer-
rilla manual. We shall continue to add
new chapters and to discard obsolete and
imperfect methods. The goal of the revo-
lutionary, however, never changes.

Gunther had his plane ticket in his pocket. It was late even by New York standards when he locked his brownstone apartment for the last time and walked to the Seventy-second Street station and stood at the local track to wait.

He had plenty of time and he wanted to make all the stops. They'd told him to rest, take some time off, go wherever he liked. He'd thought about it for days, in the afternoons mostly, on solitary walks in the park, where he'd wear his long coat and stay for hours. When he told them he wanted to leave for perhaps a week, no one objected. He was Alec Gunther again.

The train clicked and swayed to each of the stops on the route—Lincoln Center, Columbus Circle, Fiftieth Street, Forty-second Street—and Gunther sat in the second car near the brakeman's compartment. Buenos Aires would still be cold, he thought, still in its two-blanket nights, but it shouldn't take long to acclimate. His thoughts turned to Camila and the time of adjustment that lay ahead for both of them. They were both scarred survivors, but in surviving they shared a mutual loss. Perhaps together, if she let him, they could endure the odds.

Times Square and the halts between it and the Chambers Street station eventually drew out the remaining passengers from Gunther's car. He preferred the quiet, but not the loneliness. Judith had enjoyed this ride, the two of them together, whenever it was. It seemed not so long ago, yet too far in the past to recollect details. He wished he could remember them now.

Gunther was alone in the car when the train stopped, waited and finally closed its doors to the empty platforms at the Cortland and Rector Street stations. At South Ferry, where the IRT line ends, he climbed the stairs to the observation deck above the terminal. There was a slight chill in the breeze as he stood by the railing. The ferry was coming in, half a dozen people on its forward deck to watch the docking. Gunther felt the key at the bottom of his coat pocket and turned it absently between his fingers. Such a small key for so important a secret. In a day or two he would go to Camila's *Banco Central* . . . open the safe-deposit box. Perhaps it was as insane as Mackensen had said, but maybe it was time to awaken the dragon slayers.

Gunther was the Taskmaster now. If he wanted to be. He wasn't sure. It would be a new beginning and that thought pleased him. Maybe he could make it up to the losers.

The losers . . . What an absurd notion, as if it all were a contest. Victims, really. Victims of their own deceit.

Ollie Vargas was one.

Harry Phillips.

Kenneth Tripp.

John Miles.

It was a long list. Gunther might add his own name.

Camila Puentes too.

He turned his collar up against the breeze. An incessant wind tugged at his coat. He stared at the ferry. Passengers were boarding. In all his adult life as a decipherer of other men's secrets, he'd held little regard for promises. But he would keep this one. So many memories were behind him now, but Judith was not one he could forget.

Would not.

Things might have been different if he'd taken this ride with her—a hundred years ago.

He walked down to the boarding dock. There was time for organizing and planning and making strategies, but later. That would all come later when his mind was clearer.

Not now.

Now was a time to be alone. To take a boat ride. A boat ride with a memory. And he got aboard just in time.

King, Harold
The taskmaster.